Sam felt himself drifting closer to Charlotte.

Her lips were slightly parted, moist from the drink she'd been sipping. He wondered what her mouth tasted like...

"Hey, you two, come on out on the dance floor!"

He didn't know who yelled, but it was enough to sober Sam. "Would you like to dance?" He asked the question the way he'd been doing everything since Charlotte arrived at the resort—without thinking it through.

Charlotte blinked and stood up. Sam took that as an affirmative.

He rose from his chair and followed her to the makeshift dance floor, where she turned to face him. How much trouble could they get into dancing to this fast-paced Taylor Swift song anyway?

But they no sooner got into the rhythm when the song ended and a slow ballad came on.

Sam did the only thing he could think to do. He put his arms out and she unhesitatingly slid against him, as if they'd been doing this for years.

This was a very bad idea.

Dear Reader,

If you read Allie Miller's book, *Catching Her Rival*, then you'll be happy to know that this is her twin sister's story. Wondering what was in that letter Charlotte found? You don't have long to wait!

Resorting to the Truth begins with Charlotte Harrington reading that letter from her deceased mother, which turns Charlotte's world upside down. Thankfully, Sam Briton enters her life, even if they have a rocky beginning. He had a problem with Charlotte's twin sister, Allie, several years earlier, and he naturally assumes Charlotte is just as dishonest. Unfortunately, Charlotte doesn't help her case with some of the decisions she makes...

I hope you enjoy reading Charlotte's story as much as I enjoyed writing it.

Please visit my website at lisadyson.com or send me an email at lisa@lisadyson.com. I'd love to hear from you!

Happy reading,

Lisa Dyson

LISA DYSON

Resorting to the Truth

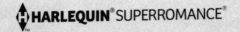

HARLEQUIN® SUPERROMANCE®

Recycling programs
for this product may
not exist in your area.

ISBN-13: 978-0-373-60940-6

Resorting to the Truth

Printed in U.S.A.

Lisa Dyson has been creating stories ever since getting an A on a fifth-grade writing assignment. She lives near Washington, DC, with her husband and their rescue dog with a blue tongue, aptly named Blue. She has three grown sons, a daughter-in-law and four adorable grandchildren. When not writing, reading or spending time with family, Lisa enjoys traveling, volunteering and rooting for her favorite sports teams.

Books by Lisa Dyson

HARLEQUIN SUPERROMANCE

A Perfect Homecoming
Catching Her Rival

Visit the Author Profile page at Harlequin.com.

For anyone searching for their roots,
may you find happiness in whatever you discover

Acknowledgment

A special thank-you to my friend
Chief David Parenti, Belmont Fire Department,
Belmont, New Hampshire, for sharing his
incredible knowledge about fire procedures.
Any mistakes are entirely my own.

CHAPTER ONE

Two months ago

CHARLOTTE HARRINGTON SAT alone in her living room, clutching the sealed envelope bearing her name, which was written in her deceased mother's handwriting. The August sun had set a while ago. The only illumination in her Newport, Rhode Island, home was the fluorescent bulb in the lamp on the end table next to her.

She had no idea how much time had passed since her recently discovered twin sister, Allie Miller, had left with Charlotte's neighbor, Jack Fletcher. They'd helped Charlotte unload her car after she'd returned from her Boston art show and wanted to give her privacy as she read her mother's last words.

Charlotte placed the envelope on her lap and wiped her damp palms on her jeans. She'd crinkled the edge of the envelope from grasping it so tightly the moment she'd found it buried in a box of ticket stubs and other memorabilia her mother had saved. If not for the phone call that evening from Felicia Malone, a woman who claimed Charlotte's mother had been seeing Felicia's husband nearly three decades ago, Charlotte wouldn't have gone searching for clues to the truth in her mother's memory box. Charlotte had stored the box under her bed to sort through later, thinking nothing of significance was inside. The way the letter had been hidden under other memorabilia, she could only assume she wasn't supposed to find it until after her mother's passing. The idea made Charlotte even more curious about the letter's contents.

During their phone conversation, Felicia had claimed that once a week, before Charlotte was born, her husband and Charlotte's mother would meet at a movie theater and then go to a hotel room afterward.

Charlotte sniffed. More than a year had passed since losing her single, adoptive mother, but the grief Charlotte thought she had under control rolled over her like a tsunami.

She ran a finger across her name on the envelope. The stationery was familiar. Her mother had obviously written the letter shortly before her passing. Charlotte had supplied the stationery when her mother had wanted to write notes to friends after her health had begun to quickly decline. Her mother had been diagnosed with pancreatic cancer and died a few months later.

Turning the pale yellow envelope over, Charlotte noticed the flap was barely sealed. Her lips twitched slightly. Mom had disliked the taste of envelope glue.

Charlotte slipped a finger under the flap and broke the seal. Even before she removed the contents, she could tell there were several handwritten pages.

She wiped her damp hands on her jeans again and pulled the pages from the envelope. She unfolded the letter, which featured a bouquet of white daisies—her mother's favorite flower—in the upper-right corner of the first page. Charlotte recognized her mother's tiny penmanship instantly. She swallowed the lump in her throat and began reading.

My dearest Charlotte,
As you read this letter, please know that my love for you knows no bounds. Even in death, which I know is imminent, my love for you will never end.

Tears welled in Charlotte's eyes, her mother's words too blurry to read. She blinked a few times and wiped away the tears running down her cheeks. Why hadn't she grabbed some tissues before she sat down?

She sniffed and continued.

I've always been honest with you about your adoption, but there are details I've left out. Details I always thought I'd have time to explain, but I don't want to add to your burden with my illness coming on so quickly. Hopefully, you are reading this after you've recovered emotionally.

You and I have talked openly about your adoption. How I brought you home as an infant, and you've been the light of my life ever since. But there are things I didn't tell you. Maybe because I selfishly wanted you all to myself. It was always you and me against the world. I have no excuse that will make up for not telling you that you have a twin sister.

She had known! Charlotte tossed the letter aside, unable to continue as the sudden anger at her mother roiled inside her. No wonder she'd hidden this letter for Charlotte to find later. Her mother must have known how betrayed Charlotte would feel.

Why had her mother kept Charlotte's twin sister, Allie, a secret? The sisters had lost out on so many years together because they hadn't known about each other.

Charlotte and Allie had met by accident at a wedding two months ago, twenty-nine years after they'd been adopted by different families. Charlotte's existence had been a huge surprise to Allie's adoptive mother, but apparently Charlotte's mother had always known.

Charlotte stood and paced in front of her sofa, clenching and unclenching her fists. Why on earth would her mother have kept such news from her? The entire time Allie and Charlotte had been looking for confirmation of their relationship, Charlotte had been positive her mother had been clueless about Allie.

Charlotte needed to know more. She picked up the letter from the sofa and continued reading, still pacing the room.

I want you to be able to find your sister, so you need to know that you weren't born in upstate New York like your birth certificate says, but in Rhode Island. The lawyer who handled your adoption, Gerard Stone, had a forged birth certificate made for you at my request. It's the birth certificate you've used your entire life, and I always dreaded the day someone would realize it was fake. But that never happened. Thankfully, it was never necessary for you to apply for a replacement.

You were born in Cranston, Rhode Island. The lawyer dealt with many female inmates at the correctional institute there who found themselves pregnant while incarcerated and wanted to put their newborns up for adoption.

I met Gerry Stone when I worked at Malone and Malone, the CPA firm in the same shopping center as Gerry's office.

Charlotte and Allie had already uncovered most of this information. The fact that it was the now-deceased Gerard Stone who had arranged for the forged birth certificate was the only new information. Allie and Charlotte had originally suspected they might be cousins and not twins because though they were unmistakably identical and born on the same day, they were born in different states.

Or so they thought until they were able to track down their original birth certificates in the lawyer's files a few weeks ago. That ascertained they were twins, both born in Rhode Island, and then confirmed by the DNA results she and Allie had received in the mail that very day.

I was well aware that Gerry did things that weren't quite legal.

No kidding. Forging a birth certificate, selling babies, separating twins. Those were probably only a few of his transgressions. Who knew what else that man had been up to?

I must admit I never would have dealt with him if not for the man who was the love of my life.

Huh? Charlotte's mother had never mentioned a man. Oh, a few she'd dated in high school and college, but no one she had been serious about. Was she talking about Felicia's husband?

Hank was a good man, a very good man, and he loved me, too. If he hadn't already had a wife and children, he would have married me. Instead, I made him choose and he stayed with them. I understood, but that didn't make it hurt any less. When Hank made his choice, I found another job because he and his wife owned the CPA firm I worked for.

This was all before you were born. I never could have adopted you without Hank's help. He gave me the money I needed for the adoption. Not a loan, a gift. That's how much he loved me. He didn't want me to be alone and knew how much I desperately wanted a child, a family, because, as you know, I have no living relatives.

Charlotte had been a parting gift. Instead of jewelry, he'd helped her mother buy a baby to ease his conscience. A thirty-thousand-dollar payoff.

Hank died a few years ago, and I sat in the back of the church during his funeral. I left before the family filed past so I wouldn't

cause them more pain. As much as I will
miss you, I look forward to reuniting with
Hank when my time comes.

Charlotte paused. She had felt that her mother
had given up after being diagnosed. Was Hank
the reason why? She could have gone through
an experimental treatment, but her mother had
decided not to explore the option.

I hope you can find a way to forgive me
for not sharing this information with you
years ago. The more time that passed, the
harder it became to tell you because I knew
you'd be hurt and angry. Losing you and
your respect would have been more than I
could have endured.

Several years ago, I began a search for
your birth mother. I thought you might
someday want to know your family medical history. Your mother's name is Barbara
Sherwood. Unfortunately, she died from a
drug overdose a few years after you were
born. She didn't name a father on your original birth certificate. I have no idea whether
you have any other living relatives or where
your twin sister is, but I hope you will take
this information and find her so you're not
alone.

Again, I hope you will someday be able to forgive me and remember that everything I have ever done was because of my love for you.

Charlotte read the letter a second time and then dropped it onto the coffee table. She put her hands over her face and shook her head.

Her mother had lied to her. Not just a little lie, but a series of lies that had continued nearly three decades.

No wonder her mother had hidden this letter for Charlotte to find after her mother's death.

Charlotte had believed her mother was the epitome of honesty. She had recently bragged to Allie that her mother would never have kept her twin's existence a secret if she'd known about it. She was the kind of person who would return to a store if she'd been given too much change, just to correct the mistake.

Charlotte's text message alert sounded on her cell phone. She picked up the phone from the dining room table. The message was from Allie.

Checking to make sure you're okay. Jack and I are here if you need us.

She'd been truly blessed to have found Allie, and their meeting had been purely accidental.

Charlotte's friend Jack had taken her to a family wedding. His cousin was marrying Allie's younger brother. After Jack confused Allie for Charlotte a few times, both he and Charlotte met Allie. Charlotte found her sister, and Jack fell in love with Allie. Charlotte couldn't be happier for the two of them. In fact, she and Allie's mother, who had warmly embraced Charlotte like a daughter, had been instrumental in getting them to face their feelings for each other.

She looked at Allie's message on her phone again. What should she say? She was too exhausted physically and emotionally to talk right now.

Thanks. I appreciate it. Will talk to you in the morning.

Charlotte sent the message and headed upstairs to bed, leaving her mother's letter on the coffee table.

CHAPTER TWO

Two months later

ALLIE MILLER SAT in her office Thursday morning and checked her calendar. A thing she hadn't done since September had rolled into October at the end of last week. It wasn't as though she had a lot on the calendar, unfortunately. One thing stood out, though. The advertising conference she'd registered for months ago was in two days. Which meant she probably had an email this morning telling her she could check in electronically for her flight tomorrow.

Damn. She'd forgotten all about it. She'd signed up for it back when she'd been optimistic about her financial future and still worked at DP Advertising. Before she nearly joined her former boyfriend in federal prison, thanks to his extortion scheme that she hadn't been aware of until after the guy's arrest. That was followed by her being unfairly let go from DP because everyone assumed she'd known about it and was somehow involved.

She sighed. The conference would be worthwhile, but she didn't want to spend a week away from Jack. Not to mention the toll it would take on her bank account. After being blacklisted in the ad industry, she had opened her own agency and didn't have much money to spare.

Allie made a few phone calls, ending with a call to Jack at his office at Empire Advertising, his grandfather's successful firm.

"Hey," she said when he answered.

"Miss me already?" His tone was teasing. "I just dropped you off." They had settled into a routine where they stayed in her Providence, Rhode Island, high-rise apartment during the week and spent the weekends at Jack's house in Newport. A bonus was having her newly discovered twin sister, Charlotte, right across the street from him.

She explained to Jack about the conference. "So I've paid for the airfare, which is nonrefundable, and the conference people told me I couldn't get a refund at this late date. I can still cancel the hotel room because I really don't want to go."

"It would be a great trip to make together," he said. "I was dealing with Granddad's health when I heard about the conference and decided I shouldn't be that far away from him." His maternal grandfather, now living comfortably in an assisted-living facility in Providence, had raised Jack. His grandfather had banished Jack's father when it was revealed that his father's latest affair with one of his college students had precipitated the argument between Jack's parents—an argument that led to his mother's fatal car accident.

"How weird would it have been if we'd met at this conference instead of the wedding?" She laughed.

"We would have lost all this time together," he reminded her. "You know, if you don't feel you can afford it, I can help you out."

"It's partially the money, since I haven't been able to snag a big-name client like John Wentworth or Raymond Foster to keep my company afloat. But truthfully, I'd miss Harvey." She was teasing about their rescue dog, but she didn't want to get too mushy by telling Jack she'd miss him terribly. Their relationship still felt too new to jump ahead too quickly.

"You'd miss Harvey?" The humor in his voice came through clearly.

"Sure. I've gotten quite attached to him."

"Glad to hear it." He chuckled. "Hey, what about Charlotte?"

"What about her?"

"You were looking for something to get her out of this funk. What about giving her the trip? She wouldn't have to attend the conference, but it's a week's vacation on an island."

"What about the plane ticket? I can't put it in her name."

He was quiet for a few seconds. "See if you

can get a credit. I'll pay for a new flight once Charlotte agrees to go."

The idea was a good one. They'd both been troubled about Charlotte's well-being since her mother's letter. Charlotte was consumed with grief and anger; her therapist had been unable to help her cope. Charlotte was determined to keep searching for their biological relatives and had emailed and left messages over social media for anyone who might know or be related to their mother, Barbara Sherwood. Allie thought her motivation was because Charlotte was still angry her adoptive mother had known about Allie and never told Charlotte.

"I'll also chip in for the hotel room," he added. "Tell Charlotte she can relax and Allie Miller will just not show up for the conference."

"That's perfect!" She couldn't believe she hadn't thought of it herself. Her sister had been so good to her since they'd met, and this trip would be a nice way to repay her. "This is really a great idea, Jack. She's been spending a lot of time searching for our other biological relatives, and I'm pretty sure she hasn't been working much. I'm worried. Her next art show is in a few weeks and I don't see how she'll be ready."

"Then make sure she accepts the trip."

"Trust me, I'll make sure she does."

"You *are* pretty persuasive," he teased and then changed the subject. "Why don't we plan a road trip to Vermont this weekend? The leaves are probably almost gone, but we could find a bed-and-breakfast and do some wine tasting and eat apple everything."

She groaned. "That sounds wonderful. You're pretty persuasive yourself. So much better than a conference by myself. I'll call Charlotte now."

CHARLOTTE SWITCHED THE phone to her other ear as she walked barefoot across her living room, through the dining room and into the kitchen. "A vacation? Now? I don't know, Allie. I'm not really in the mood for traveling."

"Come on," Allie persisted. "You'll have a great time. When was the last time you took a vacation?"

"It's been a while," she admitted reluctantly. Probably some time before Charlotte's mother had been diagnosed with cancer a year and a half ago. Charlotte didn't count the emotional weekend at the beach she'd spent with her mother after the doctors had confirmed her mom had only a few months left to live. Plenty of time for her mother to have shared what she knew about Charlotte's twin sister.

"All the more reason you should go."

Charlotte had never vacationed alone. What would she do? She didn't even go to movies by herself or dine in a restaurant at a table for one.

That's what Netflix and drive-throughs were for. "Thanks anyway. I appreciate the thought."

"Come on, Charlotte, you know you want to go. You need this. Take the time to relax and get a fresh perspective."

Could she resist such a fabulous opportunity? "I have so much to do," Charlotte lamented. "I'm showing again next month, and I still have three more pieces I want to add to my inventory. I haven't even started them."

"Wouldn't it be wonderful if you had beautiful sunset vistas, as well as birds and trees and a bunch of other stuff for inspiration?"

Charlotte realized she was smiling at the thought, and her adrenaline kicked in. She was known for her pastels, but she'd been in a creative downswing from the moment of her mother's diagnosis, stuck on charcoal as her preferred medium. The stark black with shades of gray on a white background echoed her current view of the world. Things had gotten worse after reading her mother's letter.

"Is your computer nearby?" Allie asked. "I just sent you some pics of the private island, Sapodilla Cay, off the Florida coast."

Charlotte reluctantly pulled up the pictures on her laptop. Unexpectedly, the myriad of colors in the tropical island sunset called to her. "I *have* been hoping to get back into pastels and—"

"You can have a working vacation." Allie took

Charlotte's comment as agreement. "Pack your art supplies and your bathing suit. I'll email you the ticket so you can check in. The flight leaves at noon tomorrow."

Charlotte laughed. The situation was absurd. "I don't know what to say."

"You deserve it. You've been there for me. I couldn't have gotten that Fairleigh account without your help, not to mention meeting Jack. Please let me do this for you. Let *us*—Jack and me—do this for you."

Charlotte hesitated, but the pull of the ocean views nagged her. "This is really sweet of you, Allie. You're such a thoughtful sister. I guess—"

"I told Jack I could convince you." Allie's voice came through loud and clear before Charlotte could actually agree. "Go do whatever you need to do to get ready."

"Thank you, Allie."

"You're very welcome. That's what sisters are for."

The thought saddened her again—exactly the opposite of Allie's intent. But Charlotte couldn't help thinking how many years they'd missed as sisters, thanks to her mother.

THE NEXT MORNING, Charlotte wanted to crawl back into bed. She'd barely slept after going over all the details of this crazy, unexpected vacation. Partly because she was determined to enjoy the experience and leave her grief and anger behind, but mainly because she was sure she should skip the trip and stay home.

She had stayed up way too late figuring out what to pack and what to wear on the plane. October in Rhode Island made a coat a necessity, but the temps in Fort Lauderdale and on the island would be too warm for more than a light jacket. Would the evenings on the island be cool this time of year because of the ocean breeze? She'd checked the weather app on her phone, but knew temperature wouldn't tell the complete story that close to the ocean. She settled for layers since she always froze on airplanes when they reached cruising altitude.

Not that she'd done a whole lot of flying. Occasionally, she'd needed to fly to get to galleries where her art was being shown. Beyond that, she'd traveled by car and twice by train.

Once she had sorted out her wardrobe and realized how late it was, she had been terrified she'd sleep through her alarm clock. Not that she usually did, but because of that, she had woken every hour and then had finally gotten up twenty minutes before her alarm had gone off.

Charlotte was ready early, pacing in front of the window while she waited for the driver to arrive at her small, historic home. Less than a year ago, she'd used some of her considerable inheritance from her mother to buy the home she'd fallen in love with the moment she'd seen it. Having Jack as her friend and neighbor across the street was an additional perk.

Allie had offered to drive Charlotte to the airport, but she'd declined. Allie and Jack had done enough by sending her on this trip. There was no need for either of them to drive forty-five minutes from Providence to Newport on a workday, and then drive Charlotte another forty-five minutes back to the Providence airport.

Allie had forwarded the e-ticket to Charlotte, as well as a detailed itinerary for the trip. She'd need to figure out what it had cost them so she could repay them the entire amount. Allie had offered the trip as a gift, but Charlotte planned to foot the bill herself. Allie wasn't financially stable yet, so Charlotte didn't want her sister, or Jack, to spend money on her. Between her inheritance from her mother and her successful art career, Charlotte was financially comfortable.

She checked her watch. The car was now ten minutes late. The longer she had to wait for her driver, the more she had second thoughts about the trip. It wasn't too late to back out.

But if she backed out, she'd have to explain to Allie and Jack why. She racked her brain but couldn't come up with a viable reason. Telling them she didn't feel like it wasn't going to work.

She reviewed her mental list for about the tenth time. Tickets, casual summer clothes that had been packed away for the winter, sunglasses, phone and charger, sunscreen, as well as her e-reader with several novels she hadn't had time to read. Her carry-on was filled with her art supplies to prevent loss or damage in transit. She was also careful to make sure there was nothing in her carry-on that might be confiscated by airport security.

She was about to call the car company to make sure she hadn't given them the wrong time when a black town car pulled up to the curb. Charlotte stepped out the front door onto the porch to wave to the driver. Her suitcase and carry-on were already on the porch and she started down the steps with them to the sidewalk.

"Morning, Miss Harrington. I'll take those." The driver came around the car. His hat shadowed his face as he took her bags.

"Good morning. I just need to lock my door." She smiled, slung her purse over her shoulder and locked the front door behind her.

This was going to happen. She nearly missed a step in her excitement, and she grabbed on to the wooden railing to steady herself.

Before she knew it, she was seated in a window seat on the airplane, on her way to Fort Lauderdale where she'd take a ferry to Sapodilla Cay.

For someone pretty cautious, she discovered that since there was no turning back, she was actually excited about this new adventure.

SAM BRITON STOOD on the private island's dock next to the gleaming fifty-six-foot yacht named *For My Grandkids*. The Blaise Enterprises logo was prominently displayed just below it on the stern.

"You sure you're good until Ben gets back?" John Blaise, Sam's former father-in-law slash longtime boss, yelled from the top deck of the yacht. "I can stay if you need me."

"I think we can manage," Sam replied. "This conference coming in isn't very large, about a hundred people. Between Ben's new assistant, Katie, and me, we should be able to handle them."

Sam's day had begun with the resignation of his conference manager due to his mother's illness in Liverpool, England. That was followed by a water leak in room 315 that had seeped into rooms 215 and 115. On top of that, one of the two elevators was down; a part was expected to be shipped overnight. Although, on this island, overnight shipping was hit or miss.

"I like what you told Ben about taking a leave of absence and moving his parents here. I knew you would handle the manager position like a pro." John grinned, the deep lines in his tanned face defined, and gestured up the boardwalk. "Here come the kids." Sam's children, Emma and Oliver, walked side by side, rolling their suitcases and wearing backpacks. John slipped around the corner to hide from them.

As soon as they got close enough, Sam wagged a finger at them while working desperately to hide his grin. "I expect you both to behave and don't take advantage of your grandfather."

"Oh, Daddy." At twelve going on twenty, Emma had recently decided she'd outgrown her father's sense of humor.

He slumped his shoulders dramatically and tugged on her funky striped hat. "Oh, Emma."

She huffed as she adjusted her hat.

"Papa promised we could go bowling when we get to port." Nine-year-old Oliver could barely contain his excitement. "He said there's a new place in town since the last time we stayed with him. They have lanes with bumpers, too, so I don't keep throwing glutter balls."

"*Gutter* balls," Sam corrected. "Just don't bug Papa about going. If Papa says he's too tired or wants to do something else, then no fussing. Got it?"

Both kids nodded in agreement. He had no doubt they'd have a great time. John had been widowed for almost ten years and he needed time with his grandchildren as much as they needed time with him. If not for John's help and support, Sam never could have concentrated on being a single dad while rising to the level of resort manager.

Of course, it helped that John owned the Grand Peacock chain of resorts, as well as Sapodilla Cay, but Sam had pushed himself harder than he'd thought possible to qualify for the position. He never wanted anyone to say he didn't deserve it.

John popped up from his hiding place on the boat and joined them on the dock.

"Papa!" Both kids ran into his waiting arms, Emma obviously forgetting she thought she was too old to be picked up by her grandfather.

The advantage of being a grandparent compared to a mere dad.

Sam grinned and spoke to John. "Thanks so much for taking them. Monica will be back very late Monday night, so either Monday evening or Tuesday morning would work for you to bring them back." The resort, plus a few touristy shops and sparse housing, took up most of the island, so there was no school for his kids to attend. Finding Monica to tutor Emma and Oliver, as well as a few offspring of resort employees, had been sheer luck.

"I'm glad she's working out." John pushed his nearly white hair back from his forehead where the wind had blown it.

"She's been a lifesaver. She doesn't even mind hanging around in our suite until late at night when I have to be somewhere."

"I hope she's having a good time with her parents." John rubbed his unshaven cheek. "You said it's their thirtieth wedding anniversary?"

"Yeah. She asked for the long weekend off months ago. What were the odds that Ben's parents would need him at the same time?"

"The headaches of running a resort." John waved to the kids, who'd drifted to the far end of the dock. They were pointing to something in the clear water, probably some sort of sea creature.

When they were within earshot he said, "How about handing me those suitcases, Oliver." John stowed their identical blue and pink suitcases as his grandson passed them onto the yacht.

Many years ago, John and his late wife, Rita, purchased the easy-to-maneuver boat, not wanting to give up their ability to travel by sea as they aged. They never thought death would separate them long before they expected.

Barely a few minutes later, Sam hugged his kids until they squealed, and then waved goodbye from the dock. Heading back to the resort along the boardwalk that spanned the sandy white beach, his heart constricted. He missed them and their lovable quirks already.

He checked his watch as he entered the open-air lobby. Their guests should begin arriving in less than two hours. Enough time for a final review of the week's activities with Katie and a much-needed hit of caffeine.

"GOOD AFTERNOON, FOLKS. This is Captain Jonas here." Charlotte opened her eyes and strained to hear the pilot as the entire plane quieted to listen. They'd pulled away from the gate ten minutes ago and then stopped with no explanation before now. From her window seat, she didn't see any other planes taking off, either. Maybe her flight would be canceled and she could go home. Her heart beat faster until the captain continued speaking.

"There's a storm hanging out just west of the airport, and no one's taking off. As soon as we get clearance, I'll be back to let you know. Until then, sit back and relax."

"Easy for you to say," Charlotte mumbled. The noise level rose as passengers complained. She reached under the seat in front of her to pull out her itinerary from her purse. Her flight was supposed to arrive in Fort Lauderdale at three, which gave her two hours before the ferry to Sapodilla Cay left at five. Taking into consideration that she needed to go to baggage claim and then take a taxi for the short drive to Port Everglades, this plane better take off quickly. She'd never been on a trip like this before and had no idea if there would be a security checkpoint that might be backed up.

The older woman sitting in the middle seat next to Charlotte *tsk*ed as she continued to crochet something pale pink and tiny. She glanced at

Charlotte. "Never fails. I'm always on the flight that's delayed." The woman's bright green eyes were prominant in an oval face lined with faint wrinkles. She peered at Charlotte, waiting for a response.

"You fly often?" she asked politely. She wasn't in the habit of conversing with strangers, but she reminded herself of her vow to have fun and leave her worries behind.

"Oh yes. Several times a year." The woman continued crocheting as she spoke, her hands moving rhythmically. "My grandkids live in Rhode Island. I've been living in south Florida for about ten years." She glanced at her hands, then back at Charlotte.

Charlotte checked the sky through her small window. "Looks like it's clearing over that way."

When the woman didn't comment, Charlotte stuffed her itinerary back into her purse, shoved it under the seat in front of her and leaned her head back. Her eyes drifted shut. She hoped her seat neighbor would take the hint.

"Allie?" A woman's loud voice came from the aisle nearby.

Charlotte didn't open her eyes, instead regulated her breathing and tried to block out the commotion around her.

"Allie!" The woman was insistent.

The older woman nudged Charlotte with her

elbow and said in a whisper, "I think that woman is speaking to you, dear."

Charlotte's eyes popped open to see a plump, fifty-something woman with an unruly mop of dark, curly hair and black-rimmed glasses.

"I didn't know you were on this flight." The woman's speech was quick, her silver hoop earrings bouncing randomly. "I'm surprised you're coming to the conference after the way things turned out at DP. You know, when you *left*." She used finger quotes for "left" and never seemed to stop talking long enough to inhale.

"You have me confused with my twin sister, Allie," Charlotte told her. "My name is Charlotte."

The woman pointed a finger at her and grinned wickedly. "That's a good one, Allie. I'm not sure how many people will believe you suddenly have a twin sister, but it's a nice try. I have to warn you, there are a lot of people at DP who think you knew about Jimmy's extortion plan. I'm really surprised you're going to the conference."

Charlotte opened her mouth to explain about finding Allie fairly recently, but she couldn't get a word in.

"Too bad we're not sitting next to each other." The woman turned her head quickly to look at the surrounding passengers and lowered her voice. "I'm sure you've heard all about who's going to be at the conference. Rumor has it he's looking to change advertising firms." She put her finger to her lips. "But you didn't hear it from me." The woman pointed to the front of the plane. "I'm up there on the aisle. I hate sitting anywhere else." She leaned in the row, nearly resting her ample breasts on the man in the aisle seat, to whisper, "You know how my bladder is, and I hate asking people to move. Oh, speaking of that, I need to use the facilities before they make us buckle up. So good to see you. I want to hear all about what you've been doing since you left DP. Check you later." She waved and moved down the aisle before Charlotte could say another word.

The woman obviously knew Allie from her previous job. Charlotte hadn't considered that people attending the advertising conference might mistake her for Allie. She should have, though, since they were identical twins. From their dark, chin-length hair to their matching feet with high insteps.

"I have to ask," the older woman next to her said. "Is your name Charlotte or Allie?"

"It's Charlotte. She didn't give me a chance to explain. My twin sister backed out of the conference and gave me the hotel room and travel arrangements to use as a vacation."

The woman nodded. "Sounds like you should do some investigating into this 'special guest' that's coming. I'm guessing your sister might be sorry she missed him."

The seat belt reminder dinged, and the passengers hurried to their seats to buckle up. Charlotte considered her seatmate's suggestion as the plane's engines revved.

"This is your captain again. Looks like things are moving. We're number eight for takeoff. Shouldn't be long now."

That seemed like a long way back in line, but Charlotte wasn't an expert.

Her mind wandered to what the talkative woman had said about someone important attending the conference. She should definitely call Allie as soon as she was able.

CHARLOTTE'S ROOM WAS beyond beautiful, as well as being the largest hotel room she'd ever stayed in. The furnishings were luxurious, while the room was light and airy. She crossed the hardwood floor to peer out at the ocean, drawn by the gentle breeze coming from the wall of open floor-to-ceiling French doors. The water was calm, and much to her amazement, she discovered how far out to sea she could still discern the white sandy bottom far from shore.

The first thing she did was call Allie. Her sister had already left her office for the day and her cell phone went right to voice mail. Charlotte left messages both places, but she would have to try again later.

She was about to unpack when she spotted a flyer on the bed. It was an invitation to the welcome reception the desk clerk had mentioned when she'd checked in. He'd said it was for all guests, not just conference attendees.

She checked the clock. The reception had already begun. As much as she wanted to hibernate in her room, she remembered one of the reasons she was here—to push herself beyond her comfort zone. "It sounds like fun." She spoke aloud as if trying to convince herself.

Charlotte hurried to the bathroom and brushed her teeth and her hair, touched up her makeup and applied lip gloss. She pulled a few things from her luggage, disappointed she hadn't yet unpacked. Didn't matter, this was vacation. A little food and a drink actually sounded like heaven.

She donned a long, flowing skirt and a matching floral peasant top. She retrieved her flat tan sandals from the outside pocket of her suitcase and struggled to buckle them in her haste.

She locked her laptop and purse in the room's safe. There was no need to carry a purse when she had a pocket in her skirt to keep her room key.

Before going out the door, she slipped on her little white shrug with three-quarter sleeves.

Even on the hottest summer days, most Newport evenings were cool enough to demand a light sweater or jacket, and this island in October was probably similar in climate.

Charlotte took the beautiful staircase rather than wait for the elevator. She'd noticed on her way up to her room that one elevator was out of service and she'd already taken several minutes getting herself presentable to attend the reception.

Partially hidden behind a palm tree in the lobby, Charlotte took in the gathering. The sight of food and a bar made her stomach growl. She thought she was being inconspicuous when she crossed the lobby to join the party.

"Hey, Allie!" one of the women in the crowd called out.

Just as she'd suspected, other people here knew Allie. Charlotte picked up a plate and reached for the vegetable tongs.

"Allie," said a man directly behind her. "We were all wondering if you'd be here."

Charlotte nearly dropped the tongs. She peered over her shoulder at the tall man with light brown hair, neatly trimmed facial hair and hazel eyes, who was probably in his mid- to late-twenties. She didn't know him, didn't know what to say. "I'm not—"

"I haven't seen you since you left DP." He lowered his voice. "You must be excited about our special guest."

Did all these DP people talk constantly, not allowing anyone to say a word?

Charlotte merely nodded while she put a few carrots and broccoli florets on her plate and added a small puddle of white dipping sauce. What would it hurt if a few people thought she was Allie? Probably easier than explaining constantly. Every time she told someone about finding her sister, it reopened wounds that were still raw after reading her mother's letter.

Everyone seemed to be ecstatic about someone special attending the conference. The more she heard, the more she was concerned that Allie wasn't here.

Not wanting to seem rude, Charlotte turned to face the man whose name she didn't know. "Yes, I'm very excited about our special—"

"Hi, Allie. Hi, Jared." A woman joined them before Charlotte could finish her sentence. Great. Another person who thought she was her sister. The petite woman with whitish-blond hair was about the same age as the man Charlotte now knew was named Jared. The woman held an almost empty glass of white wine in her hand.

"Hey, Veronica," Jared greeted her.

"Hi." Charlotte pretended to survey the room, figuring she'd just go along with everyone thinking she was Allie for the night. During the day, they'd be at their conference and she'd be luxuriating in the sun on the beach. She'd probably never run into them again. "This is quite a crowd."

Veronica nodded as she downed the last of her wine and set the glass on a tray with other used dishes.

Charlotte had nothing to talk about with these two. She knew nothing about them and very little about advertising. Taking a deep breath, she let it out slowly and dunked her broccoli into the dip on her plate before taking a bite.

"I'm going to take advantage of the open bar," Jared said. "Can I get either of you ladies anything?"

That sounded like an excellent idea, even if it meant she wasn't ditching either of them. Better to talk to people who thought she was her sister than stand around awkwardly by herself. "I'll come with you and see what they have." Charlotte checked out what others were drinking. A few had little umbrellas in what looked like fruity drinks.

She pointed to someone walking past the bar and told the bartender, "I'll have one of those."

"Ooh, me, too!" Veronica had followed them and now she clapped her hands like a five-year-old who'd been promised ice cream. She nudged Charlotte with an elbow. "By the way, love your hair like this. It must be so much easier than curling it."

"Um, thanks." She touched her hair. She and Allie had their dark brown hair styled in almost identical chin-length bobs when they'd met. Allie liked hers curled most of the time, but Charlotte couldn't be bothered since she worked from home and rarely had a need to get dressed up.

There was a lapse in the conversation. A perfect time for Charlotte to tell Jared and Veronica who she was.

Before she could open her mouth, their attention was drawn to a man ringing a brass bell.

SAM STOOD NEAR the food table and rang the bell to get everyone's attention. When they quieted and turned in his direction, he put his glass in the air and looked at the expectant faces in the crowd. "I'm the resort manager, Sam Briton, and I'd like to welcome you all to the Grand Peacock Resort on Sapodilla Cay. I hope you're all having a good time?" The group cheered, and he took a sip of his club soda.

He was about to begin his usual speech about the resort when the people parted. There was a face he recognized. Not a face he ever expected to see. Not one he *ever* wanted to see again.

Allie Miller.

Or, as he referred to the lying tramp from his past who'd attached herself to a boyfriend with no morals, *Alley Cat*.

CHAPTER THREE

THE MAN SPEAKING to the group stopped. He glared at Charlotte.

Her hand flew to cover her unexpected gasp, drawing more attention to herself. She had never seen this guy before, so why the loathing in his eyes?

Wow. He disliked her. Intensely.

She didn't know what to do, how to behave. People didn't usually react negatively to her, especially at first glance. He obviously thought he knew her.

Or her sister.

Her stomach flip-flopped.

The man cleared his throat. His contempt drifted away from her as he bared straight white teeth in a false smile to continue speaking.

Learning his name was Sam Briton didn't provide any answers. Allie hadn't mentioned him and he was the resort manager, not an advertising conference attendee. Charlotte watched him carefully, making sure she'd never met him, not even briefly. His deep-set, intense blue eyes would be striking, if not for his blatant animosity. He was average in height, with a strong jaw and short, dark hair. He had broad shoulders, a narrow waist, and wore his clothes well—khakis and a navy button-down shirt with the resort logo. His sleeves were rolled up, revealing the forearms of a person who stayed fit. He was definitely a handsome man she was sure she'd not soon forget.

"How do you know him?" Veronica whispered frantically as she tugged at Charlotte's elbow. "He is one *very* hot guy. Too bad he so obviously dislikes you."

Charlotte shrugged and sipped her drink. She'd forgotten Veronica stood next to her. In fact, the woman hadn't left her side since they'd first spoken. How should she answer Veronica's question? Charlotte didn't know this Sam Briton, but obviously Allie did. How *did* they know each other, and what had Allie done to earn his aversion?

Charlotte knew Allie had a troubled past, but she'd worked hard to move on. Especially since she and Jack had gotten together.

"I hope your stay here will be very rewarding, as well as relaxing," Sam was saying. "If you have any problems or questions, please don't hesitate to contact me or one of the staff. Breakfast is served from seven to nine. Enjoy your evening!" He waved, leaving everyone to talk among themselves.

Whew! This Sam person was leaving. No more caustic stares. She'd be sure to steer clear of him this week.

When he headed straight for her, she nearly inhaled a sip of her drink. She began coughing and someone took her drink from her hand. Instead of making herself invisible, she'd captured everyone's attention.

"Come with me." Sam took her by the elbow and roughly guided her away from the group. His grip tightened the farther away they got from the reception.

Unable to voice her opinion of his actions because she was still coughing, she finally jerked her elbow from his grasp. "Ouch!"

"Sorry." His apology didn't sound genuine.

He moved his hand to her lower back and his touch was anything but gentle.

They were alone in the middle of the hallway, past the sign that read Employees Only. She stopped and faced him. "Where are you taking me?" She cleared her throat. "I'm fine now. I just need some water."

He didn't speak, merely spun her around and continued guiding her to an office. The sign next to the door proclaimed Sam Briton, Resort Manager.

Resort Dictator would be a more suitable title.

She should run away, yell for help, but she had to know why he disliked Allie so much. Or did he actually know Charlotte and she didn't remember him?

"Sit." He pointed to the seat closest to the wall and in front of his desk. He closed his office door with more force than necessary. Instead of taking the desk chair, he chose the matching chair next to Charlotte's. He pulled it several feet away from her and turned it so he could face her.

Charlotte was pretty sure that if steam could truly come out of one's ears, then this would be the time she'd witness it.

For what seemed like several minutes, he didn't speak, merely stared at her with narrowed eyes. He leaned forward, hands fisted on his thighs.

"Start talking." When he finally spoke, his words confused Charlotte.

She shifted in her seat. "What would you like me to say?"

He laughed, a choking sound that lacked humor. He stood quickly and pounded a fist on his desk, making everything on it vibrate. Then he leaned in so close to Charlotte that she could differentiate the dark blue rings surrounding his lighter blue irises.

"We had an agreement." He spoke slowly through gritted teeth, but his self-control was back.

"An agreement?" Maybe she could get him to elaborate.

"Don't be coy. We both know you're too con-niving to play the innocent."

Conniving. No one had ever called Charlotte that. "Maybe you can be more specific." She kept her tone even, hoping to cajole rather than anger him. For some reason, she refused to blurt out she wasn't Allie—maybe because the details were really none of his business.

"Specific?" He straightened to his full height and paced in the small space. He stopped be-hind his desk. "You want specific? I'll give you specific. We agreed we'd never lay eyes on each other again in this lifetime." He flattened both hands on his desk when he leaned over it, his eyes venomous. "Is that specific enough for you?"

Tears built behind her eyes. She fought them with every bit of self-control she possessed. No one had ever been this angry at her before. Even if Sam thought she was Allie, at this particular moment, his rage was directed at Charlotte.

"That's easy to do." She stood, head held high, smoothed her skirt and turned to leave his office.

"Sit down!" This time he shouted. "I ought to call Security and have them detain you until I can figure out how to get you off this island."

She grabbed at the arms of the chair to steady herself and did as she was told. This was *not* the vacation she'd expected. Her heart pounded in her chest as she came to a decision. Maybe when he heard the truth, he would calm down. "I'm not who you think I am."

He snickered.

"Really, I'm not Allie Miller."

"So I'm supposed to believe you're not Alley Cat—excuse me, Allie Miller—even though you look and sound exactly like her and you're at an advertising conference?"

This wasn't going well. "She's my twin sister."

"Ha! That's a good one. Not as good as the scheme you came up with back in Charleston, but certainly worth hearing about." He sat in his desk chair, leaned back with fingers laced behind his head and spoke to the ceiling. "Go on. This should be interesting."

Scheme? What kind of scheme? Nothing Allie had shared with her. Charlotte sat dumbfounded.

"I'm waiting." Sam's tone made it clear he would brook no more deceit.

Where to begin? "My name is Charlotte, and Allie Miller is my twin sister."

"Charlotte? As in 'rhymes with harlot?'" His words burned her like acid.

"You're being unfair, as well as rude." She spoke as firmly as she was able. "Please let me explain before you pass judgment."

He went back to contemplating the ceiling. "Go on."

"Allie and I are identical twins who were adopted by two different families as newborns. We met a few months ago."

Sam guffawed.

"It's true." Charlotte cleared her throat, needing to sound truthful to both Sam and herself. "Our birth mother delivered us in a prison hospital and her greedy lawyer brokered separate private adoptions. Neither of us knew we had a sister, let alone a twin." But her mother knew. A stab in her heart from another direction.

"Nice touch, mother gave birth behind bars."

"It's the truth." She wasn't sure why she was telling him all this, since he obviously didn't want to believe her.

"Why are *you* here and not your other personality, I mean your 'twin'?" His use of finger quotes was when her patience ended.

She stood, making herself as tall as possible, her neck straining at the effort. "That's it. You have no right to keep me here. You don't believe a word I've said, so I'm leaving." She crossed the small office to the closed door.

Before she could grasp the handle, he dashed around the desk, knocking his chair back into the window ledge. He slapped his palm on his closed office door above her head.

She turned to confront him, not realizing how close he was. He hovered mere inches away. She placed her palm on his chest, planning to push him back.

Instead, she stopped when his warmth penetrated her hand, then spread up her arm and through the rest of her body. Confused, she gazed at him.

His pupils dilated. In that instant, crazy as it sounded, she knew his physical reaction mirrored hers.

Before she could protest, his mouth was on hers and his chest pressed her against the door. His kiss was angry. And erotic. Instead of fighting him, and without thinking, she slid her arms around his waist to the firm muscles of his back. She wanted him closer, as close as two people could get.

He moved his mouth to her neck, shoving her sweater from her shoulder to nibble on her bare skin. Then he hiked up her long skirt while his mouth traveled to nip sharply at her earlobe. He whispered, "Is this what you came here for, Alley Cat? To finish what you started in Charleston?"

THE WOMAN CALLING herself Charlotte struggled to push him away. Sam backed off at once. Reason had returned. What had gotten into him? His physical pull to her was unlike anything he'd ever experienced. But he'd never forced himself on a woman, and he wasn't about to start now.

He walked to the window and leaned on the sill with both hands. The sun was a mere sliver from being completely set over the calm ocean.

His office door opened and closed. He didn't need to turn around to know the woman was gone.

What was wrong with him? One minute he was angry, the next he was turned on. He'd never had that reaction to her back in South Carolina, although she'd tried her best to seduce him. That had been part of her plan. Keep him close so he wouldn't figure out what she and her boyfriend were up to.

What kind of scam was she running now? Twin sister? He laughed. That wasn't very inventive.

Why had she risked coming here? She had to know he'd be here. He'd been offered the promotion to manager at the Grand Peacock right before they'd agreed to steer clear of each other.

That had been what, four years ago? As assistant manager of the resort's Charleston property, he'd been tasked to work with Allie. Back then, she worked for a small cosmetics firm out of Wilmington, Delaware. She made regular visits to the resort's boutique that carried the cosmetics.

She'd come on to him soon after they met, insinuating she could be quite discreet. He hadn't been attracted to her, and besides, he never got involved with business associates or resort guests. His goal to rise to the top within Blaise Enterprises came second only to his children.

Allie had taken his rebuttal in stride, leaving

him perplexed and with a slightly bruised ego. Not until he discovered her real scheme did he ever think of her as anything but an attractive hustler trying to claw her way into power.

He went to his computer to see what he could find out about Allie, using her current alias. Was she using the same last name? She'd conveniently given him only a first name. He didn't find anything under Charlotte Miller that fit the woman he had just met.

There was a knock on his office door.

"Come in." Had she come back?

His assistant, Gayle, opened the door and stuck her head in. "Mr. Briton?" Her unexpected appearance outside his office was never a good sign.

"What is it?" Adrenaline made his skin tingle. Now what?

She entered his office and ran her fingers through her wavy shoulder-length, strawberry-blond hair. She blew air through her lips. "I can't believe this happened. There's a couple in bungalow 6 who are claiming his phone was stolen from their room."

"He's sure he didn't misplace it?"

"That's what I asked. They've called it. The phone goes directly to voice mail as if it's turned off."

"Did you ask if he had any location software on it?"

"He said it's a new phone and he hadn't gotten around to activating it yet." Gayle crossed her arms over her abdomen. "He wants to speak to the manager."

Sam nodded. "Is he in his room?"

"I told him you'd come to his room as soon as possible. Bungalow 6," she repeated. "Their names are Bob and Evelyn Snyder. They've stayed here several times before."

Sam recognized their names.

"I've got this. Thanks." Gayle left his office and Sam called his head of security. "Hey, George, how's it going?"

"Just fine, Mr. Briton. What can I do for you?" George was a retired New York City detective who considered this job practically a year-round vacation.

"We've had a burglary." Sam proceeded to fill George in on the situation. "So I'd like you to beef up patrols, especially around the bungalows, and monitor the video footage."

He thought about Allie's arrival bringing a whole host of problems. Broken elevator, water leak, now a burglary. How much more could happen in less than forty-eight hours?

He would definitely need to keep a constant eye on that woman.

CHARLOTTE DIDN'T WAIT for the elevator, instead chose the open staircase to return to her room.

She didn't want to run into anyone else who knew her sister. And she couldn't get away fast enough from that awful Sam Briton.

Charlotte was beyond mortified by her reaction to that Neanderthal. How dare he treat her with such disrespect. And how dare she react to his kiss as if she'd been starved for him. She'd clung to his body, matching his ardor with her own. She put her cool hands to her face, which burned with embarrassment.

Her knees were about to buckle by the time she reached her room. She settled herself on one of the two Hemingway-style chairs and propped her feet on the matching ottoman. The breeze coming from the balcony through the open sliding doors fluttered the sheers.

The phone rang unexpectedly and Charlotte jumped. She picked up the extension on the table next to her. "Hello?" Her voice quavered and she cleared her throat.

"Hi, Allie, this is Veronica. I'm sorry to bother you, but are you okay? That manager guy seemed pretty angry."

Charlotte tried to play it off. "I'm fine. It was just a little misunderstanding. In fact—"

"Misunderstanding?" Veronica wasn't going to let it go.

"He thought I was someone from his past." Charlotte wasn't about to give her more than that.

"Oh. Okay. I'm glad you straightened him out then."

If only.

When Charlotte didn't comment, Veronica said, "Are you ready for tomorrow?"

Oh no, now what? "Ready?" Tomorrow couldn't possibly be worse than today.

"For the conference. I picked up your name tag and welcome folder when I registered. I figured you'd like to see a schedule. Looks like Raymond Foster will be here Monday."

"Raymond Foster?"

"You *have* heard the news that he's looking for a new agency, right? Everyone's been talking about it. He's been with the same one since the eighties."

"I have," Charlotte answered. She decided to try again to correct Veronica's misconception. "I need to tell you something. Allie Miller is my twin sister. My name is Charlotte Harrington."

Veronica was silent for a few seconds and then she burst out laughing. "Good one, Allie. Although I don't think you'll get anyone to believe that."

"Why not?"

"Because you're known for making up things, especially to win accounts. No one is going to fall for your 'twin' story."

"But it's true."

"If you say so." Veronica didn't sound convinced.

Charlotte dropped the subject. "Thank you for registering me." Allie should be here. This account sounded like the one she needed to keep her fledgling business going.

"Not a problem," Veronica said. "I'll meet you at breakfast and give it to you."

Instead of saying no, Charlotte answered, "Sounds good." She hung up, then closed her eyes and inhaled slowly. She needed to try again to call her sister. She retrieved her cell phone and located Allie's cell number.

Once again, the call went to voice mail.

"Allie, it's Charlotte. I really need to talk to you. There's a man coming to the conference, Raymond Foster, and rumor has it he's looking for a new agency. You should be here."

She disconnected and looked at her phone. How could she help her sister? For the next hour, she called Allie every fifteen minutes with no luck.

She changed for bed, not caring that she'd missed dinner. While brushing her teeth, she looked in the bathroom mirror and suddenly knew how she might be able to help.

Everyone she'd met, including Sam Briton, thought she was Allie.

So that's who she was going to be. Honestly, it might be fun to be someone other than sad Charlotte for a change.

SAM EXITED THE main building and headed to
bungalow 6. He made a mental note to check
with Maintenance to see if the elevator part was
on its way. As was his habit, he surveyed his
surroundings as he walked down the stone path
through the canopy of palms. He watched for
landscaping that needed trimming back from
the walkway or anything else that might need
attention.

The Snyders were repeat customers now that
they were both retired, and he'd do whatever was
necessary to keep them happy. He had a difficult time believing the man's phone was stolen.
More than likely, he'd just misplaced it. The resort had rarely experienced a theft problem since
he'd been here. He had dealt with illegal activity
at the other Grand Peacock resorts he'd worked
at, but seldom at this one.

He knocked on the Snyders' door. Footsteps
became increasingly louder until Bob Snyder
opened the door.

"Come in, Sam." Bob shook Sam's hand and
gestured to where his wife was seated on the
striped sofa near the floor-to-ceiling sliding glass
doors. "You remember my wife, Evelyn."

"Of course. How are you?"

"I'm doing well." Evelyn and Bob were the
classic couple who, over their long marriage, had
come to look like each other. Short, round and

gray, with bifocals and a passion for matching outfits. Today they wore red-and-yellow floral shirts with white cotton pants.

"Good to hear." Sam took a seat on the chair across from the sofa where Bob sat next to his wife. "I'm sorry to hear you've had some trouble. Your phone is missing?"

"That's right." Bob rested one foot on his opposite knee.

"When did you notice it was gone?"

Bob looked at Evelyn. "About an hour ago?"

Evelyn nodded.

"Where did you see it last?" Sam still hoped the phone had been misplaced.

"I remember setting it down on the dresser when we got back from our walk. That was around three."

"Did anyone come to the door, or did you leave the bungalow after that?"

"Only when the front desk called."

"At least, we thought it was the front desk." Evelyn's voice trembled, and Bob patted her hand.

"What do you mean you *thought* it was the front desk?" Sam squirmed in his chair.

"We got a call asking us both to come to the front desk immediately. The man said there was a problem with some of the guests' credit cards, and we needed to bring our credit card and ID for verification."

Sam narrowed his eyes. "I never heard anything about this."

"Neither had your desk clerk. Tom, I think it was," Bob said. "He had no idea what we were talking about."

"Do you think that's when your phone was stolen?"

Bob shrugged. "Must have been. I didn't notice it was missing until quite a while later, but that's the only time we were away from it."

"Is there anything else missing?"

"Everything else of value was already locked in the room safe. The phone call made it seem urgent that we complied, so I didn't think about my phone. I only had it out to be sure we didn't get a text from our son. He and his wife are expecting their first child in a few weeks."

Sam got up and walked around the room, checking the windows and French doors leading to the private hot tub. Whoever took the phone must be an employee—or working with one of them—to have gotten into the bungalow without breaking in. The front door automatically locked when it was shut, so a person would need a master key to get in. Sam couldn't imagine any of his staff taking such a risk. Someone must be desperate to have pulled a stunt like this.

A few minutes later, after assuring the Snyders he would take care of the matter and reimburse them for a new phone, he also promised them two free nights at the resort.

Sam walked back to the lobby, trying to wrap his mind around the blatant theft that had taken place during his watch. He needed to get a written warning out to all guests and employees as soon as possible.

And definitely keep a close eye on Alley Cat. Her arrival on the island coincided with this theft, and he wouldn't put it past her to be up to her old tricks.

CHARLOTTE ROSE EARLY the next morning, her head foggy and her eyes barely able to focus. Sleep had eluded her, so she had given up and dressed in shorts and a T-shirt to run on the beach to clear her head.

She'd tried several more times to call Allie last night, with no success. She left her sister messages each time. Charlotte finally left a message on Jack's phone, too, which he also wasn't answering.

Charlotte kept a steady pace down the beach. The weather was gorgeous, sunny and not too hot with a constant, gentle breeze. Rhode Island rarely provided mornings like this except for a few weeks in the summer. Definitely not in October.

Unfortunately, she wasn't the only one with the idea to run on the beach.

He was coming toward her, still a few hundred feet away. Although she'd met Sam barely twelve hours ago, she recognized him immediately from his body shape and the way his long legs ate up the ground.

Without warning, both her mind and body recalled the tension in his well-developed, muscular arms, and the expert way his mouth had reduced her to a quivering idiot.

Should she run past without acknowledging him? Look the other way? Nod at him? Wave?

Her heart rate increased. She sucked in more air and got a stitch in her side, but no way would she slow to a walk with him approaching her. She fought hard against the urge to stop and double over in pain.

He wouldn't see her distress, no matter what.

His eyes were hidden by his sunglasses, making it impossible to tell if he looked at her as he ran past. His pace was smooth and effortless. He was shirtless and had the sculpted physique to do so.

No words were spoken by either of them.

As soon as he passed by, she stopped short and grabbed her side, sucking in oxygen in small bursts. What was wrong with her? She ran at the gym on a regular basis and rarely had endurance problems.

"Are you okay?" Sam had doubled back. His

unexpected question startled her, doing nothing for her already spiked vitals.

"I'm fine." Her choked words contradicted her statement.

"Straighten up." He came around behind her and pressed a warm hand to her left side.

"Ouch." She tried to move away from him, away from his touch. Especially the heat transferring from his body to hers.

"I'm trying to help." He pressed again, massaging gently. "Right here?" At her nod, he added, "Take deep breaths from your belly. Slowly. That's it. Now exhale and take another deep breath."

Deep breathing was nearly impossible with him so close.

The pain slowly subsided and he moved away quickly. She was left standing there with nothing to say but, "Thank you."

He nodded.

"This never happens to me at the gym." Why was she explaining?

"It's easy to overdo it here on the beach. The great scenery makes you forget how far you've gone."

That was the first friendly thing he'd said to her in their short acquaintance. At least he had no clue that his sudden appearance was what made her pulse and breathing go haywire.

He glanced at his watch. "I need to get going. Are you okay now, Allie?"

She swallowed, straightening her back. "I'm fine." Her words were sharper than she intended, but it bothered her that he still thought of her as Allie. Even if she *had* decided to be Allie for the week, he wasn't aware of it.

He turned to take off again.

"You really still think I'm Allie?"

Her words stopped him and he faced her.

His brow furrowed, but she couldn't gauge his eyes through his sunglasses. "You've given me no reason to believe you're anyone other than Allie Miller. Can anyone verify your identity? Do you have some ID to prove it?"

"Of course I have ID, but it's in my room. I'll bring it to your office later, if I must." Telling him to check the hotel computer would only confuse him more. Allie had added Charlotte's name to the room without removing her own. For all he knew, she could be either one of them.

"Isn't there anyone at the conference that will vouch for you? I could ask around."

"No!" Charlotte shouted, reaching out to him. She stopped before she actually touched him. "No, please, don't say anything."

He cocked his head at her vehemence. "So if—and I say *if*—you aren't really Allie, then why are you here and not her? Are you in advertising, too?"

She couldn't answer. After deciding to pretend to be Allie, she should probably let Sam believe that's who she was. Even if deep down she wanted him to know the real Charlotte.

He laughed, the same humorless laugh from last night. "You're losing your touch, Allie. You used to be a much better liar." He took a step in the direction of the resort.

She grabbed his arm to stop him, releasing him a second later. "Please…promise you won't mention this to anyone. Everyone believes I'm Allie and I've decided I'd rather keep it that way."

He didn't answer at first. What she wouldn't give to see those eyes of his behind the dark lenses. "Somehow I'm not surprised you're still scheming. We'll see what happens."

"What does that mean? You already think I'm Allie. I'm simply asking you to keep thinking that."

"You need to prove yourself to me before I can make any promises." He checked his watch again. "Now I really do need to go."

He ran off before she could organize her thoughts and ask how he expected her to prove herself to him.

CHAPTER FOUR

SAM QUICKLY DRIED off after his shower. Running into Allie this morning had destroyed his concentration. What was it about her that had him physically reacting like a horny teenager? He never should have touched her. Massaging her side stitch away had been excruciating. He'd never been the least turned on by her when they'd met several years ago. What had changed?

Could she actually *be* Allie's long-lost identical twin the way she claimed?

He laughed. That was preposterous.

Then he shook his head. If she *were* Allie's twin, she had identical genes and was bound to be as untrustworthy. No matter what, she was bad news.

By the time he made it to the lobby, conference attendees were everywhere. Breakfast was ending and workshops would begin soon. His gaze stopped at Allie, her still-damp hair falling in waves to just below her chin. His mind automatically wandered to what she might have looked like in the shower, his body craving her wet, soapy curves.

He shook his head. This madness needed to stop.

Then he saw her name tag. He could barely make it out from where he stood, but it was definitely Allie Miller. If she were truly her twin, then why wasn't she using her real name? Charlotte something. Wasn't that the name she'd given him?

Sam checked his watch. He filled a cup with coffee from the buffet and followed his assistant conference manager down the hall toward his office.

"Everything going okay?" Sam asked Katie, who remained in his doorway after he entered his office.

Her head bobbed excitedly, making her light blond ponytail swing. "So far, so good." Her excitement was contagious.

"Let me know if you need help with anything and I'll get you some." Sam walked around to the other side of his desk. With Ben in England taking care of his parents, Sam would need to make sure Katie could handle things by herself. Ben had complete confidence in her, but she was fresh out of college and had worked at the Grand Peacock less than a year. Sam reached for the messages on his desk and sipped his coffee.

"I might need an extra person directing peo-

ple for meals," she told him. "I already recruited
Tom to help me decorate for Sunday night's gathering. They'd like karaoke set up, too."

"Sounds good." The less he was required to
be near Allie, the better. He was also pretty sure
their desk clerk, Tom, had a major crush on Katie.
So he'd do whatever she needed.

"I better make certain everyone gets to where
they're supposed to," Katie said.

"Good luck!"

Her chuckle came from down the hall.

He turned his attention to the message his
chief repairman had left on his desk. Sam was
pleased to see the elevator part should be in-
stalled by late that afternoon.

Next, he checked his email. George, his head
of security, needed to talk to him. Sam called
him immediately, hoping there had been no further burglaries.

"Hey, George, Sam Briton. Give me some
good news."

"I wish I could, sir. I'm afraid there's a problem with the video footage from yesterday's burglary."

"A problem?" Having cameras along the outdoor paths leading to the bungalows was always
a challenge, thanks to the unpredictability of nature, which was why they checked the cameras
daily. They were mostly there for the safety of
the guests in case someone got hurt. Criminal

activity was seldom a problem, so the cameras weren't monitored 24/7.

"There are four minutes and nineteen seconds of palm fronds waving in the wind," George reported. "Someone moved the cameras."

"Moved them? Can you tell who did it and how?" No way could someone pull something like that off and not get caught. They'd have to get up in the palm trees to get access, which would probably require a ladder.

"Looks like whoever did it knew exactly where the cameras were located. And they avoided the path. The footage shows what I assume is the couple staying at bungalow 6 walking toward the main resort. Shortly after that is when the camera is tilted and the trees are all that can be seen."

"The Snyders," Sam clarified. "Retired couple, matching outfits."

"That's them. After the four-plus minutes, the camera is aimed back where it's supposed to be."

"So it was deliberate," Sam concluded. "No chance a bird or animal bumped it."

"Correct. I'm headed out there now to see if I can find footprints off the path, evidence of a ladder or any other clues."

"Good," Sam said. "Let me know what you find."

CHARLOTTE SAT AT a small table in the lobby, sipping a cup of coffee that was upsetting her already roiling stomach. Could she pull off this act? Make everyone believe she was Allie? She told herself it would be easy because no one believed she was Allie's twin, no matter how many times she repeated it.

Her sister still hadn't returned her calls and neither had Jack. Charlotte had awoken in the middle of the night and remembered that Allie and Jack had planned a trip this weekend. A New England trip, Vermont, she thought they'd said.

Charlotte could have emailed them, but figured if they weren't answering their phones, then they weren't checking email, either. She also surmised they might be in an area with poor cell coverage because Allie was always good about calling Charlotte back. And hearing that Raymond Foster was coming would surely pique her interest. According to what Charlotte read on the internet last night, he owned a conglomerate of most of the food brands in her fridge and pantry.

Veronica and Jared were seated across from Charlotte. From their constant chatter, they were either super relaxed or super nervous. She couldn't tell which.

"Don't you just adore this place?" Veronica was saying. "I'd love to bottle that salty ocean breeze and take it home with me."

Home. That's where Charlotte should be. Not conducting a ruse that could go wrong at any moment. Her stomach flipped again. What if she ruined things for Allie instead of helped her?

Jared laughed at Veronica's suggestion. "That would just make me miss this place more."

They continued their discussion on how to take the island home with them until the young woman in charge—Katie—informed them breakfast was over and workshops would begin in a few minutes. She gave directions to where things were located, reminding them that they'd received a resort map in their registration materials.

Charlotte felt confident about knowing the names of a few people. That was a decent start in pretending to be Allie. Her memory for names was pretty good, thanks to her inner artist that kept accurate pictures of people stored in her brain. Just never ask her what she ate for breakfast yesterday.

She'd checked the schedule for the workshops. Raymond Foster would be doing a two-hour presentation Monday morning with regards to what a client wanted and how to win big accounts. Charlotte thought she should attend that one so she had an idea of what to tell Allie if her sister wanted to pitch to him.

That gave her two days to get Allie to return her call.

SAM LEANED BACK in his desk chair and studied the week's schedule Katie had provided. Nothing out of the ordinary, but he could see a few holes where he might be needed with Ben gone.

His phone rang.

"Sam Briton," he answered after the first ring.

"Hey, Sam," his father-in-law greeted him. "Just checking in to let you know the kids and I arrived safely in Fort Lauderdale."

"Good to know," Sam said. "Are my munchkins behaving?"

"Of course they are," John answered with a chuckle. "How's it going there? Are you managing okay without Ben?"

"Katie's doing a great job, so far," Sam told him. "There's been only one hiccup." He decided on the fly that John would be a good person to talk to about the Allie Miller situation since he was fully aware of her Charleston trouble.

"A big or little problem?"

"Not sure yet," Sam replied. "Allie Miller is an attendee at the conference we're hosting."

"Allie Miller? Why is that name familiar?" Before Sam could answer, John continued, "You mean the little schemer who got caught up in that mess in Charleston?"

"The one and only."

"Is she causing trouble again?" There was agitation evident in his tone. "You better keep a close eye on that woman."

"Believe me, I am." Sam swallowed, trying not to focus on how he had been closer to *that woman* than he should have been. "We've also had a burglary." He gave John the details, including the movement of the video camera.

"Funny how it coincides with Allie Miller's appearance," John said.

That's what Sam thought, too. "Yeah, real funny." But Sam wasn't laughing.

They chatted a few more minutes about what the kids were up to and then Emma wanted to talk to Sam.

"Hi, Daddy," she greeted him.

"Hey there, cutie. Whatcha' up to?"

He could tell by what she called him what kind of mood she was in. "Dad" was her usual form of address, and "Daddy" meant she wanted something. Look out if she called him "Father." Just thinking about that superior tone gave him the willies.

"Nothing much. Papa's cook made us chocolate chip pancakes for breakfast, and later we're going bowling so Oliver will shut up about it."

Sam grinned. He missed them, even their bickering. "That sounds like fun."

"I guess so." She paused. "Daddy, I was wondering if I could get an advance—"

"I knew you wanted something." Sam kept his tone light. "An advance on your allowance? For what?"

"Oh, Dad." Emma's disdain came through loud and clear. She lowered her voice. "I found a birthday gift for Papa. It's his birthday next week, you know. There's a half-off coupon on-line, but it expires tomorrow."

Sam had completely forgotten about John's birthday. Thankfully, he had a wonderful daughter to remind him. "Tell you what, send me the link and I'll pick up the tab. No need to get an advance on your allowance."

"Really? That would be great! You're the best, Daddy." She went on to tell him about the deal she found to have a book made of family photos.

"That sounds like the perfect gift," Sam agreed. "We can gather pictures when you get home. Is Oliver around? I need to get back to work or your grandfather might replace me."

Emma laughed as expected and then said, "There's one more thing."

"Sure, what is it?"

"I heard Papa talking to you and he mentioned that lady's name. Allie Miller. Isn't she the one who caused all that trouble a few years ago?"

Emma had an outstanding memory. She'd been about eight at the time of Allie's appearance in their lives. Old enough to be aware there was a problem, but too young to process the details. "One and the same," he said, "but don't worry. I'm keeping an eye on her." A very close eye. Maybe too close.

"Okay." Her answer was hesitant, then she added, "I really don't like her." She spoke in earnest. "But I'll help to watch her when Papa brings us back to the island. I'm not going to let her cause trouble again."

He was about to tell his daughter that he could handle Allie without her help, but Oliver grabbed the phone to tell Sam all about Papa's new 3-D television.

As soon as he finished speaking with Oliver and disconnected, Katie showed up in his office doorway. "I have a list of conference attendees. All but two people have checked in."

"Is one of them Allie Miller?" If the woman he kissed was really Allie's twin, then Allie would be one of the missing.

Katie checked her list. "No, she arrived and checked in." She consulted her notes. "We got a call about Peter Reynaud. He had a family emergency, but Jerry Cummings is a no-show." She handed him the list.

The truth stared him in the face. Allie Miller was attending the conference, not her twin. He should have known when he had first seen her, and again when she'd worn the name tag. She'd lied about having an identical twin. But why? What was she up to this time?

CHARLOTTE SPENT THE morning in a teak lounge chair on the beach while everyone attended workshops. There were two or three workshops taking place at the same time, so she figured no one would miss her. They'd think she had attended a different workshop than them.

She'd brought her camera and sketch pad, but after taking several pictures of the resort behind her and the ocean view in front of her, she'd packed them away in her tote bag. Then she'd luxuriated in the sunny day and the peace she had found with the sounds of the ocean and the various birds calling as they'd flown over the water searching for food.

"There you are!"

Charlotte turned to see it was the woman from the plane. When they'd checked in together, Charlotte had learned her name was Mona. She stopped next to Charlotte's chair, hands on her hips and her long, flowing skirt flapping in the breeze. "If I didn't know better, I'd think you were avoiding me. I haven't seen you since we checked in."

Charlotte smiled kindly. Mona *did* know better. "I've been around. I needed a break to clear my head." Charlotte quickly changed the subject. "How are you?"

Mona grabbed her floppy brimmed hat, which was about to blow off her head. "Wonderful! Were you in that workshop about transfer?" She didn't wait for an answer, pulling her hat down over her mop of resistant curls. "It wasn't just about transfer, but other techniques, as well.

Most of them I've heard of or used before, but it was a good refresher."

"I missed that one." Charlotte had no idea what transfer was, but filed it away to look up later. Hopefully, Mona wouldn't ask her what workshops she *had* attended. The woman was probably a very nice person, but Charlotte needed time to get used to her big personality.

Veronica and Jared were more Charlotte's speed.

"Anyway," Mona continued, adjusting her sunglasses, "Katie has been looking everywhere for you."

"Me?" Charlotte pointed at herself. "Why?"

"How should I know?" Mona said on a shrug. "But I'll take your lounge chair since you're getting up."

The woman didn't sugarcoat her thoughts and feelings, Charlotte would give her that much. You knew right where you stood with her.

Charlotte rose from her chair, unhappy to be leaving the salty air and sunshine behind. Not to mention the peacefulness of the ocean. At least before Mona interrupted.

As Charlotte made her way across the sand, carrying her sandals in one hand and her tote bag in the other, she puzzled over why Katie wanted to speak to her. Had she figured out Charlotte wasn't Allie? But why would she care? The conference fee was paid and Katie worked for the hotel, not the company that coordinated the conference.

The lobby was deserted when Charlotte arrived, except for a young woman at the registration desk. "Do you know where I can find Katie?" Charlotte asked.

The young woman gave her a friendly smile and pointed in the direction of the hallway leading to Sam Briton's office. "She's probably in her office back that way."

Charlotte nodded. "Thank you." She turned in that direction and paused ever so slightly. She had no wish to run into Sam again. Not only was her body remembering what happened between them in his office, but on the beach, as well. Her hand touched her side where he'd massaged her cramp away.

Her head held high, she took the plunge and headed to Katie's office. The door was open, but her office was empty. Now what?

Just as she was about to look for paper and pencil to leave a note, Katie came up behind her. "Ms. Miller?"

Charlotte spun around. Her pulse rate accelerated as if she'd been caught doing something illegal. "Yes," she said breathlessly, then continued in a stronger tone, "I was about to leave you a note. You were looking for me?"

Katie smiled. "Yes, I was. It's actually Mr. Briton who wants to speak with you. He was dealing with some other issues and asked me to locate you."

Charlotte's stomach revolted. She didn't want to talk to Sam Briton...ever. If she'd known Sam was the one who'd requested her presence, she would have stayed on the beach.

Wow! Where did that come from? Maybe the beach air was giving her the courage to stand up for herself, even if it was only in her head. Although, *thinking* she'd stay on the beach and actually *staying* there to spite Sam were two different things. After all, he was in charge of the resort. He could easily make trouble for her.

"Please step into my office, Ms. Miller." The male voice coming down the hall was already intimately familiar. Instead of allowing Sam to intimidate her, she straightened her shoulders and tried not to be too annoyed by his tone.

Without speaking, she did as he requested. His presence was tangible as he followed her into his office. Thankfully, he left the door open as they took positions on either side of his desk. She didn't need a repeat of last night's regrettable incident or their chance meeting on the beach this morning.

Now if only she could erase the unsettling images from her mind. Even in the bright light of day, the ghostly impression of last evening's intimate clinch remained front and center in her brain.

"Have a seat." Sam's tone was commanding as he lowered himself into his chair.

She looked at the chair next to her. "I prefer to stand." Was she channeling Allie's self-confidence? This could be habit-forming. Standing up for herself felt pretty good. Especially when it was out loud and not merely in her head.

He shrugged, but his eyes narrowed as if he didn't like her newfound strength. Not that preferring to stand was actually a definitive issue. He probably didn't care.

He reached across his desk for a piece of paper that looked as if it contained a list. His shirtsleeves were rolled up to below his elbows and Charlotte found herself fascinated once again by his well-developed, tan forearms. Her gaze traveled to his large hands with their long, slim fingers and neatly trimmed nails.

"Allie?" From Sam's tone, Charlotte suspected it wasn't the first time he'd addressed her.

She lifted her chin a millimeter. "Yes?" She needed to get used to answering to her sister's name if she had half a chance at fooling anyone, especially that big client.

"So I guess the jig is up."

"Excuse me?"

"Last night you tried to convince me you're not Allie, but her 'twin' sister." He used air quotes, which she disliked immensely, and his mouth twisted as if to mock her. "Charlotte. Isn't that the name you used?"

Before answering, she sat down in the chair and pulled it closer to the desk so they were eye to eye. She chose her words with deliberation. "My name *is* Charlotte, and Allie Miller *is* my identical twin sister."

He slammed the paper down in front of her. "Then why is Allie Miller on this list of conference attendees and not *Charlotte*? Why are you wearing your sister's name tag?"

She put a hand to her name tag and swallowed with difficulty. People in the art world didn't speak to her like that. "I'm going to trust you'll keep this between us."

He stared at her, and she had trouble finding her voice, as well as the words. Where was that self-confidence now?

She spread out her hands on the desk. "Here's the deal. When I arrived, I found out there's a man, a presenter, who is looking to switch advertising agencies. I can't get in touch with my sister to let her know, but I'm hoping to talk the man into allowing Allie to pitch to him. She needs a large account like his to keep her business going. Meanwhile, everyone thinks I'm Allie, no matter how many times I've told them I'm her twin. They just think I'm lying." *Exactly like you do.* "So I'll use that to Allie's advantage."

"I'm not surprised." He turned his back to her

and faced the ocean through the window. "Just another lie to protect yourself."

"What!" Charlotte leaned toward him, hands flat on his desk. She spoke to his back, wishing she could face him eye to eye. "Why won't you believe me? I'm telling the truth!" She sucked in a breath—she should have just shoved her ID in his face when they'd first met. But at this point, she almost didn't care what he believed. *Almost.* "I'm *not* Allie. I'm Charlotte." It took a lot to make her mad, but she was almost there. "Is that why you summoned me here? To ask why I'm wearing my sister's name tag? You could have had Katie ask me."

He was silent for so long, she thought maybe their conversation was over. Then he asked, "Do you know how to climb a palm tree?"

"What?" The question was so far off topic that she nearly laughed. "Why would I climb a palm tree?"

He spun around to face her. "Never mind." He tapped a pencil on his desk. He didn't look at her when he said, "We're done here, *Allie.* I don't know what your game is, but I expect you to stay out of trouble this week."

Charlotte's eyes widened and she stared at him for a long moment. Talking to the jerk was a worthless cause. She stomped out of his office and headed directly to her room. She needed time alone to get her emotions back under control. The man made her ridiculously angry and frustrated. So unlike her true self. She rarely found someone who irritated her that much.

She ripped off her name tag lanyard and threw it on the bed. Then she opened the French doors leading onto the balcony, choosing to stretch out on the lounge chair overlooking the ocean. Breathing deeply and closing her eyes, the peacefulness of her surroundings slowly, but effectively, calmed her.

Several minutes later, she rose from her chair and stood at the iron railing to watch the ocean. She smiled. The sunlight reflecting on the water inspired her to grab her camera.

Feeling rejuvenated after capturing many different angles through the lens, she checked the time to see that lunch had already begun.

Charlotte threw the lanyard over her head and reached the lobby a few minutes later. She helped herself to the food set up on long tables.

Carrying a water bottle under her arm, a green salad in a bowl and a plate with a half sandwich and tropical fruit, she stepped outside to the lanai and peered at the square tables to locate a free seat.

She'd have been happier taking her food onto the beach or to her room for some more alone time, but instead she gravitated to the chair Jared and Veronica had waiting for her as they had promised at breakfast.

"Thanks for saving me a seat," she said and meant it sincerely. These two were the bright spots in this trip, as well as her only information about what to tell Allie regarding Raymond Foster.

"I assume Katie found you," Veronica said before Charlotte could sit down. "She was asking everyone if they'd seen you." At Charlotte's nod, Veronica asked, "So what did she want?"

Charlotte set her plate down and pulled out her chair. "Turns out, it wasn't Katie who wanted to see me. It was the resort manager, Sam Briton."

Veronica choked on her sudden intake of breath. "That hot guy who dragged you to his office last night like a caveman?"

"That's the one." Charlotte was glad she hadn't confided in anyone about what actually happened in his office. She had merely told her new friends that Sam had mistaken her for someone he knew back in South Carolina. Someone he didn't care for.

"What did he want?" Jared took a bite of his sandwich.

"He wanted to apologize again for last night." That seemed like a credible reason. She congratulated herself for coming up with it so easily.

Before they could ask Charlotte more questions, Katie rang a bell to get everyone's attention.

"This is your fifteen-minute warning," she

said in her perky voice. "Lunch is almost over and workshops will continue until five o'clock. Please read your provided schedule for times and locations. I'll be around to answer any questions." She glanced at the paper she held. "Dinner will be served at six o'clock, followed by some entertainment I'm sure you'll enjoy. The bar will be open until midnight." At the crowd's obvious delight at her last statement, Katie waved and retreated into the lobby.

Fifteen minutes passed quickly as Charlotte, Jared and Veronica discussed which workshops to attend. Charlotte made sure to pick a different one from them. Then they scrambled to finish lunch and get to their chosen workshop. Charlotte went along with the hurrying, thinking she could hide out on the balcony of her room for the afternoon.

That was one place she could definitely avoid running into Sam Briton.

CHAPTER FIVE

ALLIE AND JACK left early Saturday morning for Devonshire, Vermont, a small town on the north side of the Green Mountain National Forest. They had just exited US 91 in Vermont when Allie said, "I hope Charlotte made it okay. She was supposed to text me when she got there." She turned to Jack, who was driving. "Have you heard from her?"

"Not that I know of." He pointed to his phone. "Is there anything on my phone?"

She picked it up from the center console and pressed the button to wake it up. "There's a missed call from Charlotte. I wonder why she called you and not me." Allie dug through her purse for her phone. "My phone's dead. No wonder I haven't heard from her."

"Why don't you call her back on my phone," Jack suggested.

"Good idea. I'll have to charge mine when we get to the B and B. How much longer till we arrive?"

"About an hour and a half according to the

GPS," he said. "You okay waiting for lunch? There are supposed to be some nice places in town."

"That's fine. I'd rather get there sooner than later." They'd left Allie's apartment in Providence around nine and it was about a three-and-a-half-hour drive.

"I wish the leaves hadn't already dropped," she said as she navigated Jack's phone to find Charlotte's number. "I also wish I knew how your stupid phone works."

He laughed. "Just go to missed calls and her number will be there."

She found it and the call went through. Unfortunately, she got Charlotte's voice mail. "Hey, Charlotte, this is Allie on Jack's phone. Mine's dead. Will charge it at the B and B. I'm guessing you made it to the island. Have fun! Talk to you soon."

She disconnected and turned off Jack's phone. "Now that we're pretty sure she made it okay, we should turn off our phones so we're not distracted."

Jack glanced at her, his eyebrows dancing and his eyes gleaming. "Sounds good to me." He turned back to concentrate on the road. "I talked to Granddad this morning and he's fine. We can turn the phones on every few hours just to check for messages."

"Deal."

Allie put their phones into her purse and sat back to enjoy the view. "Have I mentioned what a wonderful idea this was?"

Jack grinned. "We haven't even gotten to the good part yet."

CHARLOTTE AWOKE WITH a start. It took a few seconds before she realized where she was.

She must have drifted off to sleep while enjoying the peacefulness of her balcony. The lounge chair was ever so comfortable and the sounds of the ocean had calmed her into oblivion.

She checked her cell phone for the time and saw a missed call from Jack. That must have been what woke her. She listened to Allie's message. Darn! Why didn't her sister say anything about Raymond Foster? Had Allie's phone been dead since Charlotte first called late yesterday afternoon? She obviously hadn't listened to Charlotte's messages yet.

She quickly hit the button to redial Jack's number and got his voice mail. She disconnected without leaving a message. Then she tried calling Allie with the same result. She left a message this time, mentioning Raymond Foster's plans and asking Allie to call as soon as she got the message. Then Charlotte set her phone aside. What was she going to do now? She hadn't a clue how to put a presentation together. That was Allie's field of expertise. What a shame it would be if she went to all the trouble of pretending to be Allie and then her sister wasn't able to follow through to impress the client.

Popping up from her chair and heading back inside her room, she decided to look at the workshop schedule again. Maybe there was a workshop that would help her.

She'd left her tote bag and purse on a chair, but now her purse was open and things had spilled out of it. Her heart pounded. She dug into her small purse to find her wallet gone. She dumped her purse on the bed, making sure she hadn't missed it.

"Where could it be?" She spoke aloud to her empty room and looked around to see if her wallet had somehow fallen out of her purse.

No sign of it. Then she dumped out her tote bag, which she only carried to make it appear she was attending the conference. The workshop schedule drifted out.

She looked under the chair and opened the door to the hallway to see if her wallet was out there. Nothing. And nobody. Even the cleaning people were gone for the day.

She closed the door and locked the dead bolt, then stood in place for several minutes assessing the situation. She needed to report it to the hotel.

Which probably meant dealing with Sam again. He'd no doubt blame her for not securing her door with the dead bolt and then sleeping through a robbery.

She swallowed and crossed to the room phone. "I'd like to report a theft," she said when the front desk picked up.

"I'm so sorry to hear that," the man said. "Can you give me details?"

"My wallet was stolen from my purse. It was on a chair in my room while I was on the balcony. There wasn't much cash, but there were two credit cards and my driver's license."

"Is there anything else missing? Any electronics or jewelry?"

Her breath caught. She hadn't considered that. Then she realized she'd locked her laptop in the safe and her phone had been with her on the balcony. "Not that I know of."

"I'll report this to the manager and someone will be in touch with you soon."

"Thank you." She hung up, wondering which was worse—the theft or dealing with Sam. Maybe he'd send someone else since he didn't seem to like being around her any more than she liked being around him.

She got out her laptop to get a phone number for her credit card companies. By the time she'd made the calls to report the theft, there was a loud knock on her door.

Checking the peephole as a precaution, she opened the door to Sam.

"Come in." She moved back so he could do just that, unable to stop herself from breathing in his now-familiar scent.

He turned to her as she closed the door and faced him. "You had a theft?"

His businesslike attitude was actually a relief. She didn't need more threats and accusations.

"Yes." She repeated what she'd told the desk clerk.

He looked at the bed and must have noticed that her purse contents were strewn all over.

"I dumped my purse to make sure I hadn't missed my wallet."

He nodded. "And nothing else was taken?" He surveyed the room.

"I had my laptop locked in the safe and my phone was with me on the balcony."

"And you're sure you didn't leave your wallet somewhere? A pocket? Your suitcase? The safe?"

His question made her doubt herself, but for only a few seconds. "I'm sure. I know I didn't leave my purse open and things strewn about when I went out to the balcony."

"You read the note that was delivered to everyone about keeping valuables locked up?"

"Yes." The man could infuriate her in an instant. "I didn't think that meant they had to be locked up while I was still in the room."

He ignored her jab and made a few notes on

a pad he pulled from his pocket. "Why weren't you at the workshops?"

His question startled her. She was mentally exhausted trying to convince him of her identity and now he was questioning her every move. "I was learning how to climb palm trees instead."

His glare said he didn't appreciate her humor.

"I had a headache and decided to come up here to rest." Lying didn't come easily to her, but the fib wasn't far from the truth. Her pulse now pounded in her temples.

"I see."

Was he turning this on her? Blaming her for the theft? "You see what?" Her tone was sharper than she intended.

He looked up again from writing on his pad. "I *see* that you weren't feeling well and decided to skip the afternoon workshops." He stared at her and finally added, "Is that correct?"

"Yes, it is." She'd been put in her place. She straightened and asked, "What are you going to do about the theft?"

He pocketed his pad. "I'll alert our head of security and have him check the video of the hallway outside your door."

"Oh!" That was great news. "So you might be able to find my wallet?"

"That's my hope." He surveyed her room. "Let me ask you something. Had your room been cleaned before you returned or was it done during your nap on the balcony?"

"It was already done when I came up here after lunch."

He pursed his lips.

"Why does that matter?" she asked.

"Because unless your door wasn't shut tight, the only people who could have gotten in would have been staff, which includes Housekeeping. Your door was secure?"

She thought back to when she looked out into the hallway. "It was closed tight after I noticed the theft, but I can't say for sure about before." She narrowed her eyes. "You aren't trying to blame me for this, are you?"

"Not at all," but he didn't sound convincing. "I'm gathering the facts. Even if your door had been left wide open, there's no excuse for the theft." He walked to the door, his hand grasping the handle. "I'm very sorry about this, Ms. Miller. I'll be in touch."

So it was Ms. Miller, now, was it? Her frustration threatened to spill over, but she kept it in check. Without her ID, she couldn't prove who she was. Why had she been so stubborn? She should have simply waved her ID in his face the first time he'd asked for it.

He was out the door before she could say another word.

SAM LEFT ALLIE'S ROOM, wondering how she was involved in the burglary. Was it a coincidence that the thefts began with her arrival? Had she purposely made herself a victim to throw him off, or had her wallet actually been stolen? Such a coincidence to have her wallet stolen after he'd asked her for ID to prove she was Charlotte and not Allie.

He returned to his office to discover a message about another theft. Someone attending the conference hadn't locked their laptop in their safe and it was missing. He immediately dialed his head of security.

"Hey, George, we've got more problems." He filled him in on the thefts. "I'm going to talk to the guest whose laptop was stolen, but I'd like you to take a look at the video from the third-floor hallway. Both thefts were from the same floor."

"I hope we don't have the same problem we did with the outdoor video," George said.

"Same here. Also, see if there's any footage of a woman around thirty with dark, chin-length hair, either before or after the time of the thefts."

"Sure thing."

Sam disconnected and went to find Katie.

He found her in the lobby. "Make sure all the conference attendees know they need to lock up their valuables every time they leave their rooms."

She frowned. "Wasn't there a flyer distributed to the guests to make them aware of the theft?"

"For all the good it's done." He smirked.

"Has there been another problem?"

"We've had a couple of thefts in the past two days. I'd like to make it as difficult for the thief as possible."

Katie nodded. "I'll make the announcement at dinner, both before and after. That will be the next time most of them will be together."

"Sounds good." He headed back to his office. He wasn't there more than a few minutes before his phone rang. "Sam Briton."

"It's George," his head of security said briskly. "Just as we suspected. The video camera was moved again."

"Damn it! How is someone doing this without being seen?"

"Could be a group instead of an individual," George suggested. "Someone to be a watch while others do the actual dirty work."

"True." Sam rubbed a hand across his cheek. "Now the question is, what are we going to do about it? I can't keep having these thefts occur. It'll ruin the resort's reputation." As well as his own.

"I'd like to hire a few temporary people to beef up security," George said.

"But we need help now. It would take too long to find qualified people and get them to the island."

"I already have two who are living here. One is Gayle's husband. He's an ex-army MP who deployed twice to Iraq. Then there's Hayden, a former small-town Georgia police officer who works in landscaping."

"Really? I had no idea they had backgrounds like that. Go ahead, get them on board. They're both upstanding guys." He'd met Gayle's husband at their holiday party last year, and Hayden had worked for the resort since before Sam arrived. "I'm also going to call a staff meeting with my department heads to let them know they need to be more vigilant about security."

After they disconnected, Sam called the resort florist. "This is Sam Briton. I'd like a flower arrangement sent to room 323. Have the card read, 'Please accept our apology for the theft that took place at our resort.'" He paused. "Sign it 'Sam Briton.'" He wasn't sure why he was only sending flowers to Charlotte and not the other burglary victims. He also didn't know why he hadn't signed it "The Management," which was his normal procedure when an apology was necessary.

He obviously wanted her to know the flowers were from him and not a faceless corporate entity, but why?

SATURDAY-NIGHT DINNER was a festive affair. Charlotte arrived at the lanai to find a tropical extravaganza. There were fresh flower blossoms floating in clear water containers, interspersed with lit candles along each long table. There were also lights strung around the perimeter, giving a romantic feel to the area.

"There you are."

Charlotte turned at Veronica's voice. "How was your afternoon?"

"Pretty good. Where did you end up?"

She decided to be as honest as possible so she could keep her stories straight. She used the same excuse she'd given Sam. "I had a headache and went to my room."

Veronica's eyebrows rose. "Are you okay?"

Charlotte nodded. "Except that someone broke into my room while I was asleep on the balcony and stole my wallet."

The other woman slapped both hands over her open mouth, her eyes wide. "Are you kidding?"

"I wish I was. I reported it to the hotel, but I'm not sure they'll be able to recover it. It sounds like they've been having a problem with thefts recently." Charlotte purposely left out that Sam was the one who'd taken down her report, as well as the one who'd sent her the most gorgeous flowers as an apology. She didn't want to put too much emphasis on him so Veronica wouldn't pick up on the number of times Charlotte and Sam had interacted. She shrugged. "So that's all I can do, I guess."

"What about your flight home? How will you

be able to get through security without your driver's license?"

Charlotte stared at Veronica and the blood pounded in her ears. "I never even thought about that." She needed to get back to Rhode Island. She couldn't afford more than one week away from home with her art show coming up. How could she get a duplicate driver's license that fast? How long would it take? "What am I going to do?"

Veronica shrugged. "I don't know, but you better call someone at DMV to find out."

"Good idea. I'll do it later since no one will be there on a Saturday evening." There wouldn't be anyone in a DMV office until Monday morning, she was sure. As much as she'd like to run back to her room to check the DMV website for the procedure, she had plenty of time before then.

"Let's get a drink and grab seats so we can sit together." Veronica led the way to the bar and they each ordered the same umbrella drink as last night's.

The same drink Charlotte had choked on before being unceremoniously corralled into Sam's office for a verbal battering. She stopped the memory there, before she softened her opinion about Sam by remembering how hot his mouth had been on hers.

Her entire body heated at the memory anyway. She took several deep breaths to cool down.

Tonight she was determined to put her worries and her unwilling attraction to Sam behind her and enjoy her surroundings. She'd already called about her credit cards and there was nothing she could do about her license until after the weekend. She couldn't seem to get in touch with Allie to tell her more about Raymond Foster, and he wasn't on the island yet anyway. Everyone here thought Charlotte was Allie, so she might as well act more like her sister and enjoy the evening.

They'd barely settled into their seats when Jared joined them. Before Charlotte could say a word, Veronica blurted out about Charlotte's theft.

"That's terrible," Jared said. "I hope they find out who's responsible."

"Me, too."

"May I have your attention?" Katie held a microphone near the end of the lanai, right in front of the buffet tables, and waited for everyone to quiet down. "Thank you." She glanced at the paper she held and made a few announcements about changes in the workshop schedule for Sunday afternoon.

"I'd also like to remind you to keep your valuables locked up. We've had a few unfortunate thefts in the past two days and we're hoping to put a stop to them. If you have any information that might help us, please come speak to me or to the resort manager, Sam Briton."

A neon sign in Charlotte's brain flashed *BE-WARE* at the mere mention of Sam's name.

Katie continued with the menu for the evening. "Our chef has prepared quite a feast. I hope you enjoy the food, as well as the karaoke planned for later."

Charlotte sipped her drink through a long straw and sat back in her chair. Nothing was going to bother her tonight.

Then, from the corner of her eye, she saw him.

Sam Briton had stepped out onto the lanai. Under other circumstances, she might have gone over to speak to him, maybe flirt a little. Laugh at his jokes. Touch his arm.

He searched the hundred or so people seated at the long tables as if looking for someone in particular.

His gaze stopped when it reached her.

SAM STOOD OFF to the side of the tables, taking in the guests seated there. His attention focused on Allie, who was watching him watch her.

What was she up to? He was determined to find out. After hearing that the video camera on her floor had been moved so two more thefts could be carried out, he decided to keep an eye on her himself. He'd show up when she least expected it.

He focused on Allie and realized she was scowling at him. He'd get nowhere if he went at this in a combative way. Maybe he could earn her trust and then determine if she was involved in the larcenies.

Sam watched as Katie sent tables to go to the buffet line. The food looked delicious, and he was pleased to see his staff replenishing near-empty chafing dishes quickly.

When everyone had been through the line, Sam picked up a plate and filled it with his own dinner. The chef rarely delivered a less-than-outstanding meal for their guests, and it saved him the trouble of cooking for himself. With the kids gone, he hated to bother.

He took his plate and walked to the lobby, then sat down to eat dinner. From his seat, he watched to see if Allie would leave the other conference attendees and come inside.

He didn't realize how hungry he'd been until his plate was empty in a matter of minutes. He wiped his mouth on a paper napkin and walked his plate to the kitchen. "Great meal," he told his chef, Armand, who smiled at the compliment. They were lucky to have the classically trained, award-winning chef on the premises.

"We're having a security problem, a few thefts," Sam told Armand. "I'm going to call a meeting tomorrow afternoon for department heads and I'd like you to attend. We need to put a stop to the problem immediately."

Armand nodded. "I'll be there. Anything I can do?"

"It appears to be an inside job, so if you have any information or suspect an employee or employees of being involved, let me know. Also, anyone who might be dissatisfied and looking to exact revenge."

Armand looked thoughtful. "We had to let a busboy go a few weeks ago. I've heard he's still on the island because he has family here."

Sam nodded. "I remember that. He was chronically late. Text me his name so I can let George in security know. He can check the guy out."

Sam left the kitchen and walked through the lobby to the lanai where the noise level rose significantly. Plates were being cleared and desserts were being set up in place of the entrée. As good as Armand's entrées were, his desserts were better. Tonight it looked like Key lime pie and some sort of apple crumble.

He'd have to run an extra mile tomorrow if he indulged tonight. Deciding it was worth it, he helped himself to a piece of pie.

His fork was halfway to his mouth when he realized Allie's seat was empty. Her two buddies that she'd been sitting with were still at the table, but he didn't see Allie anywhere.

He put his dessert plate on a serving tray with other dirty dishes and went in search of her. The ladies' room was his first thought, but he didn't want to hang outside the door too long or someone might wonder if he was a pervert.

He spied Katie coming in his direction and he grabbed her arm, speaking in a low tone. "Come with me. I need you to do something."

Her eyes narrowed, but she did as he requested. "What is it?"

"Check the ladies' room and see if Allie Miller is in there. She's about thirty with dark hair to about here." He put a hand to right under his chin to demonstrate. He didn't add that she had a killer body and a sharp wit.

"I remember her. She's the one you wanted to see this afternoon. Okay, be right back." Katie was gone only a few seconds. "No one in there at all."

Sam nodded. "Thanks."

"Does this have something to do with the thefts?"

"Possibly. She's someone I knew in Charleston, South Carolina, and she was a load of trouble back then. It seems coincidental that the thefts began when she arrived."

"Interesting. I'll keep an eye out for her."

"I'd appreciate that. Thanks for your help." He left Katie and headed back to the lanai. Allie was in her seat. If she'd been in the bathroom, she would have passed him.

So where had she been? Pulling off another burglary? He didn't want to believe it, but he couldn't help but be suspicious, based on her past behavior.

CHARLOTTE ADJUSTED HER chair and crossed her arms to rub her upper arms with her hands. "I'm still a little chilly even with this sweater on." She'd waited until she was done eating dinner before running to her room to retrieve the garment.

"I'm pretty comfortable," Veronica said as she adjusted her lightweight shawl on her shoulders. "I'm glad I remembered to bring this. We'll have to make sure we dress appropriately once the sun goes down."

Charlotte nodded. "I had the feeling it would cool down once it got dark, but I didn't realize we'd be eating outdoors."

"Dessert's out," Jared announced. "Want me to get you something?" He looked back and forth at both women.

"I think I'll stick with my hot tea," Charlotte told him.

"I'll go with you to see what's there," Veronica said as she rose and pushed her chair under the table.

Charlotte didn't know the other people around her, so she sat quietly, listening to conversations. Just as she realized she should be more outgoing as Allie, there was a tap on her shoulder. She jumped.

"I didn't mean to startle you." She recognized Sam's voice before she turned her head in his direction.

"You didn't," she lied, inhaling his clean scent.

He didn't say anything right away, so she asked, "Did you want something?"

"I was thinking we got off on the wrong foot yesterday, and I'd like to make it up to you."

Was this the same man who'd accosted her and refused to believe a word she said? "Why?" Maybe he thought his flower arrangement made up for everything he'd done and said.

He smiled. Not a big toothy grin, but more of a twitch of his lips. "Because I owe you an apology."

She didn't know what to say. "An apology?" He certainly did owe her one, but she never thought she'd get it in this lifetime. "You sent flowers to apologize. They're beautiful. Thank you." She'd taken out her camera to get some close-up shots of them to put with the other photos she'd collected. Too bad the pictures had to wait until she felt up to using pastels again.

"You're welcome." He sounded sincere. "I'm sorry for assuming you're the same person I met back in Charleston. We've both changed since then, and I'd like to give you the benefit of the doubt." Not quite an acknowledgment that he believed she was really Allie's twin sister.

"You would?"

"I would. Now, is my apology accepted?"

She shrugged. "Sure." She thought that would

be the end of it, but he still hovered over her. "Was there something else?"

"I was wondering if you'd like to take a walk on the beach later. After dessert is over. Unless you're planning to participate in karaoke?"

She disliked karaoke. She wasn't a singer, didn't want to sing in front of anyone and she didn't enjoy listening to other nonprofessionals sing, usually way off-key.

But she didn't want to spend time with him, either. Not if he didn't trust her yet to tell the truth. Considering the pros and cons, she decided it might be best to see what he was up to. He couldn't possibly be apologizing, could he? She needed to find out.

"Why not," she said before she realized what she was saying.

CHAPTER SIX

SAM HAD TOLD Allie he'd be in the lobby when she was ready to head to the beach. Their walk would be dark, as the sun had already set, so he'd grabbed two small flashlights from his top floor apartment.

Now he was back in the lobby, wondering why he was about to do such a foolish thing. What was he doing purposely spending time with the woman he'd vowed to never associate with again? Then he reminded himself it was better to remain close to your enemies and know what they were up to.

"Hey, Tom," he greeted the guy behind the reception desk. "How's it going?"

Tom looked up from the computer screen he'd been concentrating on. "Hey, boss. Pretty good."

"Have you had any more guests get a fake call from the front desk?" The only one Sam knew about was the call the Snyders had received.

"Not a one," Tom told him. "Hopefully, that flyer stopped whoever was behind the calls."

They chatted a few minutes about the thefts before Sam's attention was caught by Allie's approach.

"All set?" she inquired. Her expression was pleasant, but not as warm as her outfit was making him. Her skinny jeans rolled up at the ankles accentuated shapely legs, and her long-sleeved V-neck T-shirt hinted at her curves and revealed the barest amount of cleavage.

He nodded to her and said to Tom, "Just make sure when people check in, you—gently—remind them to be cautious and call the front desk to verify any calls they might receive." Sam had purposely said that when Allie was within hearing distance so he could broach the subject without her wondering if he suspected her involvement in the thefts.

"How many thefts have there been besides mine?" She asked the question as they crossed the lobby.

"Half a dozen," he replied.

"Does this happen often?"

"Almost never, especially at this Blaise property," he said. "This is very unusual, and we're using all of our resources to stop them and find the culprits." He wanted her to know they were taking the situation seriously. Even calling in the mainland police wouldn't accomplish anything more than what his security team was already doing.

"You think there's more than one person involved? Like some kind of gang?"

"I don't know for sure, but my guess is that one person couldn't do it all alone."

They had followed the six-foot-wide boardwalk path from the lanai to the beach, and now were about to step down onto the sand. "We can leave our shoes here," he said as he took off his boat shoes and set them on the side of the boardwalk. He'd changed into khaki shorts while in his apartment getting the flashlights, so there was no need for him to roll up his pants to avoid getting them wet.

He automatically reached out to steady Allie when she started listing to the right while unbuckling her sandal.

"Thanks," she said, her voice a little shaky, reminding him that he wasn't unmoved by their physical proximity, either. "Maybe I should sit down on the edge of the boardwalk before I fall and hurt myself." She smiled and did just that, removing her sandals quickly. She stood up, brushed off the back of her jeans and looked at him expectantly.

"Let's go." He veered left to walk down the beach, and she fell in next to him.

After a few minutes of walking parallel to the ocean in silence, seemingly out of the blue, she asked, "Why did you invite me to come on a walk with you?"

He shouldn't have looked at her because she wet her lower lip with her tongue. *Because I want to kiss you again to make sure I didn't dream the heat between us* was not the thing to say. Neither was anything having to do with her being guilty of the thefts, because he had to admit he was having his doubts about her involvement.

He should have had an answer prepared and it took him a few seconds before speaking. "I felt bad we got off to a rough start." That was certainly true for several reasons, including the kiss they'd shared. It had been anything but perfect as a first kiss, but definitely hot.

"Why?"

Couldn't she take his explanation for what it was? He'd told himself he'd asked her on this walk to gain her trust, but he couldn't exactly say that, either.

"Because you're a guest at my resort and it's my job to make sure you enjoy your time here." Before she could ask more questions, he asked his own. "Why did you accept my invitation? You can't possibly want to spend time with me after I've been so hostile."

She didn't answer at first. "You're right. I'm not used to people being so mean to me. Especially when I've never met them before. Maybe I wanted to give you a second chance."

Hadn't met him before? She sounded sincere.

She continued, "I thought this walk would be our chance to set things straight."

"Like how you're Alley Cat's twin sister?" The sarcastic words were out of his mouth before he could stop them.

She was no longer next to him. He turned to see she'd stopped walking and put her hands on her hips.

"I don't appreciate you calling my sister names." Her tone was uncharacteristically authoritative. More like Allie and unlike the twin-sister act she'd been trying to convince him of since arriving on the island.

"I'm sorry," he said and meant it. "It just slipped out. Don't be mad."

She gasped. "Don't be mad? You call my sister names and I'm supposed to be okay with it? I don't need this. I never should have agreed to take this walk with you. The two of us will obviously never see eye to eye." She did an about-face and kicked up sand when she walked quickly to the boardwalk.

He watched her a few seconds and then took off after her. He told himself he needed to keep her close and that would be impossible if she couldn't stand to be around him. The truth was, he liked being near her.

"Wait!" he yelled.

She slowed her pace, but didn't stop. He caught

up to her and gently touched her elbow. "I'm sorry," he said. They both stopped walking and she looked at him, her eyes tear filled.

"I don't know what happened between you and Allie in the past," she said quietly. "I haven't known her long enough to hear her entire life story." She paused, wiping a single tear that escaped down her cheek. "I *do* know that, if not for her, I wouldn't be here on this island."

"What do you mean?"

Again she paused. Was it because she was overly emotional or was she trying to come up with a plausible story? She finally said, "I've been through a personal tragedy and Allie offered me this trip to help me get back to normal."

Allie gave her a trip? That didn't sound like the conniving woman he knew at all. If this woman was truly Allie's twin named Charlotte, then Allie must be getting something in return from this, too. Sam's experience with her wasn't anything close to what Charlotte described. "I'm sorry about whatever you've been through," he said sincerely. "And I'm sorry for insulting you and your sister. If you say you're Allie's sister, then I'll take your word for it." Right now he was more confused than ever, which meant he should probably tread cautiously. Twins shared the same DNA. Did that mean they shared the same personality traits, like dishonesty?

"Thank you. I appreciate it." She brushed a hand over her cheek.

He nodded. "Are you still up for a walk?"

"I guess so. It's a beautiful night. I wish I had my camera with me."

"It's pretty dark to take pictures."

"You'd be surprised at the points of light you see at night, especially when the moon is full."

They turned and walked in the direction they'd just come from, farther and farther away from the boardwalk near the resort. From his pocket, he pulled out the two small flashlights he'd brought with him. "Here." He handed her one.

"Thanks." She turned it on and shone it on the beach in front of them.

He didn't bother with his own since one seemed enough light.

"You're a photographer?" he asked.

"Not professionally, but I take photographs of things like sunsets to capture them to create later."

"So you're an artist?"

"I am." She paused. "I've been working in charcoal recently."

"I guess I assumed you were in advertising." He looked at her and said, "How do you create a sunset in charcoal? Aren't the colors the point of capturing the moment?"

She opened her mouth as if to answer. Then her eyes widened and she said, "Look out!"

Before he could turn to see what she was warning him about, he stepped down on air instead of sand, and fell, landing hard on his hands and knees.

"ARE YOU OKAY?" Charlotte asked as she carefully climbed down into the three-foot hole someone had obviously dug during the day.

"Ouch," was his muffled reply.

She grabbed hold of his arm, feeling the play in his biceps. "Let me help you up." Right after they'd kissed, she'd vowed to ignore his sexuality. A lot of good that vow was.

"Thanks, I'm good." He stood and brushed off his hands and legs.

She shone her flashlight over him. Blood dripped down his shin. "You're bleeding!"

He leaned over to check it out. "I must have cut my knee on a shell. I'm fine."

"No, you're not. Let's get you back to the resort to clean it up."

He grinned at her.

"What?" she asked. Didn't he see he could get an infection if it wasn't taken care of? "Is your tetanus vaccine up-to-date?"

"I've never seen you like this before." He cleared his throat and sobered. "I mean, you're not like your sister at all."

"What does that mean?"

"I can't see her caring whether I've had a teta-nus shot or not."

So maybe she and Allie were different in many ways, but Charlotte couldn't imagine her sister wouldn't care about someone if they were hurt. "Allie isn't as coldhearted as you think."

He wisely didn't reply. Instead, he pulled her close and covered her mouth with his. She heard a sound and realized she'd moaned. This kiss was so much better than their first. Just as hot, but without the anger.

When she came to her senses, she pulled back slightly to look him in the eye. Even lacking il-lumination, she could see the passion.

"I'm sorry," he said, releasing her.

"You are?" She rubbed her upper arms, chilled now that she wasn't in his embrace.

He hesitated. "Yes and no."

Interesting answer. "Go on." She bit the inside of her cheek to keep from smiling.

"I've wanted to kiss you again to make sure…"

"Make sure of what?" She wasn't going to let him off the hook easily after some of the things he'd said to her since they met.

"Make sure our first kiss wasn't a fluke."

This time she hesitated. "Oh."

"Oh? That's all you can say? I'm crushed that

you weren't curious, too." His fake hurt tone was punctuated by his mime of stabbing his heart.

"I didn't say that." Her tone was equally as playful.

"Oh." The single syllable was about as sexy as she'd heard in a long time.

They stared through the fading light at each other until Charlotte broke the silence. "Come on," she said, "let's get you back to the resort." She was about to put an arm around the back of his waist for support and thought better of it. "Can you walk okay?" The less touching between them, the better. She wasn't sure she could resist him now that she knew he'd been thinking about their kiss as much as she had.

"I'm fine," he said and they both made their way out of the hole. "You're making too big a deal about a little cut."

She pointed to his shin. "A little cut doesn't bleed that much. You might need stitches. Is there a doctor available?"

He chuckled. "I don't need stitches. Antibiotic cream and a bandage will do. I have those back in my apartment."

"Then let's get you fixed up." They began walking, Sam able to make it on his own with only a slight limp. When they reached the boardwalk, they stopped to put their shoes back on. "I wish I had a tissue," she said. "You're going to bleed onto your shoes."

He brushed the blood away and wiped his hand in the sand. "All taken care of."

He wasn't taking his cut seriously, and she didn't like it. She would need to go home with him to make sure he treated it.

They reached the resort lobby where the slightly off-tune strains of "Midnight Train to Georgia" drifted in from the lanai. She was glad she hadn't stuck around for karaoke.

"I can take it from here," Sam told her. "Thank you."

"I'm not going anywhere. Come on." She sounded uncharacteristically bossy, even to herself. Maybe she was successful at channeling a bit of Allie's personality.

Sam shrugged. "If you insist." He led her to the elevator, inserting his key.

"My floor is off-limits to resort guests."

She nodded, having already assumed that.

They rode the elevator to the fourth floor, and the doors opened directly on to his apartment. Sam exited the elevator first, turning on a dim lamp in the darkness.

"This is gorgeous," Charlotte said as she stepped out. The walls were mostly floor-to-ceiling windows, allowing the occupant to see out to the ocean from anywhere in the large open space.

"I enjoy it," he said, turning on another lamp. "One of the perks of being the manager. I'll go get my first-aid supplies."

While waiting, Charlotte walked around the different areas in the large room. There was a kitchen in one corner, connected to a dining area, and then the living area with comfortable seating that enabled one to either watch the television mounted on the single solid wall or take in the stunning scenery outside.

A buffet in the dining area held framed pictures. There were several of a girl and a boy at different ages, and then one of Sam with them. Another photo showed Sam, the children and a woman who was obviously related to the children. The three of them shared the same slightly turned-up nose and high cheekbones.

Was Sam married? Charlotte looked around the room. Was his wife here now?

She sucked in a breath and put a hand to her open mouth. He'd kissed her. Twice. Was he the kind of guy to fool around on his wife?

"What's wrong?" Sam walked toward her and had clearly heard her gasp.

"Oh, nothing," she lied. "I was just looking at your pictures. These are your children?"

He nodded, a proud smile blooming on his face. "Emma is twelve, going on twenty. And

Oliver is nine and thinks he's the same age as Emma. They're visiting their grandfather in Fort Lauderdale."

"Oh." She wanted to know about his wife, but didn't know how to ask. "Did their mother go with them?" That seemed less harsh than asking why he'd kissed her while married.

"No. She died several years ago."

Charlotte almost sighed with relief that she hadn't enjoyed the kiss of a married man. "Oh, I'm so sorry." She truly was. "That must have been very difficult for all of you."

He didn't say anything. She had no doubt touched on a delicate subject.

Charlotte's eyes moistened as she thought of her own mother. Losing her had brought tremendous grief, as well as frustration, knowing her mother had deliberately kept the truth from her. The lies would never be explained to Charlotte's satisfaction.

She turned her head away from Sam so he couldn't see the tears. "Let's get your knee fixed up and I'll be on my way."

Sam turned her to face him. "What is it? What's wrong?" He wiped a tear from her cheek with the pad of his thumb.

"It's nothing." She shook him off and slightly adjusted the family picture on the buffet.

"I don't believe you. No one cries about someone else's loss for no reason. You didn't even know my ex-wife."

"Ex-wife?"

He nodded. "We were divorced at the time of her death." He pulled out a dining chair and propped his leg on another chair. "It's a long, depressing story." He looked at her with narrowed eyes. "You thought I was married, didn't you?" His question startled her. "You think I'm the kind of guy who kisses women when his wife isn't around. Takes walks on the beach in the dark with them. Don't you?"

"No, no. I didn't think that." Even though that was exactly what she'd thought.

"That's why you gasped earlier when you saw the picture of the four of us, isn't it?"

He was intuitive, she'd give him that. "Okay, I was mistaken. You would have thought the same thing." Then she added, "Just like the way you jumped to the conclusion that I'm Allie and not Charlotte."

"Touché." He wiped the blood from his leg with the wet washcloth he'd brought with him. "Let's call it even. Two subjects that don't need to be discussed."

Charlotte understood. She didn't want to talk about her mother's passing, either. She opened the first-aid kit he'd put on the table. It contained antibiotic cream and a large gauze pad and tape that would cover the cut better than an adhesive bandage. Now that she could see the actual cut with the blood wiped away, it didn't look as bad as she'd first thought.

"I can do that," he said when she opened the small individual package of antibiotic cream.

"I'm sure you can," she said. "I just don't trust you'll do it." She smiled to soften her words, though she did mean them.

"I wasn't going to forget about it," he told her. "I'm a big boy who can take care of himself."

"And when did you say you last got a tetanus shot?" She raised her eyebrows at him.

He smirked. "Probably two years ago when I had a physical and updated my shots for this job."

"Probably?"

He rolled his eyes and laughed. "I'll double-check the files tomorrow morning. I don't want to bother tonight. Will that make you happy?"

"Yes, it will." She added a last piece of tape to the gauze pad. "There. That wasn't so bad, was it? Much better than losing the leg from an infection."

He chuckled. "Thank you, Nurse." He rose, testing his knee by taking a few steps.

"I guess I should go," Charlotte said.

"You don't have to." He gestured to the seating area by the windows. "Would you like something to drink? It's the least I can do to thank you for tending to my wound."

This time *she* laughed. "I'd love some water."

She followed him to the kitchen area. "You make it sound like I'm Florence Nightingale and you've been wounded in battle."

He grinned. "Hole on the beach, foxhole in battle. Same thing."

He handed her a glass of ice water and gestured with his own for them to sit down. "So how did you and Allie find each other?"

His question came from nowhere and she was taken aback. "It was completely by accident," she said.

"You weren't looking for each other?"

She shook her head. "Neither of us had any idea that we had a twin. I had just begun looking into finding my birth mother to get my medical history, and Allie didn't want to know anything about our birth parents." She sipped her water and settled into the cushions of the love seat. "My neighbor Jack asked me to be his plus one for a family wedding. His cousin was marrying Allie's brother. At the wedding reception, people kept telling me I had a doppelgänger. I never did run into Allie until the end of the evening. That's when we compared notes and realized we were related, but didn't know how."

Sam's brows furrowed. "You couldn't figure out that you were twins? Weren't you born on the same day?"

Charlotte swallowed the lump that had formed in her throat. Her mother's lies had surfaced again. "That's true. We were born on the same day, but according to our birth certificates and what we always believed about ourselves, Allie was born in Rhode Island and I was born in New York. At that point, we thought we might be cousins. It was only later that we found out my mother had lied about me being born in New York. I was born in Rhode Island just like Allie." She wasn't sure how much longer she could talk about this without falling apart.

"Why would your mother do that?" He cocked his head to the side. Her distress must have shown on her face because he leaned forward and said, "You don't have to talk about it if you don't want to."

She swallowed. It was a painful subject, but talking about it might help. She rose from her seat and began pacing. Except for Allie, Allie's parents and Jack, Charlotte hadn't confided in anyone since reading her mother's letter. She wasn't sure why she was ready to pour her heart out to Sam, but he seemed truly interested.

She inhaled and began telling him about her mother's death, as well as the letter explaining about the married boyfriend who'd given her the money to buy baby Charlotte. "My mother knew all along I had a twin sister—unlike Allie's mother who didn't have a clue. My mother wanted to keep me to herself. We have no other relatives and she was afraid she'd have to share me with a sister if I ever found out."

"That sounds pretty self-centered." Sam's tone was matter-of-fact.

Charlotte nodded. "I agree. And I can't seem to find a way to forgive her."

"Do you need to?"

"Of course. How else will I be able to move forward?"

"Tell yourself it doesn't matter now. You have your sister."

"But we lost all of those years together, thanks to my mother." She couldn't simply get over her hurt and anger as he suggested.

"And you're making up for that time now."

"That won't make up for the years we didn't know each other."

"Trust me. Being angry at someone doesn't help. I learned that from experience. Thankfully, my kids needed my full attention when my ex-wife caused us all grief, even before her death."

"I'm sorry you went through such a difficult time." Charlotte wanted to hear more, but wasn't sure she was up to it. She took her glass to the kitchen. "I really should go."

He got up from his seat and put a hand on her arm. She shouldn't have been surprised by the warmth that suddenly spread through her. "I didn't mean to bring up such a difficult subject," he said. "I'm only trying to make you see that because your mother's gone, you'll never have the chance to tell her how her lies made you feel. So you can either move past them and enjoy the sister you found, or you can spend the rest of your life being angry and hurt, with no outlet to vent."

She thought about his words for a minute. "You sound like a psychologist."

He shrugged and put his glass in the sink. "I guess they've rubbed off on me."

"You've been to more than one?"

He nodded. "Several. You're not the only one who has anger issues with someone who's not around anymore to defend themselves."

Before she could ask him more about how he had been able to recover, his cell phone rang.

He pulled the phone from his pocket and looked at the screen. A smile lit up his face. "Excuse me. I need to take this." He hit the button to connect and put it to his ear. "Hey, baby." He chuckled and turned away from Charlotte. "I know, I know. I'm sorry."

Instead of sticking around to hear his private conversation with what sounded like a girlfriend, Charlotte headed to the elevator and pushed the button to call it. She turned to wave when the elevator door opened. Sam waved back and whispered, "Thanks for the help." Then he laughed at something the person on the other end said.

So Charlotte hadn't been kissed by a married man. Just by a man with someone in his life he called "baby."

WHEN SAM DISCONNECTED from his phone call, he was still smiling. His daughter always made him feel good. Especially when he pretended to forget and call her "baby" the way he used to until she'd decided she'd outgrown the moniker.

From what he understood from both Emma and Oliver, it sounded as if the kids were having a great time with their grandfather. They'd even made a trip to the Everglades where they saw baby alligators.

He went to the kitchen sink and put his and Charlotte's glasses in the dishwasher.

Charlotte.

That's the first time he'd unintentionally thought of her as Charlotte and not Allie. Maybe it was because he couldn't see Allie ever worrying about a little cut on his leg.

Surprisingly, he was nearly convinced that Charlotte was telling the truth about who she was. If she was lying, then she was a damn good liar. She'd been very credible when telling him how she and Allie had found each other at the wedding. There was more she wasn't telling, but he wouldn't push her. He had his own secrets. She'd opened up enough to let him see that she had more integrity than Allie.

Her emotions seemed real, too. Crying on command took real talent, and he'd swear her tears had been real.

All in all, tonight had been a success. They were getting along and she'd confided personal information about herself.

No matter what, he'd still be on guard. He had trusted Allie back in Charleston, but she'd fooled him completely. Luckily for him, he'd had an assistant who'd clued him in about what she'd overheard in the ladies' room. That had been the beginning of the end for Alley Cat in Charleston.

So even if Charlotte was telling the truth about everything, that didn't mean she had no ulterior motive.

He picked up his cell phone and placed a call to Charlotte's room. "It's Sam," he said when she answered. "I wanted to make sure you made it back to your room."

"Oh." Silence. "Thank you."

He continued. "I also appreciate your concern when I stupidly fell into that hole."

She laughed. "I could have fallen in just as easily as you did."

Except that he'd been too busy looking at Charlotte to watch where he'd been going. "I doubt that. I also wanted to apologize for not walking you back to your room. I can't ignore calls from my daughter."

"Your—" She cleared her throat. "Your daughter?"

"Yes, she wanted to discuss her grandfather's birthday."

"Oh." A long pause. "Not a problem. Of course your daughter comes first."

She sounded different. He wished he was having this conversation in person. That would have allowed him to see her expression, as well as give him half a chance at a good-night kiss. A thought came to him. "You thought I was talking to a woman, possibly a girlfriend, didn't you?" He grinned at the idea.

"Oh, n-n-no," she stuttered, convincing him he was right. "I didn't think about who you were talking to."

She was not as good a liar as her twin, because he didn't believe her, but he decided not to push the issue. "To be clear, I'm not seeing anyone. I'm not the kind of guy who takes walks on the beach or kisses other women when I'm involved." And with that he ended the call.

CHAPTER SEVEN

SUNDAY EVENING, WHILE she and Jack were driving home after a spectacular weekend in Vermont, Allie pulled her phone from her purse. She looked to Jack, who was driving. "Wow! My phone has been off all weekend. I guess after hearing that Charlotte made it to the island okay, I completely forgot to check it."

He grinned and squeezed her leg just above her knee. "I think you had your mind on other things."

Her face heated. "I think you're right." They'd had a fabulous weekend, both in and out of bed. She pressed the phone's power button and waited for it to turn on. There were several voice mails. She opened the phone app to listen to them. "I hope everything's okay," she told Jack. "Charlotte left me a lot of voice mails."

Jack glanced her way. "That's not a good sign."

Allie turned up the volume and played the first message so Jack could hear it, too.

"Raymond Foster!" Allie could barely breathe after listening to Charlotte recount who was coming to the conference. "I mentioned him to you the other day. He's my dream client and he's looking to switch agencies." Jack already knew that because he'd heard Charlotte's message, too, but saying it aloud made it all the more real. "What am I going to do? I'm registered for the conference, but I can't possibly get a presentation done *and* fly down there in time. Besides, I have a big meeting Tuesday morning. I've already postponed once. I can't do it a second time." She slumped in her seat, hoping a strategy would magically appear.

Jack patted her arm, keeping his eyes on the road. "It's not the end of the world. Maybe Charlotte can make an appointment with him and explain that you're the one he should talk to. Then you can fly to wherever he is in a few days or whenever he's got an open slot."

She considered it. "But what if he thinks that's too much trouble and it just makes him not want to hear from me? He's been known to be unpredictable. I can't believe he's actually firing his current firm. They're one of the top agencies in the country and he's been with them forever."

"It does seem odd. Why don't you call Charlotte and find out what's going on? Maybe this is a rumor floating around. You know how these things escalate."

Allie was already pressing buttons to connect to Charlotte. "Hey, Charlotte, how's it going?"

"Allie! Where have you been?" Charlotte sounded flustered, very unlike her. "I've been trying to reach you ever since I got to the island."

"Tell me exactly what's going on."

Allie listened as Charlotte told her how everyone thought she was Allie, and when she heard about Raymond Foster coming and couldn't get in touch with her twin, she decided to pretend to be Allie.

"That's brilliant," Allie told her. "How did you manage that?"

"It wasn't difficult. I kept trying to explain that I was your twin sister, but no one took me seriously. They thought it was some scheme of yours because of the DP Advertising mess. So I finally went along with it when I heard about Raymond Foster changing agencies."

Of course there were people from DP at the conference. Allie should have considered that and warned Charlotte. "I'm sorry I didn't prep you on who would be at the resort. I honestly didn't think about it since you wouldn't be attending the conference."

"Well, I am now," Charlotte said. "Thanks to Veronica and Jared."

"Who?"

"They're DP employees. They seem to know you."

Allie thought a moment. "I think I know who

they are. Tall guy and a little blonde woman, both a few years younger than us?"

"That's them."

"I wasn't really friends with anyone I worked with at DP."

"Well, Veronica was nice enough to sign me in at the registration desk, even before I decided to pretend to be you."

"That *was* nice of her. I wish I could fly down and take your place so I could get an appointment with Foster."

"So you're not coming down? I was really hoping you could."

Allie hated to disappoint Charlotte. "I can't. I have an important meeting Tuesday morning that I have to be here for."

"I hate to see you miss this opportunity."

So did Allie. "I don't know what else to do."

"What if I see if I can make an appointment with him for when he gets home? Then you could fly to wherever he is."

"That's what Jack suggested, too, but the guy's reputation makes him out as some sort of flake. I'm afraid he'd be turned off by me if I asked for a favor like that."

"I can understand."

"I guess I'll have to miss out on this opportunity." Allie tried to sound upbeat, but knew she wasn't succeeding. "Thanks for letting me know, though."

Charlotte was silent for so long that Allie wondered if their call had been dropped.

"This might sound crazy," Charlotte finally said, "but what if I continue to pretend to be you and get that appointment with Mr. Foster?" She paused. "Can you put together a presentation and email it to me? I won't be able to present it as well as you, but I'll do my best."

Allie didn't know what to say. "You'd do that for me?"

"Of course," Charlotte said. "You're my sister, and I'd do anything for you."

Allie was overwhelmed by Charlotte's generosity. "I don't know what to say." She turned to Jack and whispered, "She offered to pitch to Raymond Foster for me."

Jack looked skeptical. "Is that a good idea? She has no experience."

"I heard that," Charlotte said with a nervous laugh. "I'm hoping your talent will upstage my inexperience. Make me a presentation that will knock his socks off."

"As soon as I get home, I'll start on a presentation for him and email it to you. I can coach you on what to say."

Charlotte didn't say anything. Allie looked to Jack, who glanced at her and then back to the road. He shrugged and whispered, "Tell her I'll help coach her, too. She'll be great."

"I know she will," Allie whispered back and

then related Jack's offer to Charlotte. "Are you sure you want to do this?"

"I'm sure."

"Getting Raymond Foster's business would be the best thing that could happen to my firm," Allie said. "I'll owe you a huge debt."

"You won't owe me anything. But you have to be specific. What should I say? What should I wear? Oh, gosh, I don't know if I have the right clothes with me to make this presentation."

"Don't worry about it. You're on an island and anything nice will do."

Allie asked about the rest of Charlotte's time at the resort and couldn't believe it when she said, "My wallet was stolen with my ID and credit cards. Luckily, I left my other credit cards at home since I wouldn't need them on the island. I called the credit card companies, but I'm worried about my driver's license. I can't call until tomorrow morning and I have no idea how long it will take to get a replacement."

"That's terrible," Allie said. "What is Management doing to help you out?"

"They've had a rash of thefts over the past few days, so they're pretty busy. I'm worried about not being able to fly home at the end of the week with no ID."

"Good point." Allie wondered how she might be able to help her sister. "Let me know what DMV tells you tomorrow and we'll go from there. Maybe they can issue a temporary or something. I could overnight it to you if I can pick it up at one of the branches. I'm guessing they would issue a duplicate with your picture on file, but I don't know for sure."

"I hope so," Charlotte said. "Speaking of the resort management, there's something else I need to ask you about. What's the story between you and Sam Briton?"

"Sam Briton?" Allie's throat tightened and Jack glanced her way. She hadn't thought of him in years. "Does he work there?" What should she say about him? She'd made mistakes in her past and even though both Jack and Charlotte knew about some of them, they didn't know everything.

"He's the manager here," Charlotte told her. "He thought I was you and he wasn't very happy about it."

Allie didn't doubt it. "Did he tell you how we met?"

"Only that you were both in Charleston a few years ago and had some kind of difficulty. What happened?"

Allie swallowed. "It's not a big deal." She glanced at Jack and then stared straight out the front window at the road. "He was the assistant manager of the Blaise property in Charleston, and I was there from time to time selling cosmetics to the resort's boutique." She paused, feeling completely exposed to the two most important people in her life. "He discovered the cosmetics my coworker delivered were counterfeit—poorly made—when several people complained about getting a rash."

"Why would he be upset with *you* if it was your coworker who brought the cosmetics?"

Why did it have to be Sam Briton who managed the resort? Allie never would have had to explain otherwise. Kept her past in the past and all that. "I was involved with the coworker at the time, but I had also befriended Sam to keep the account at the boutique. He took that as a complete betrayal."

She ignored Jack's reaction. She'd seen his head swivel her way from the corner of her eye.

"But it wasn't you who delivered the cosmetics."

"I couldn't make Sam believe I didn't know about the fakes. He was adamant about never seeing us again or he'd turn us both in." Allie didn't see a need to go into any more detail. Charlotte now knew the pertinent facts.

"I've witnessed how stubborn Sam can be," Charlotte said. "I'm glad he didn't turn you in, but it explains why he's been so unfriendly to me."

CHARLOTTE STOOD ON her balcony, enjoying the breeze while speaking with Allie. "Tell me about your trip. Did you enjoy it?" She was afraid she'd be tempted to tell Allie more about her interaction with Sam. Her face heated as she thought about their kiss.

"We had a great time," Allie said. "We ate at a quaint restaurant in town Saturday night. The bed-and-breakfast was cozy and the food was to die for. The innkeeper baked the most delicious apple tarts the night we arrived, and then she provided a smorgasbord of goodies for breakfast, both savory and sweet."

"Sounds great," Charlotte said.

"We're planning to go back to ski when there's snow. You should come, too."

"I might just do that, although I could really get used to the sun and sand here."

They spoke for a few more minutes before hanging up. Charlotte captured the scenery in front of her as a snapshot in her head, so different from a snowy mountain. The sun had set a while ago, but once again the moon was nearly full. It shone bright in the sky, reflecting on the water. She loved being at the resort, no matter how many difficulties she'd encountered. A sense of peace came over her when taking in her surroundings.

She'd spent a relaxing day taking pictures and sketching different places on the island. She hadn't unpacked her pastels yet, sticking to her charcoals. She remained hopeful that soon she'd feel the need to use color again in her artwork, but it needed to come naturally. Not forced.

It didn't help that now she was stressing out about this presentation for Raymond Foster.

Why had Charlotte suggested it? "I don't know how to give a presentation," she said aloud to the ocean below. Allie was persuasive and good at her job. She was not only skilled at selling a product, but selling herself and her ideas, as well. Charlotte couldn't compete with that or with anyone else who would be pitching to Raymond Foster.

She and Allie might look identical, but they certainly didn't share all of the same personality traits. Selling herself or a product wasn't something Charlotte was comfortable with. Talking about her art? Now, *that* was a different story.

Charlotte had recounted her time at the resort to Allie, but hadn't gone into detail about Sam. Her sister didn't need to feel guilty about sending Charlotte down here. Hearing details about how Sam had initially treated her—including that angry kiss—weren't necessary. That would only ruin Allie's mood after what sounded like a wonderful weekend with Jack.

Charlotte touched her lips, thinking of Sam. She had been inexplicably relieved to hear the call had been from his daughter and not a woman. And she'd been embarrassed when he'd realized it, too. She shouldn't care if he had a girlfriend or not. She wasn't interested in him or in any kind of relationship until she came to terms with her mother's deceit. Certainly not a relationship with someone who didn't trust her implicitly. He might act as if he believed her, but she saw the doubt in his eyes. Besides, she didn't need to be involved with someone long-distance. After this week, she'd probably never see him again.

That was, *if* she could get a replacement ID so she could leave the island.

A loud knock sounded on her door. She checked the peephole to see it was Veronica. "Come in," Charlotte told her, unlocking the dead bolt and opening the door wide.

"I came to see how you're doing," Veronica said with a giggle. "I haven't seen you all day."

"I'm fine." Charlotte grinned at the woman's effort to walk through the doorway without wobbling. "But I'm not sure I'm as fine as you are."

Veronica giggled again. "We've been at the bar," she said superfluously and hiccuped.

"I can see that," Charlotte quipped. "We?"

"A bunch of us from DP." She leaned on the corner of the dresser to keep her balance. "You should come down, too."

"I'm not sure that's a good idea." Charlotte gestured to the chairs by the glass doors. "Would you like to sit down?"

Veronica took her up on her offer and plopped into a chair. "Why would you think that?"

Charlotte considered telling Veronica the truth—from her identity to giving Allie's presentation. Maybe Veronica could provide tips on being successful when she met Raymond Foster. But, then, maybe Veronica was going to pitch to him, too.

Charlotte sat in the other chair and faced Veronica, ignoring her question to ask, "What do you do at DP?"

Veronica's face scrunched. "You know what I do. I'm an account executive." She held up her pointer finger. "I guess I was still a junior account executive when you were at DP."

"So tell me what your job entails."

Veronica cocked her head. "These are odd questions, Allie. Why are you asking me such basic questions?"

"First, tell me if you're planning to pitch to Raymond Foster."

Veronica shook her head. "No, we've got one of his biggest competitors as our client and going after him would be a conflict of interest. You already know that."

Charlotte went back and forth in her head before speaking. "I have something to confess."

Veronica's eyebrows shot up and she leaned forward, swaying slightly to the right. "Spill it."

"I need you to keep this our secret. Even from

Jared." Charlotte wasn't sure what the relationship between Veronica and Jared entailed, but
the more people who knew the truth, the more
chance there would be that things might fall
apart.

Veronica nodded vigorously.

"Remember how, when I first got to the island,
I told you my name was Charlotte Harrington?"

Veronica nodded again.

Hoping Veronica wasn't too drunk to com-
prehend, Charlotte continued. "Well, that *is* my
real name. I was telling the truth about having
a twin sister." She then explained how she had
decided to go along with everyone's perception
when she'd heard about Raymond Foster needing a new advertising agency. "So for my sister's
sake, I let you think I was Allie. I'm very sorry."

Veronica was quiet for an uncomfortable
amount of time. "I don't believe you. Prove it."

Charlotte was stymied. "I'd show you my ID,
but you already know it was stolen."

"That's convenient." Veronica had suddenly
sobered. She surveyed the room. "Maybe you
have it hidden somewhere so you can say you
have no proof."

Charlotte was shocked. She gestured around
the room. "I'm not lying. My ID and credit cards
were stolen. Feel free to search if you'd like. I
thought I could trust you with this, but I guess
I was wrong."

Veronica stared at Charlotte, then looked around the room, then back at Charlotte. Her lips turned up in a grin. "Ha! Gotcha! That was a test. Of course I believe you're not Allie."

"You do?" Charlotte's eyes widened as she tried to keep up with Veronica's thinking.

"Sure I do. The real Allie would never have treated Jared and me so nicely."

"What do you mean?"

"When we all worked together, you—I mean, Allie—never had time for us. No matter how many times we invited you—your sister—to have lunch with us or when we brought her a muffin in the morning, she was always too busy." She pushed her hair back from her face. "We knew that meant we weren't good enough for you. Her. You—sorry, your sister—couldn't even remember our names."

Charlotte didn't know what to say. Although that tracked with Allie's reaction when Charlotte mentioned Veronica and Jared. "I'm sure there's more to it than that. I know my sister works very hard, but I can't believe she would purposely be rude to you."

"Maybe not." Veronica didn't sound convinced.

"I hope you'll accept my apology for not telling you sooner that I'm not Allie."

"We didn't really give you a chance. I thought

you were making up a story since you—sorry, *your sister*—left DP on such bad terms."

"I know. I can see why you would think that." From what Charlotte knew of Allie's past, telling people she was her twin sister to avoid conflict might be something she would actually do. "So how bad is it? Does everyone at DP still dislike Allie?"

"Actually, no one has mentioned her as far as I know. At least until we got here and saw you. I think there were a lot of rumors floating around right after you—Allie—were fired, but that died down pretty quickly."

"I'd still like to keep my true identity under wraps," Charlotte told her. "I talked to Allie and I've offered to do her a huge favor since Raymond Foster will be here."

"What's that?"

"I'm going to set up an appointment with him to pitch Allie's company. She'll put a presentation together, but I'll need to pitch it." Charlotte rubbed her hands together. "I'm having second thoughts about whether I can pull it off."

"Of course you can," Veronica said enthusiastically. "*Giving* the presentation is the easy part. Allie will be doing the hard part."

Charlotte hadn't thought about it that way. For her, creating her artwork was what came easy and natural. Standing in front of people to sell it would be where she would fall apart. "That's easy for you to say. You must do it all the time."

"Get up in front of people? Yes. Is it easy? No." Veronica's answer was surprising.

"So you get nervous speaking to people?"

"Of course, most people do. But you learn to push past that nervousness and concentrate on what you're saying. You use the nervous energy as a positive."

"That makes sense," Charlotte said. "But I don't know anything about advertising or how to sell an idea. I'm an artist."

"You are?" Veronica's eyebrows rose. "Professionally or as a hobby?"

Charlotte smiled. "Professionally. I'm one of the lucky ones."

"Wow! That's great. What's your medium?"

A sore subject in Charlotte's mind. She hated admitting she used to use pastels and now only used charcoal. She rose from her chair. "I have some pictures on my phone I can show you."

"These are gorgeous," Veronica cooed as she scanned Charlotte's older pastels. She stopped at a more recent picture and looked at Charlotte. "Why did you switch to charcoal? Your pastels have such depth to them."

How much to tell her? She could bring the conversation—and herself—down by talking about her mother's death. Especially since her mother's letter was a downer in itself.

Charlotte inhaled. "I lost my mother about a year and a half ago. Charcoal has been my medium of choice since then."

There. She'd spit out the truth with no sign of tears or a meltdown. She took a calming breath anyway.

"I'm so sorry," Veronica said. "Is your father still living?"

Charlotte wasn't asked very often about her father since she'd become an adult, but she did her best to answer. She ended with, "That's why meeting Allie was such a life changer for me. Much more so than for Allie, who has several other adopted siblings, as well as two living adoptive parents." An entire family who immediately accepted Charlotte as one of them.

As their conversation progressed, Charlotte felt more and more comfortable with Veronica. "So tell me about yourself. I know nothing about you."

"There's not much to tell. I grew up as a military brat, living all over the United States and even a few years in Germany."

"How exciting! I've never been outside the United States." Charlotte vowed to change that as soon as possible. There were so many interesting things to do and see outside her small world, and she needed to experience them. "How did you end up in...? I can't remember where DP is headquartered. I know Allie has mentioned it. Somewhere in Connecticut?"

Veronica nodded. "Yes, I'm living in a small town in Connecticut, outside of New York City. Way too expensive, but convenient to our offices, as well as close to everything the city has to offer."

"That sounds exciting. What about your family? Where are they now?"

"My parents are retired outside of DC. My dad's last military tour was there and we'd lived there once before. I have one sister and she just graduated from Virginia Tech with an engineering degree."

"Impressive. How did you decide to go into advertising?"

"Quite by accident." Veronica smirked. "My parents wanted me to do something more like my sister. Be an engineer or go into the sciences. But I never had an interest in all that math and science stuff. I spent my free time in high school— this is going to sound really geeky—creating comic books."

"No wonder you went into the field if you're that creative."

Veronica blushed. "They kind of got me into trouble. The comics featured my teachers and some of the things they would do or say."

Charlotte laughed. "And I suppose one of your teachers found out?"

"An ex-boyfriend stole one and conveniently slipped it into the teachers' lounge."

"It had your name on it?" Charlotte asked.

"Thanks to the ex-boyfriend, it did." Veronica laughed. "I can joke about it now, but it was devastating when it happened. I was so embarrassed."

"But look what happened. That was the beginning of your advertising career."

"Actually, it was an art teacher who heard about my secret and came to me when she saw what I'd done. She thought I had talent and suggested a career in advertising or something like that. She said art was a tough field to break into, but advertising would give me an income to fall back on until then."

"So, are you doing anything artistic on the side? Any more comic books?"

Veronica shook her head. "No. I figure someday I'll get back to it, but for now my job takes up too much time."

Charlotte nodded. "As long as your job makes you happy."

"It does. I wasn't sure at first, but now that I've been promoted from junior to account executive, I'm not spending most of my time ordering lunches and taking coffee requests. I'm heading a team and interfacing with clients."

"That does sound a lot better."

"Let's get back to your presentation for Foster," Veronica said. "I'll do whatever I can to help you."

"Thank you so much!" Charlotte exclaimed. "So what do I do first?"

Veronica hesitated, as if considering the best strategy. "I think the first thing you do is go to a few workshops and learn what you can about the industry. They're set up in beginner, advanced and other tracks."

Charlotte rose and pulled out the workshop schedule. Veronica marked the ones she thought would be most beneficial. "I thought going to the one Raymond Foster is giving would be good."

"I guess you haven't heard. He's not getting here until Wednesday night, so they've canceled his workshop."

"Bummer. Well, I really appreciate your help," Charlotte said. "I wish I could do something to help you in return."

Veronica cocked her head. "There *is* one thing you might be able to help me with."

"Name it."

CHAPTER EIGHT

SAM HAD EATEN a quiet dinner in his apartment and he couldn't explain exactly why, but he felt the need to go downstairs. As he walked through the lobby, he told himself he wasn't looking for Charlotte. However, he wasn't disappointed when he found her on the resort's lanai.

An impromptu gathering had taken place. Small groups of people laughed and talked together. Nothing had been scheduled for the evening, so they were on their own. They were drinking, but not so much as to cause concern.

Charlotte sat at a table with a few people. Her legs were crossed and a friendly smile brightened her face. He vaguely recognized the one woman she was with as someone he'd seen her with several times. Same with the lone man at the table. The rest of her group wasn't as familiar to him.

So it wouldn't seem as if he was checking up on her or anxious to spend time with her, even though he was, Sam walked to the far end of the lanai to greet the people seated there. "How's everything going over here?" he asked a group of three men in shorts and polos. "I'm Sam Briton, the resort manager."

"We love the resort," one man about Sam's age of thirty-four said.

"Yeah, we were wondering if we could extend the conference about another week or so," another said, making everyone laugh, including Sam.

"I'd love to accommodate you, but I'm afraid you're out of luck," he said with a grin. "We're all booked up next week, but we'd love to have you back another time." He and the men chatted for a few minutes before he moved on to another group and asked the same question.

Not long after that, he was left with only Charlotte's group to speak to. He'd surreptitiously watched her from the corner of his eye, unable to stop himself. Each time her dark hair blew into her face, she carefully brushed it back and tucked it behind her ears. She was dressed casually, as were all the others on the lanai. Her long navy shorts came to just above her knee and her tailored, button-down plaid shirt showed a hint of a navy tank top that dipped low over the swell of her breasts.

Okay, so he'd really checked her out. What was it about her that caused him to constantly look and think about her? Something more than his suspicions about her possible involvement in the thefts. He couldn't help it. She and the thefts had been simultaneous, and she was closely related to Allie Miller. They shared DNA, so he would be crazy to ignore that.

Sam reached Charlotte's group, and he placed a hand on the back of her chair, careful not to touch her, though he wanted to. "How's it going over here?" He reintroduced himself to this group, like all the others he'd spoken to.

"This is so relaxing," the man of the group said.

Charlotte smiled at Sam, and his body heated inexplicably. "How's your knee?" She looked down to where he'd been cut and then back up. "Did you check on that tetanus shot?"

He grinned. "Knee's fine. Shots up to date."

"Would you like to join us?" she asked.

Standing over her, he realized he had a bird's-eye view right down her neckline. He didn't think he looked more than an instant before realizing it, but it was long enough for one of the other women to repeat Charlotte's question.

"Um, no, that's okay, but thank you," he stammered, feeling like a teen with raging hormones. "I'm just making sure everyone is enjoying their evening. Is there anything we can do to make your stay better?" Now he was back to feeling like Manager Sam and not Creepy Sam.

"Some dance music would be nice." Charlotte looked at him expectantly.

"We do have speakers out here," Sam said. "Let me see what I can do."

He left to find someone more knowledgeable about their music system, and then returned to the group with an update. "We should have it working in a few minutes. We get satellite radio here. What would you prefer? Current hits? Classic rock? Eighties? Nineties? Country? Jazz? There's a station for everything."

The members of the group glanced at each other and shrugged. "I don't really care," Charlotte's friend said, and the others agreed. "How about some current hits? I could go for some Taylor Swift, Gaga and, oh! Usher." She patted her heart in a fake swoon.

Sam grinned at her dramatics. "Coming right up."

He was walking away when he heard one of the women—not Charlotte—say, "Be sure to come back and join us."

"I'll see what I can do." He waved while walking away. He wasn't in the habit of socializing with guests, but this was an opportunity to be around Charlotte, and he couldn't turn it down.

What was he supposed to call her in front of other people? Did they know she wasn't Allie, or was she still keeping her true identity a secret from everyone?

By the time he made it back to the lanai with a ginger ale in his hand, several people were dancing and bouncing to an Iggy Azalea hit. Some of the others he'd spoken to had joined the group on the makeshift dance floor.

"You're not dancing," he said to Charlotte, stating the obvious. She was the only person seated at her empty table.

She shrugged. "I'm fine right here. Besides, this is all for Veronica." She pointed to an empty chair. "Have a seat."

"How's that?" He sat in the offered chair and set his drink on the table.

Charlotte brought her chair closer. He assumed it was because the music was loud and she didn't want to yell over it. Their knees were so close he could feel the heat coming off of her. He wanted to touch her leg, run his hand up her thigh…

He stopped his lascivious thoughts and concentrated on her words.

"Veronica has a crush on Jared." She pointed to the woman he'd recognized as Charlotte's friend and the lone man in their group on the dance floor. "She wants my help getting his attention."

Sam nodded. "Another talent of yours? Playing Cupid?"

She laughed. Hard to hear over the music, but a delight to watch. "Hardly. Although if you count my sister and her boyfriend, I'm batting a thousand."

He grinned, but wondered if she had a boyfriend back home. "Speaking of Allie, have you heard from her yet? I know you were worried about getting in touch with her because of the guest speaker coming in."

Charlotte's eyes widened in excitement. "Yes, I finally talked with her earlier this evening. She's very excited about the opportunity."

"So she's flying here?" That would certainly prove beyond a doubt they were twins if he saw them both at the same time.

Charlotte shook her head. "No, I wish she could. She has business to conduct there."

How convenient. "So I guess that means she has no chance at this new client."

"Not quite. I offered to continue to pretend to be her and do the presentation, as well, so she's going to email it to me."

"You did?" His first thought was that Charlotte was as deceitful as her twin. "That doesn't sound like a good idea."

"We didn't know what else to do. Getting this account would save Allie's fledgling company."

"What if this guy figures out who you are? He won't like it if he finds out he's been tricked." Sam could guarantee that's the way he'd feel if he were in that guy's place.

"I guess that's a chance we have to take." She narrowed her eyes at him. "Why are you so against it?"

"I'm not a fan of deceit."

She didn't say anything at first, and he thought she might be upset with him. "I'm not a fan of deceit, either," she finally said. "But I love my sister and, unless you have a better idea, this is what I need to do."

He nodded and decided not to say anything more about it for the moment.

Charlotte grabbed his forearm and leaned in. "Can I confide in you?" He had no time to answer before she continued to speak. "I'm scared to death to do this presentation! I don't have a clue about what I'm doing."

His mouth went dry and he gulped at his drink, trying to ignore his body's reaction to her touch. "You'll do fine." He couldn't remember the last time he had such a strong physical reaction to a woman.

"But I've never done a presentation like this. I could screw up, and then Allie's company would lose its chance at this huge account."

Without thinking, Sam laid a hand on Charlotte's that still grasped his forearm. "She wouldn't let you do it if she didn't have faith in you."

She looked directly into his eyes. "I guess you're right. Thank you."

They stayed like that, eyes locked on each other, until Sam felt himself drifting closer to her. His gaze moved to her mouth. Her lips were slightly parted, moist from the drink she'd been sipping. He craved the taste of her mouth.

"Hey, you two, come on out on the dance floor."

He didn't know who yelled the invitation, but it was enough to sober Sam immediately and realize what he'd been about to do. "Would you like to dance?" He asked the question without thinking it through.

Charlotte blinked and stood up. Sam took that as an affirmative.

He rose from his chair and followed her to the makeshift dance floor.

How much trouble could he get into while dancing to this upbeat Taylor Swift song anyway?

She leaned forward and said something to him, but he couldn't hear her when they were this close to the speakers.

He stepped closer, her body within his grasp. "I can't hear you," he said loudly. He shrugged and she moved in closer to him. She was killing him. Slowly but surely.

She spoke directly into his ear. "I said, the music is pretty loud." Her breath on his ear was nearly his downfall.

He turned her head to speak into her ear, but his words came out as a whisper when his lips grazed the shell of her ear. "I agree." But he didn't want to move away from her to turn down the volume.

They continued dancing, their movement close enough that their bodies occasionally brushed. An elbow, a forearm, her lovely breasts against his chest. Sam squeezed his fists, ignoring the growing urge to grab Charlotte and hold her and kiss her until they were both satiated.

Then a sexy Sam Smith ballad started playing.

"I love this song," he heard Veronica say next to them before slipping into Jared's arms to slow dance with him.

Sam glanced at Charlotte and did the only thing he could think to do. The only thing he'd been dying to do. He put his arms out and she slid her entire body against him as if they'd been doing it for years.

This was a very bad idea.

That was all Charlotte could think as she luxuriated in Sam's embrace while they swayed to the music.

Ever since Sam had kissed her last night, she'd been thinking about how it felt to be held by him. How long had it been since she'd been in a man's arms? Too long.

Her mother's illness and death had taken a toll on all aspects of Charlotte's life, including her love life. When her mother had needed full-time care, Charlotte had provided it. The guy she'd been casually dating at the time had wanted more attention. He'd given her an ultimatum, and she had chosen her mother over him.

No great loss. She barely remembered him now.

Charlotte had initiated the dancing for Veronica's sake, not knowing she would benefit, too. According to Veronica, Jared seemed oblivious to her feelings, but he didn't seem to mind slow dancing with her. Charlotte could see them over Sam's right shoulder, and they appeared lost in each other.

Repaying the favor to Veronica might have been easier than Charlotte had expected.

"You're pretty quiet," Sam said softly next to her ear.

Or maybe enjoying Sam's embrace was a bigger price to pay than she first realized.

His words startled her. "Oh, sorry. I was just thinking about those two." She nodded at Veronica and Jared.

"Gee, thanks." His words were thick with sarcasm.

She chuckled. "I didn't mean it that way."

He turned them around a hundred and eighty degrees. "Now you won't be distracted and I can have your full attention."

Oh, he had her attention, all right. Every cell in her body was aware of him.

"So what shall we talk about?" she asked.

Floating silently in his arms was good enough for her.

"I don't know. Pick a subject. Literature, foreign policy, favorite last meal."

She laughed, sounding nervous to her own ears. Better that than sounding as if she wanted him to take her right there on the dance floor. "That's quite a range."

The song ended and she reluctantly said, "Let's sit down. I think it'll be easier to talk away from the speakers." She didn't want to stop dancing with him. She merely needed to remind herself that now was not the time or place to seduce him or be seduced by him.

"Good idea." His agreement was a disappointment, but at least he still held her hand. She liked holding hands, the way fingers were made to intertwine.

She rubbed the sudden chill from her upper arms when he released her hand as they reached their table. "What time is it?"

He checked his cell phone. "Almost eleven. You're not going to tell me you have a curfew, are you?"

She smiled. "No, I was just thinking that the air is cooling off and I'd like to go get a sweater from my room. I'll be back in two minutes."

He pulled out a chair and sat down. "I'll be right here waiting."

SAM HAD A few minutes to himself to go over what Charlotte said about Allie, since everyone who'd been at their table was still dancing.

He'd bet money that Allie had told Charlotte part of the Charleston story, but not all of it. He doubted Charlotte knew how he and Allie had become friends, having coffee together whenever she came to the resort. He'd been shocked when she'd come on to him in order to get him to not turn her and her sleazy boyfriend in to the authorities. If Charlotte knew about that, he didn't think she'd have been as comfortable dancing so intimately with him.

He checked his cell phone. Charlotte had been gone for five minutes. As he wondered if he should refill their drinks, the fire alarm sounded inside the resort.

He jumped up from his seat and pulled his radio from his belt. He spoke directly to his head of security, "What's going on? This a false alarm?"

"I'm checking it out," George said. "Give me a minute and I'll get right back to you. Better get an evacuation going just in case. I'll make sure the chem truck is in position."

"Right." With no fire department on the private island, their small security team was cross-trained as firefighting personnel. They kept a chemical truck, about the size of a dump truck, garaged for emergencies.

Sam put the radio back into its holder and faced the people on the lanai. The speakers still blared music, but the loud, pulsing alarm nearly drowned out the tunes. They watched him, waiting for direction. "We need to evacuate the resort." He pointed toward the beach as he yelled loud enough to be heard. "I want all of you to take your things and head that way. I'll send someone down when we have the all clear."

Everyone spoke at once.

"I have a job to do," he said in a raised voice. "Please move away from the building for your own safety."

He realized Charlotte hadn't come back down. Had she decided to retire for the evening? She must have heard the alarm going off all over the building. Surely she'd follow the directions over the loudspeaker telling everyone to evacuate.

He jogged into the lobby and saw Tom, who worked at the registration desk, directing people outside as they came downstairs. "Good job, Tom. I'm going to start on the third floor and make sure everyone is out of the building."

"Do you know what's going on?" Tom asked. "People keep asking me."

"George is investigating. I don't smell smoke, but that doesn't mean this is a false alarm. The resort is pretty spread out."

Sam ran to the back stairs, where people were

evacuating from the upper floors. They moved over quickly to let him through.

"What's going on?" several people asked on his trek to the third floor.

"We're checking it out," he repeated each time. "We'll let you know as soon as we know something. Please keep going down to the lobby, where you'll be directed outside."

He got to the door for the third floor at the same time Charlotte was about to descend. "I wondered where you got to," he said breathlessly, still not smelling any smoke.

"It took me longer than I thought," she said, shakily adjusting her sweater on her shoulders.

"Go downstairs to the lobby and someone will direct you. I'll find you as soon as I make sure everyone's out."

She nodded, focusing on his every word.

He'd no sooner stepped into the third-floor hallway than he got the all-clear from George. "It was a small fire near a storage closet in the hallway leading to the kitchen. It's out, but there's damage from the sprinklers going off."

"How the hell did that happen?" Sam asked. Thankfully, the sprinkler system was set up in zones, so there would be water damage only in the fire area.

"I'm pretty sure the fire wasn't an accident."

"Someone set it?" Sam nearly stopped breathing. First thefts, now fire. What would come next?

He couldn't help thinking they all happened after Charlotte had stepped foot on Sapodilla Cay.

Coincidence? He truly wanted to believe that, but common sense said otherwise.

CHARLOTTE'S HEART WAS beating as fast as she'd ever felt it. "A fire!" she said to Veronica when they caught up with each other near the beach. "I wonder what happened." The last time she'd been evacuated from a public building had occurred when she'd lived on campus in college.

"I haven't heard a thing so far," Veronica said as someone from the resort gave them permission to return. "It must have been a small fire if they're letting us go back in so quickly."

"Or a false alarm," Jared suggested.

The women nodded their agreement.

"Well, that was certainly exciting," Charlotte said as her heart rate finally slowed down to normal. "I heard the alarms go off when I was touching up my makeup in my bathroom and then the announcement to evacuate came. I nearly forgot the sweater I went up there for in my haste to get out."

"I'm so glad it wasn't a bigger emergency," Veronica said as they reached the lanai. "I was really having a good time before those alarms went off." She looked at Jared. "What about you?"

He shrugged. "Sure." He glanced at his cell

phone. "It's getting late and I need to be up early. I think I'm going to head up to bed. I'll see you ladies tomorrow."

Veronica stood in silence for several minutes, watching Jared leave.

"I can't believe he just left like that," Charlotte said to Veronica. "You two looked like you were having such a good time before we were evacuated."

Veronica's mouth turned down. "I thought we were, too."

"I guess we'll have to put our thinking caps on and come up with a new strategy tomorrow."

Veronica's eyebrows shot up. "Well, whatever you're doing with the resort manager seems to be working."

"You mean Sam?" Charlotte's face heated, recalling how turned on she'd been even before she'd stepped into his arms.

"Sam, is it?" Veronica teased. "Yes, I'm talking about him. You two were burning a hole in the dance floor. The heat coming off of you could have warmed a three-bedroom house in Alaska."

"It was that obvious?"

"Absolutely."

So she hadn't imagined it. "The music is still playing. Let's relax with our drinks and decompress before going up to bed."

"Sounds good," Veronica said. "I'm too wound up to go to sleep."

So they did just that, joining a few others who had the same idea. About thirty minutes later, the group started breaking up and Charlotte headed to her room. She made it across the lobby to the stairway when Sam suddenly appeared.

"That was exciting," Charlotte said by way of greeting. "Was there an actual fire?"

Sam nodded. "Not big, but there was damage near the kitchen from both fire and water from the sprinklers."

"That's too bad. Was it electrical or something else?" She had no idea what might have caused it and that was her only guess.

"Not electrical." His expression was dead serious. "The fire was deliberate. Someone set it."

SAM WATCHED CHARLOTTE'S eyes widen in surprise. If she knew anything about the fire, then she was excellent at pretending she didn't.

"Someone actually *set* the fire?" she asked.

"That's right. You can smell the accelerant as soon as you get near the site."

"Why would someone do such a thing?" Then she gasped. "Whoever did it put all of us in danger."

"That's true," Sam confirmed. The people in his care had been put in a hazardous situation, which made him both angry and vengeful. "I'm not sure the way the fire was set would have caused the entire building to go up. The sprinklers pretty much put it out and a fire extinguisher did the rest." Almost as if it were the work of bored teenagers, but there were none staying or working here at the time.

"Whew! That's good. I'm sure there's quite a mess to clean up, though."

He ignored her comment and asked the question burning in his gut. "Do you know anything about how the fire started?"

This time her eyes nearly popped from her head. "Me? Know anything about the fire? Of course not. Why would you even ask me that?"

"I'm asking everyone," he covered. "I need to know if you saw or heard anything when you were going upstairs for your sweater."

"No. Nothing at all." She lowered her voice. "If you want to know what took me so long, I spent most of the time in front of the bathroom mirror. I realized my mascara had smeared, probably in the heat of dancing, so I was touching up my makeup. I didn't see or hear a thing."

Her answer seemed logical, since he'd run into her on the third floor, but he was still wary. Nothing but trouble had arrived since she'd stepped foot on the island.

"If you discover anything that might be useful, please let me know. We've never had this much illegal activity in the time I've been here."

She seemed to consider his words carefully. "You said the thefts started a few days ago. Do you suspect the thefts and the fire are related and that it might be someone who arrived when I did?"

"That's certainly possible. I'm not ruling anything out yet." Although he'd been so focused on Charlotte because he thought she was Allie... He hadn't looked at others who'd arrived when she had.

"But why a fire?" she asked. "I can see the thefts, but not the reasoning for starting a fire. Maybe it was an accident?"

"Not likely with the accelerant. And I haven't figured out yet why the fire."

"To draw attention away from something else, maybe?"

Sam certainly hoped that wasn't the case.

Just then his radio at his waist sounded. "Briton," he answered.

"It's George. We've had two more thefts, boss."

He met Charlotte's eyes. "Damn." He should have known the fire was a cover-up. The sprinklers had caused more damage than the fire itself. And anyone who knew anything about the resort knew that all security personnel would be called in to fight a fire, leaving the hotel wide open for anything to happen. "Meet me in my office in five to give me details."

Sam replaced his radio on his belt and turned

back to Charlotte, who had obviously heard what happened.

"So the fire *was* meant to divert attention." She wasn't asking, merely stating the obvious. "And you're thinking I know something about it." Her eyes widened. "You think I'm involved."

He didn't say anything, waited for her to continue.

"Why would I do anything like that? Is that what you think of me? That I'd put hundreds of people in danger?" Her tone increased in volume the more she spoke.

"Can you blame me for questioning you? After your twin sister used me like she did?"

Charlotte frowned. "Used you? How?"

He lowered his voice. He didn't need anyone else to know how Allie had played him. "She didn't tell you how we became friends over those few months that she was coming to the Charleston property to deliver her pirated cosmetics? How she came on to me when I found out what she was doing in hopes of not turning her in?" He sucked in a breath. "Is it any wonder that I suspect you might be involved in the incidents here after being played like a fool by your identical twin sister?"

She stared at him, not saying a word. This was obviously news to her.

"It's going to be a long night." He spoke

brusquely. "Make sure you lock up your valuables and dead bolt your door."

She nodded ever so slightly, and he headed to his office.

Certainly not the end of the evening he'd had in mind when the two of them had been dancing earlier.

CHAPTER NINE

CHARLOTTE ROSE EARLY the next morning, eager to get through her to-do list before spending the rest of the day working on building her inventory for her upcoming show and then relaxing on the beach. She preferred the morning light to work in, but today she had too many things to take care of first.

She'd had a terrible night's sleep, dwelling on what Sam had told her about his past relationship with Allie. Charlotte had been struck dumb by his account and unable to ask any questions or comment. His revelation did make it a little easier to understand why he was hesitant to trust her.

She quickly showered while mentally reviewing her to-do list. First, she needed to figure out how to sign up for an appointment with Raymond Foster. That was one thing she hadn't talked to Veronica about.

Then she needed to call the Rhode Island Department of Motor Vehicles to see if they could quickly issue her a replacement driver's license and overnight it to her. Otherwise, she had no clue how she'd fly home without any ID.

She and Veronica had decided she should attend two beginner workshops, one this morning and one after lunch, and then Charlotte would be free to enjoy the fresh air while hopefully completing the charcoal drawing of a starfish she'd come across on her meanderings on the beach the other day. She'd taken several photographs at different angles before the tide had picked it up and carried it back into the ocean.

She donned a long, diagonally striped yellow-and-white skirt with a fitted yellow tee, and then headed down to the breakfast buffet. Veronica waved as Charlotte reached the lobby, and Charlotte remembered the other thing she needed to add to her to-do list: come up with a new plan to get Veronica and Jared together.

"Good morning," Charlotte said to Veronica with a smile and began filling a cup with coffee. "Any sign of Jared this morning?"

"Nope." Veronica seemed less cheerful than usual. "I haven't seen him since last night."

"I'm sure he'll be around. He's certainly not going to stay in his room all day." Charlotte patted Veronica's shoulder. "Besides, isn't there some kind of party tonight? Another chance to sidle up to him."

Veronica shrugged. "I guess so."

"Come on. Let's get some breakfast and you'll

feel better." Charlotte led the way from the coffee kiosk to the buffet. "Maybe he'll come join us for breakfast like he's been doing since we arrived."

As it turned out, that wasn't the case. Jared never showed up for breakfast and never answered his cell phone when Veronica called him.

"Maybe I should go check on him," she said.

"Why don't you try his room phone," Charlotte suggested and pointed to a far wall. "There's a hotel phone over there."

"Good idea." Veronica left Charlotte with their empty breakfast dishes. Her coffee was cold and she decided to get some more.

Sam was filling a to-go cup when she arrived at the coffee station. "Good morning," she greeted him, not expecting a reply. She couldn't help admiring his well-fit khaki pants and navy polo shirt. His short sleeves showed off his well-defined arms.

"Morning." His greeting wasn't as cheerful as usual, either. Even on this island, Monday morning was not a good time for people. Especially after their last confrontation.

"More trouble?" she asked, because she didn't like the way they left things last night.

"You mean, besides a thief and an arsonist on the loose? No. Unless you count the complete mess the fire and water caused. On top of that, I need to call our insurance carrier and my father-in-law to let them know what happened."

"Your father-in-law?" Charlotte repeated.

Sam nodded. "He's John Blaise, CEO of Blaise Enterprises that owns the resort."

"Ah! Now I get it. And he's the one who has your kids?"

Sam's lips twitched and his expression softened. "He does." Amazing what the mention of his kids did to his disposition.

Charlotte suddenly realized she hadn't been watching the time. She pulled out her cell phone. "Oh, good, it's only eight forty-five," she said and then explained to Sam, "I'm going to a nine o'clock workshop and don't want to be late."

He grew serious again. "So you're really going ahead with this plan of yours to do the presentation?"

Charlotte nodded. "I am. There are two workshops today that Veronica thought might be beneficial."

"And if this guy figures out who you really are? What then?"

Charlotte didn't like being on opposite sides of yet another argument with Sam, but held her ground and stood up for her sister. "I guess that's a chance I'll have to take. If Allie is okay with it, then so am I."

"I was beginning to think you were different from her," he said stiffly. "I guess neither of you know right from wrong."

Charlotte straightened. "Please don't speak

like that about my sister. You were very clear last night about what happened between the two of you in Charleston. If you can't say anything nice about her, then don't say anything at all." She knew she was pushing the limits by pretending to be Allie, but Charlotte didn't like hearing how much he didn't like her sister. "Maybe we should just stay away from each other."

He stared at her a few seconds and then said, "Have a nice day," before heading off across the lobby.

She'd stuck up for herself and for her sister, something that didn't come naturally. Then why did she feel so unhappy about it?

WALKING TO HIS OFFICE, Sam found himself incredibly irritated by Charlotte's insistence on pretending to be Allie to get an advertising account. She had seemed so different from Allie. Maybe he shouldn't have given her the benefit of the doubt after all.

If not for him being so inexplicably physically attracted to her, especially this morning in her sunny yellow, curve-hugging outfit, he probably never would have begun to allow himself to believe Charlotte was the opposite of Allie.

Thanks to his ex-wife and her deceit, he nearly always saw the bad in people before the good. Even knowing that about himself, he couldn't help feeling that was better than being naive and letting people run all over you.

Sam reached his office and sat down behind his desk. He was checking email when the assistant conference coordinator appeared in his office doorway.

"Hi, Katie. How's it going?"

Better than what he was dealing with, he hoped.

She smiled. "I think everything's going well. The fire caused some problems around the kitchen, but the chef is confident that the luau this evening will go well. He's been roasting the pigs on the beach and he's planning to cook most of the rest of the feast over an open flame outside."

People always seemed to enjoy when they put on a Hawaiian luau, despite being on an island off of Florida's east coast. His chef did an excellent job of duplicating true Hawaiian cuisine.

"Breakfast go okay?" Sam asked. He'd eaten a bowl of cereal in his apartment, delaying his departure because he hadn't been looking forward to starting his day.

Katie nodded. "The staff has use of the kitchen and though there was damage to one of the pantries, the chef's able to make do with mostly food in the fridges. He's sent someone to the mainland to replace the necessary supplies instead of waiting for our next delivery."

"Good. How's everything else going?" Sam only wanted good news.

Katie had nothing bad to report so when George popped his head into Sam's office, Katie left.

"What's the news on your end?" Sam asked his head of security.

George had nothing new to tell. He reiterated what he'd told Sam the night before. There had been two more thefts during the fire. The victims had left their rooms quickly and hadn't taken the time to lock up their valuables. They'd played right into the thief's hands. One iPad had been stolen, along with some expensive jewelry.

"Do you think we need to call in some more security?" Sam asked.

"It's beginning to look that way. Even bringing in two more guys to patrol the resort hasn't helped."

"Let me call John Blaise and see what he thinks." Sam picked up the phone receiver and George stood up to leave. "Maybe he's run into this kind of situation before. I'll call you as soon as I hang up."

George gave a silent wave and left Sam alone in his office.

"Hey, John, it's Sam."

"Sam! Good to hear from you. I was about to call you."

"You were?" Had he already heard the news?

"Yes, the kids decided coming home tonight would be better than in the morning."

"They did? Why? What happened?" They never wanted to leave early from their grandfather's house.

John laughed. "I have an unexpected board meeting at nine o'clock tomorrow. So it was either leave here with the kids before dawn or bring them back tonight."

Sam grinned. "Ah! Now I understand."

"So what's up with you? Or maybe you called to talk to Emma and Oliver?"

"That would be nice, but I have business to discuss with you first."

"More trouble?" John asked.

"I told you about the theft in one of the bungalows. Since then, there have been seven more, plus two more last night when a fire was set in one of the kitchen pantries. No one was hurt and the fire was put out quickly, but I need some advice on how to handle this situation."

"Damn! I'm glad no one was hurt, but I hope that fire doesn't raise our insurance rates."

"That's my next call," Sam told him and then asked his advice on adding more security.

"That sounds like a good idea. The more manpower the better. In fact, I can bring some reinforcements with me since we're coming your way tonight."

"That's perfect," Sam said. "I need to stop this rash of illegal activity."

AFTER CHECKING WITH Veronica about Jared, who finally answered his hotel phone and admitted to oversleeping, Charlotte signed up for an appointment with Raymond Foster for Thursday afternoon. Then she found her way to the first workshop with little trouble. She entered the room from the back and took a seat in the last row. She didn't want anyone to speak to her so she wouldn't have to lie about her identity. She kept her head down, writing a to-do list in a notebook for her upcoming art show.

"We're about to begin." The room was about half-full when someone began speaking at the podium. Charlotte's head shot up at the voice. It was Mona from the plane. The DP employee who knew Allie.

Charlotte maneuvered herself behind the woman in front of her and slunk down so Mona couldn't see her.

"Good morning," Mona said. "My name is Mona Livingston from DP Advertising. We've had a change in your program. Harold Bartholomew is unable to be here today because of a family emergency, but I'm pleased to introduce a woman who is not only an expert on today's subject, but she's also my boss. Please welcome Donna Patterson."

Donna Patterson? Owner of DP Advertising? Allie's former boss? The one who must have fired her? This was not good. Not good at all.

Charlotte scooted down farther in her seat, wishing she could crawl out of the room with no one the wiser. She eyed the distance to the door, but her chances of being noticed and making a scene were too great.

She kept her head down as if taking copious notes while Donna Patterson taught a very informative workshop on Presentation Skills: Communicating with Impact.

"Now I'd like you to take five minutes and put together a quick pitch for a product, either real or imaginary. Then we'll choose partners and you'll present to each other, using the tips I just outlined. We'll follow that with a thumbs-up or thumbs-down on whether you'd buy your partner's product and why or why not. If we have time, we'll have a team or two come up front to present their pitches."

Charlotte had no idea how to put a pitch together. Instead, she devised a plan to leave. Otherwise, people would certainly question why Allie Miller couldn't come up with a simple pitch. Charlotte didn't even know where to begin. She dealt in images, not words.

She waited, looking busy as she wrote on her pad, until the five-minute prep time was over and the time to pair up came. While the room was in chaos, Charlotte headed directly to the rear door and escaped without looking behind her. A little way down the hall, she plastered her back against the wall and caught her breath, letting her racing heart return to normal. Going to that workshop had not been the best idea, even if she did learn something about presentations.

The meeting room door suddenly opened and Donna Patterson stormed out. "Ms. Miller." Donna was directly in front of Charlotte before she realized what was happening. She had nowhere to go but to press her back more firmly against the wall.

She cleared her throat. "Yes?"

"What the hell are you doing here?" Donna Patterson was taller than she'd appeared behind the podium. She was close to six feet tall with a large build and eyes that could burn holes in someone. Right now, they were aimed at Charlotte.

She straightened to her full height, bothered immensely by this woman's tone. "I'm attending this conference like everyone else." She tried for indignant, but not sure she succeeded.

"I didn't mean that," the woman said smartly. "Why were you attending my workshop?"

"I didn't know you'd be teaching it."

"Even if Harold had taught the class, it's too basic for someone with your skills and experience."

Was she actually speaking nicely about Allie?

"Thank you."

Donna stared at her, waiting for an explanation.

"I'm trying to refresh my skills. Go back to

basics. That kind of thing." Charlotte sucked in a breath, hoping she didn't sound as nervous as she felt.

"Go spend your time in workshops that would actually help you." She raised one eyebrow. "Ethics, maybe." The woman who'd gone from scary to nice had ended with a jab that hurt Charlotte as much as it would have hurt Allie. Unfortunately, Donna Patterson had turned away and returned to the workshop before Charlotte could come up with an appropriate retort.

Feeling unwelcome and not expecting to get much more from Donna's workshop, Charlotte headed to her room to both calm down and to call the DMV to find out about getting a replacement driver's license.

"I'm happy to pay for the overnight postage," she told the brusque woman on the other end who had told Charlotte they could certainly issue her a replacement license, but it could take up to forty-five days. "I need it much quicker than that."

"It'll probably only take about ten days, but you can never be sure." The woman told her to fill out the forms online, have the one form notarized and then gave Charlotte the address.

"I saw all that on the website," Charlotte said. "But I need the replacement quicker than that. I need to fly home on Friday and have no ID. Besides, I don't have those documents with me."

Who traveled with documents like their birth certificate or proof of residency?

"I'm sorry, ma'am, but there's nothing more I can do."

SAM SAW CHARLOTTE coming down the main staircase from across the lobby, where he had just poured himself a fresh cup of coffee. He put a plastic lid on his disposable cup and headed in her direction.

He hadn't left things with her in a good place, and decided to remedy that. He couldn't keep a close eye on her if she didn't want him within ten feet of her. "Charlotte."

She turned to look at him, and, from the expression on her face, he realized she was upset. "Yes?"

He closed the gap between them. "I wanted to apologize for earlier. I'm sorry for what I said about Allie. It's not an excuse, but I'm pretty worked up about what's been going on around here. I'm sorry I took it out on you."

She shrugged. "Whatever." She proceeded to walk away.

"Wait!" He touched her upper arm and she raised her eyebrows. He dropped his hand. "Would you like a cup of coffee?" That was pretty lame, but he didn't like seeing her sad.

"No, thanks." Again she was about to leave.

"Is everything okay?" he asked.

She looked at him as if questioning whether she should confide in him. Finally, she spoke. "No, everything's not okay."

"Is there anything I can do to help?" He surprised himself by his serious offer.

"I doubt it," she said glumly. "Besides, why would you want to?"

He gave her an honest answer. "Because I'd like us to get along. So I'll keep my opinions about certain things to myself." He left out how he couldn't get her out of his head, no matter what he thought about her actions or her sister.

"Oh." She paused. "Well, I spoke with the Rhode Island DMV, and they can't overnight a new license even if I pay the postage."

"That's ridiculous."

She nodded and explained about the documents she needed in order to verify her identity and be able to fly home. "I don't know what I'm going to do. I was headed down here to see if I can extend my stay until I'm able to go home."

He rubbed his jaw. "This will make you feel worse, but I know for a fact we're booked up for the rest of the month."

She seemed to wilt in front of his eyes.

"I'm sure we can come up with a solution," he said when her eyes filled with moisture.

"I appreciate that," she said in little more than a whisper, "but I need to get home. I have an art show coming up and a lot of stuff to do at home for it."

He had a thought. "Is there anything Allie can do to help? Can she get into your house and then take the documents to the DMV and get a duplicate? Then she could overnight your license." He raised a finger. "Although...we don't get things overnight here. It's usually two-day delivery, so she'd need to get on it right away."

Charlotte's face brightened. "That's a great idea. I don't know why I didn't think of it. She already offered to do whatever I needed to get a replacement license. And Jack—her boyfriend and my neighbor—has a key to my house."

Didn't sound like the Allie he knew, but Charlotte swore the woman had changed for the better. Maybe she was right.

"Where are you going?" he asked when she started climbing the stairs.

"I need to go call her," she said over her shoulder. "Thanks for the idea."

He stood in silence, with no clue about how to keep her from walking away from him.

And no clue as to why he wanted her to stay.

CHARLOTTE DID, INDEED, speak with Allie. She was thrilled that Charlotte had procured an appointment with Raymond Foster. Allie had no problem going to Charlotte's house to get the needed documents and take them to the DMV.

Relieved after their conversation, Charlotte used the resort business center to print the forms she needed to fill out. Luckily, the resort had a notary. When she was done, she faxed the completed documents to her sister. Now it was up to Allie.

After lunch, Charlotte attended the other workshop Veronica had recommended. How to Develop and Hone Your Strategic Skills was informative, but a little more information than she would need to do Allie's presentation.

Too bad Charlotte hadn't stuck around to actually practice a pitch in Donna Patterson's workshop. That would have been helpful, but Charlotte never could have come up with a pitch. Her mind didn't work that way, so she would have had nothing to practice with.

Late in the afternoon, Charlotte lounged on a beach chair. She loved the sound of the wind blowing and the waves lapping at the shore. The birds flying overhead provided a chorus all their own.

She'd been alone for most of the afternoon, so when she heard the sound of children, it surprised her.

She opened her eyes and turned her head. A boy and a girl were laughing as they ran around, chasing each other and throwing a ball more to hit the other one than to have them catch it. Charlotte smiled at their antics.

As they came closer, she recognized them from the pictures at Sam's. His children were home. She tried to recall their names. Emma and Oliver, she thought. That sounded right.

"Hi," she said to them when they came within hearing distance.

"Hi," Oliver said politely. "We just got back from our papa's house. He got a *huge* new TV." The boy stretched his arms out as wide as they would go. "We watched some 3-D movies on it and it was like being at a movie theater."

"I'll bet that was fun," Charlotte said.

Oliver began telling her about their trip to the Everglades, but Emma interrupted him. "Let's go, Ol. You know Dad doesn't like us to talk to strangers."

"I don't think your dad would mind," Charlotte told her. "He and I know each other."

Emma was very serious. "I know. I remember you, too."

Charlotte's eyes narrowed. "How could you remember me? We've never met before."

Emma's mouth twisted. "I remember you from when we lived in South Carolina. You're not a nice person."

Allie had obviously made quite an impression on this little girl, and not a good one.

"I'm not who you think I am," Charlotte began. "My name is Charlotte Harrington and you met my twin sister, Allie Miller."

Emma stared at her in silence. The girl was good at intimidation.

"It's true," Charlotte said, desperately looking for the words to explain. "Allie and I are twins, but we didn't grow up together. We were both adopted by different families. We just met each other a few months ago." Charlotte brushed her windblown hair back from her face. "I know she caused problems in Charleston, but she's changed since then and she's trying to make up for her mistakes."

Emma smirked, reminding Charlotte of Sam.

"It's true." Why was she trying so hard to convince this preteen? In a few days, Charlotte would be home and she'd never see these people again.

From down the beach, Sam called for them.

"Oliver, Dad's calling," Emma said.

Oliver turned to go and must have realized Emma wasn't following him. She had taken a step closer to Charlotte. "Aren't you coming, Emmy? Dad probably wants us home for dinner." He looked at Charlotte and rubbed his stomach. "I'm starving. And he promised to help me put together the kite Papa bought me. We're going to fly it together, too."

Charlotte grinned. He didn't seem to care about what happened in Charleston. Although he was probably too young to remember. She

remembered Sam telling her that Emma was
twelve and Oliver nine.

"I'll be there in a minute," Emma told her
brother and gave him a gentle shove in the right
direction. "Go on. Tell Dad I'm coming."

When Oliver was out of hearing range, Emma
faced Charlotte. "I don't know who you are for
sure, but I'm warning you to not make trouble while you're here. My dad was in a really
bad mood when all that trouble happened in
Charleston and I don't want him to go through
that again."

Big talk for such a young girl. Charlotte envied
her bravery. She was obviously sticking up for
her father and brother. Quite a tight-knit group.

"Your dad and I have talked about all of this
and I think if you speak to him, you'll realize
who I am and that I'm not here to cause trouble."

Emma considered Charlotte's words. "I *will*
talk to my dad about you," she promised. "But
that doesn't explain about what I heard him say
to my grandfather."

Charlotte's heart sped up and her mouth went
dry. "What did he say?"

"I shouldn't repeat it."

"I'd really like to know. I can't refute it if I
don't know what was said."

Emma paused. She looked at where her dad
and Oliver stood, then turned back to Charlotte.
"He told Papa he has someone doing a back-

ground check on you." Emma put her hands on her hips. "So if he trusts you so much, then why is he doing that?"

Emma spun around and took off, leaving Charlotte with no chance to respond.

Not that she had an appropriate answer.

CHAPTER TEN

AT DINNER THAT EVENING, Sam enjoyed catching up with Emma and Oliver. Sam made it a habit to have dinner with them upstairs in their apartment as often as possible. He was missing the luau, but his kids came first. Especially since he hadn't seen them in several days.

He'd ordered food delivered so he wouldn't have to cook. Later, he would get Emma and Oliver settled for the night and then head downstairs to check things out. He had no babysitter for the evening, but he would be right downstairs and a radio or phone call away if the kids needed him. He didn't like doing that with the problems going on, but he couldn't stay with them all evening. He needed to patrol the resort and keep an eye out for possible thieves.

"So what's the homework situation?" The kids had finished telling him about the baby alligators they'd seen on their airboat ride through the Everglades. He hated to bring the conversation down by mentioning homework, but life got back to normal tomorrow when their tutor, Monica, returned.

"I did mine," Emma said quickly. "I finished it before Papa got here. I only have my half hour of reading to do before bed."

Of course she'd done her homework before they'd left. Sam smiled. She was a chip off the old block.

"I have spelling to do," Oliver said glumly.

"Okay!" Sam clapped his hands once and stood. "Let's get to it. Clear your plates and I'll put the leftovers away."

Since it was their normal routine, they did as he asked.

Before they settled into bed for the evening, Sam told them his plans. "I shouldn't be late, but I have some work to do. You each have a walkie-talkie next to your bed, as well as a phone extension. If you can't get me on the radio for some reason, dial zero and someone at the front desk will answer."

"We know, Dad, we know." Oliver rolled his eyes, while Emma merely gave him a look that said, "We've got this, Dad."

Sam tucked in Oliver first and then went to Emma's room across the hall. He stood in the doorway to watch her in the midst of the hearts and flowers she'd used to decorate her girlie but funky room. She sat up against the pink bolster in her bed, a book clenched in her hands as she read. She'd recently discovered a new young-adult mystery series, and she went through them faster than she'd read the Harry Potter books.

Unlike Oliver, who preferred physical activities to being forced to read for thirty minutes every day. Sam had tried all sorts of books to grab the boy's interest, but so far, no luck.

"Hey," Emma finally said to him in acknowledgment.

"Hey," he said in return. "Must be a good book."

She smiled. "Oh, Daddy, it's *so* much better than good. I can't wait to read the next chapter."

"Well, don't stay up too late reading. You have school tomorrow."

"I won't."

Sam sat on the edge of her bed to give her a kiss on the forehead and a good-night squeeze. "Good night, baby." She stiffened and he chuckled. "Sorry. Good night, Emma." He kissed her again, a loud smack on her cheek that made her groan in agony, which turned into giggles.

He rose to leave, but she called him back. "Daddy?"

He spun around. "Yes?"

"We ran into that woman on the beach today."

"That woman?" As soon as he voiced the question, he knew who she was talking about. "What about her?"

"She told me she was the twin sister of that bad woman in South Carolina. Is that true?"

"Yes," he answered. His daughter sounded as suspicious of Charlotte as he had been.

"I heard you say you were doing a background check on her, so you must not trust her, either."

He hesitated. "I'm checking out several people who are staying here. Everyone who arrived when the thefts began." She already knew a little about the trouble they'd been having, so it wasn't new information. He'd filled both kids in earlier so they would be extra diligent about their safety, as well as their possessions.

"I'm not going to trust her," Emma said with absolute confidence.

"That's fine, but I doubt you'll run into her. She's part of the conference that's going on this week and she'll be pretty busy." *Pretending to be someone she wasn't.*

"Well, if I do see her," she said vehemently, "I'm not going to believe a single word she says."

Sam's lips curved up slightly. She couldn't be more like him if she tried. Trusting the wrong people can hurt. His daughter had learned that lesson the hard way when her mother was still alive. Oliver had been too young to understand or recall the pain his mother had caused them all.

If only he could remember to guard himself

around Charlotte when he was standing in front of her and drawn to her sweet mouth and sexy curves.

WHEN CHARLOTTE JOINED the luau that evening, she was presented with a lei made with actual flowers, not the artificial ones she'd seen in the party stores at home. The sweet smell of the fragrant petals surrounded her, relaxing her and taking her cares away.

She quickly located Veronica, holding an umbrella drink in a hollowed-out pineapple. "Hey," Charlotte greeted her new friend. "This looks like it'll be fun." Even for an introvert like herself who didn't get out much.

"Uh-huh." Veronica sipped her drink.

"Something wrong?"

Veronica shrugged. "Jared."

Charlotte looked around and didn't see him. "Where is he?"

"That's the million-dollar question. I haven't seen him all day."

"Not even after you woke him up when he overslept this morning?" Veronica had finally spoken to him when she called his room from the house phone in the lobby.

She shook her head. "Nope. Nada."

"I'm sure he'll come down for dinner." Charlotte pointed to the tables in the distance overflowing with food. "He's certainly not going to miss this feast." From what she'd witnessed since arriving, Jared could eat more than she and Veronica combined.

"You're probably right," Veronica said. "Let's get some food and we can save him a seat. Looks like they have tables set up on the beach near the food."

They trekked to the beach and began filling their plates. If not for the signs in front of the serving dishes, indicating the food and ingredients, Charlotte wouldn't have known what she was about to eat. Among the offerings was kalua pua'a, which was spit-roasted shredded pork with sea salt and green onions. Then there was Hawaiian poi, a starch made of taro root, something Charlotte had always wanted to try. Lomi lomi salmon was a tangy salmon salad that the chef said went well with the poi. Poke, a raw-fish dish she'd only heard of on a cooking show, as well as many other unfamiliar dishes, were available to try. A few of the fruits looked exotic to Charlotte. Lychee turned out to be one of her favorites when she nibbled at it from her plate.

They found seats across from each other at one of the long tables. Veronica quickly changed the subject of their conversation from food to Jared.

"Do you think he's sick?" Charlotte suggested when they'd nearly finished their food and Jared hadn't appeared. "Maybe he's in his room because he doesn't feel well?"

Veronica's mouth formed an O. "I hadn't thought of that. Maybe you should check on him."

"Why me?" Charlotte asked. "I think it would be better if you checked on him. He'd know you're concerned about him."

Veronica tilted her head. "I guess you're right. I just don't want him to think I'm stalking him or something."

"You're his friend. You're concerned."

"I don't know," Veronica said. "He's just been a little off since we arrived on the island."

"Off how?"

"It's hard to explain." Veronica paused. "He's been right beside me, but I feel like his mind is a million miles away."

"Is he dealing with personal problems? Worried about someone or something back home?"

"If he is, he hasn't shared it with me."

Charlotte had a sudden thought. "Did you ever consider he might have feelings for you but doesn't know how to deal with them?"

"That's ridiculous. Jared is usually so open, at least with me. If he has feelings for me beyond friendship, then he's been excellent at hiding them."

"I don't know," Charlotte said. "I've seen him look at you. I would bet my next art commission that he's got more than friendship on his mind when it comes to you."

Veronica blushed and put her hand to her cheek. "I hope you're right. He's the only guy I want and if he doesn't feel the same…"

Charlotte patted Veronica's hand. "He does. I'm sure of it." She looked around for the bar. "Now, you go find him and don't stop until you do. Meanwhile, I'm going to get me one of those drinks." She pointed to Veronica's umbrella concoction.

"Yes, ma'am." Veronica gave her a mock salute and began walking in the direction of the resort's main building, while Charlotte headed to the bar set up on the beach.

The bartender handed her an umbrella drink and she'd barely thanked him and turned away when Sam came into view. Her heart pounded at the mere sight of him. He was headed straight for her. He moved with ease, his long strides covering the distance between them quickly. She recovered her senses enough to remember she was upset with him.

"Just the person I wanted to see," he said before requesting a soda from the bartender.

"I can't say the same," Charlotte said.

His eyes widened in surprise and then he sipped his drink before saying anything. "I'm sorry to hear that."

Charlotte straightened. "And I'm sorry to hear

you're checking up on me. I thought you believed me."

Sam looked panicked and his gaze shot around.
"Come over here." He took Charlotte's elbow and
led her away from the bar, as well as other people.

"This is like déjà vu," Charlotte quipped with
dripping sarcasm.

She remembered the first time he'd dragged
her away from people and into his office. He'd
kissed her like she'd never been kissed before.
Her temperature rose at the mere idea of it. If he
did it again, she might enjoy it. And she couldn't
have that.

"I've apologized for what happened that first
night," he said when they were far enough down
the beach and away from everyone. "I need to
explain about the investigation and I don't want
anyone else to overhear. I'm guessing your run-
in with my daughter is how you found out about
the background checks?"

"That's right. She doesn't believe I'm Allie's
twin, either." Like father, like daughter.

"Don't worry about her," he said. "And don't
worry about the background check unless you're
hiding something."

"Of course I'm not hiding anything. But all
you had to do was ask."

"You're not the only one we're investigating.
Everyone who arrived the day the thefts began
is under scrutiny."

That actually made her feel a little better. But then she had a thought. "What if that's what the thief or thieves want you to believe?"

He narrowed his gorgeous blue eyes at her. "What do you mean?"

"Maybe they chose that day, knowing many people were arriving and that would throw suspicion on everyone and not the real culprits." She was surprised he hadn't thought of that himself.

"You have a point." He was as serious as she'd ever seen him in their short acquaintance. "I need to revisit our plan of action."

CHARLOTTE RETURNED TO the luau after their conversation, and Sam mulled over her idea. He finally concluded they should consider that people other than the Friday arrivals could be guilty.

Sam glanced around. The luau was beautiful. The tiki torches had been lit before the sun set, and the conference crowd appeared to genuinely enjoy the demonstrations of both the Hawaiian hula and traditional Tahitian dancing. The dance troupe had been coming since before Sam arrived at Sapodilla Cay, and he never tired of hearing how much people enjoyed the entertainment. He grabbed a piece of his favorite dessert—coconut pie—from the dessert table and headed upstairs to check on his kids for the third time that evening.

The first time, Emma had still been awake

and hadn't appreciated being checked on. The next time, she was asleep and he didn't have to make up a story about needing something from the apartment.

While in his apartment this time, with the evening winding down and no problems with the resort, Sam decided a late-night soak in the hot tub would be nice. He finished his pie and then changed into his swim trunks. He added a T-shirt and slipped on his boat shoes before grabbing a towel.

At the last minute, he poured some wine into a plastic cup and rode the elevator to the first floor.

The raised hot tub was located directly outside the far end of the main building, right next to the pool with a swim-up bar and a fountain, which usually drowned out all other noise. The fountain was turned off and the bar wasn't open this late, so no one was around. He stripped down to his bathing suit and turned the timer on to start the motor for the bubbles, eager to enjoy a peaceful soak.

Not much time passed before he heard footsteps. He opened his eyes and saw Charlotte wearing a skimpy cover-up that begged to reveal what was underneath. It was a gauzy thing, knotted at the bust, and left her shoulders bare. The cover-up barely covered her butt cheeks.

"Oh," she said when she saw him. "I didn't mean to interrupt."

"You didn't," he lied, but couldn't say he wasn't glad to see her. His hardening erection, which was, thankfully, concealed under a layer of bubbles, wasn't unhappy about her arrival, either. "Come on in, the water's fine."

She paused. "That's okay. I don't want to disturb you."

"I'll leave then," he offered. "I can tell you don't want to be here at the same time as me—"

"That's true."

"Ouch."

She held up a hand. "I didn't mean it that way. Well, maybe I did. You haven't been exactly welcoming." She pulled her cover-up so it hid more of her bare skin. "It's just that you looked so peaceful in there. You're under a lot of stress with everything that's going on, so you should go back to relaxing."

"I insist," he said, moving to a seat farthest from the stairs. It wasn't until he added, "Please," that she seemed to consider it.

"Okay," she finally said.

His mouth watered when she turned away from him and removed her cover-up, revealing a modest two-piece bathing suit in a rainbow of colors. It was sexier than a string bikini. She laid the cover-up and her towel on a nearby chair and removed her sandals. When she walked toward the hot tub stairs, he could barely breathe. Her exposed skin, and there was a lot of it, was slightly tanned and glowed in the dim lights surrounding the pool and hot tub. He clenched his fists under the water to avoid reaching for her.

She'd gotten to the top step, and was about to step into the water, when she tilted forward. Sam rose from across the hot tub, putting his arms out to catch her. Everything happened in slow motion, as rising and moving through the bubbling water wasn't easy.

He caught her by the waist and she avoided doing a belly flop. She held on to his shoulders and he pulled her to him, water splashing around them. They were wet skin to wet skin before he could consider what they were doing.

He slowly lowered them both down into the water until he sat and she was on his lap at a ninety-degree angle. He ran a hand up her arm to her neck and cupped her face. Her lips were slightly parted and he couldn't wait any longer to taste them again.

"Hey," he said.

Her mouth curved into a smile. "Hey," she countered.

"Are you okay?" he asked.

She nodded without saying anything, her focus on his mouth.

"What is it about you that makes it so that I can't stay away?" Not having or expecting an answer, he covered her mouth with his own.

CHARLOTTE DIDN'T KNOW what happened. She must have slipped on the top step of the hot tub. Before she knew it, she'd tumbled forward and was in Sam's arms. The truth was, she was enjoying every minute of it, no matter how clumsy she must have appeared.

His mouth was hot and insistent, just the way she'd remembered. She'd thought of his kiss more times than she'd like to admit. This repeat performance was more than living up to her memory.

Although she'd felt his physique through his shirt the other times he'd kissed her, having access to his wet, well-formed body was completely different. His chest was mostly smooth, except for a light smattering of hair along his breastbone. His biceps were well defined, and she could run her hand along his smooth upper arm and over his shoulder and never tire of it.

With a groan, Sam pulled back and wiped his free hand over his damp face. "I'm sorry. I don't know what got into me." He lifted her easily and set her on the seat next to him.

Charlotte didn't know what to say. What had she done wrong? He seemed to be enjoying their interlude as much as she was, so what happened? She waited for him to explain.

"You're a resort guest and I'm an employee," he explained, peering around the pool area. "I'm sorry. Again. I was out of bounds."

Charlotte swallowed, relieved to know she

wasn't the actual reason for him stopping. She'd begun to wonder if she'd been so out of practice kissing that she'd become bad at it. "Is there some corporate rule against it?"

"Nothing in writing," he said. "But I'd hate to have my employees see us and think it was okay to fraternize with the guests."

She smiled. "Fraternize? Is that what we were doing?" She blushed when she realized she was flirting.

He grinned. "Something like that."

"So now what?" she asked and pointed to his plastic cup. "Does sharing whatever you have in that cup come under the heading of fraternization?"

He picked it up from the far edge of the hot tub where he'd set it. He passed it to her and held her gaze. "Pinot Grigio. A fraternization-free grape."

She took a sip of the cold wine, watching him as she did so. "Refreshing," she pronounced as she handed it back. "Definitely no essence of fraternization."

His fingers grazed hers as he took the cup and turned it to drink from the exact spot she had. Her blood reached its boiling point. As she had done, he watched her as he drank and then put the cup on the far edge of the hot tub.

She squeezed her legs together, trying to still the desire building within her core.

They sat back in their seats, still looking at

each other. Charlotte's insides were melting, and not from the hot water. They weren't even touching. What would happen the next time they did? Or would they?

Her question was answered quickly when Sam reached for her hand under the water and intertwined her fingers with his. He squeezed gently and she squeezed back.

"How did we get ourselves into this?" she asked. "I came here for a relaxing week at the beach and look at me now."

He grinned and his gaze lowered to her barely showing chest. Then it lowered to her body below the water, even though she knew he couldn't actually make out her form under the bubbles. "Yeah, I've *been* looking. That's part of the problem." He moved their clenched hands to his thigh and rubbed his thumb along hers.

Her face heated again from his comment. It had been so long since she'd been seen as attractive. Or felt like a sexual being.

"So now what?" He voiced the question that was on the tip of her tongue.

She shrugged. "I don't know. Maybe another sip of that wine?"

With his free hand, he passed the cup to her. She took a drink and passed it back. This time he didn't take a drink but instead put the cup back, released her hand and grabbed her by the waist so she could straddle him.

His mouth covered hers and when she wiggled into a more intimate position on his lap, he groaned. She felt the power she had over him and luxuriated in it, knowing from both his groan and his erection pressing into her that he wanted her as much as she wanted him.

His splayed hands roamed her naked back and moved lower to cup and gently squeeze her backside, pressing her even more intimately against him.

He tasted like the wine, and his mouth was hot as his tongue parried with hers. Her breasts ached for his touch, even while they were pressed against his naked chest. The feeling was so sensual she could barely breathe.

The hot tub bubbles stopped. Charlotte's heart leaped to her throat, while Sam merely held her close and leaned his forehead on hers.

"I guess the timer ran out," he said on a chuckle. "I'd suggest turning it on again, but maybe this is a sign."

"Oh. Right." Charlotte was flustered, taken by surprise at his ability to control his ardor like a light switch. "Yes, I'm probably turning into a prune. And it's getting late."

She began to remove herself from his lap, but he pulled her back into place. He nudged her chin until they were eye to eye. "When I said sign, I meant maybe we shouldn't be out here in such a public place."

"But what about not fraternizing with the guests?" *Please say you don't care about that. Tell me that being with me is more important to you than a rule that's not even written down.*

He kissed her quickly on the lips. "I think we can work around it." His expression grew serious. "It's been a long time since I've felt such a strong connection to someone. I'm not sure I can ignore it and let you walk out of my life at the end of the week without exploring it further."

"Oh."

He kissed her again. "That's it? Oh?"

She shook her head, as if that would straighten her thoughts. "No, there's a lot more than 'Oh.' I just don't know what to say."

"Tell me you want to explore this connection. Tell me you don't want to miss out on what this might be."

She nodded. "I do." She kissed him this time. "I really do."

"Let me check on my kids, grab a quick shower and I'll come to your room." He paused. "Are you okay with that?"

Truthfully, it sounded both wonderful and scary at the same time. "Yes. I am," she whispered.

CHAPTER ELEVEN

ALL THE WAY up to his apartment and during his shower, Sam questioned what he was doing.

He'd never slept with—never even kissed—a guest before. He didn't count the time Allie had kissed him, since she also had an ulterior motive, wasn't a resort guest and he hadn't been interested in what she was offering.

So what was it about Charlotte that made him forget his ethics? She was the exact physical duplicate of Allie. For all he knew, beneath that killer body could also be the identical duplicitous personality.

He turned off the water in the shower and dried himself. He could call Charlotte and say he'd changed his mind. Tell her this was a bad idea. Or make something up, instead of being so blunt. A resort emergency wouldn't sound unbelievable after the past few days of mayhem.

Then he remembered how utterly sexy Charlotte looked in her bathing suit. How she felt in his arms, the smoothness of her skin, the subtle curves that made her all woman. The way she kissed him with complete abandon.

Damn. He was in big trouble. This was a situation he didn't know how to deal with, and there was no one he could confide in.

Even as he reviewed the pros and cons, he was continuing to get ready to go to her room. He dressed in shorts and a T-shirt, collected his cell phone, his radio...and condoms.

No denying he was about to listen to his body and ignore the warnings in his head.

His kids were both still sound asleep when he left his apartment. He stood in front of Charlotte's door for several minutes before knocking. He knew he'd be on the video footage, but as long as nothing untoward happened on this level to make someone view it, his rendezvous would remain his own secret.

Both he and Charlotte were free to pursue a physical relationship, he reasoned. His former father-in-law had not so subtly hinted several times that Sam should move on, find someone who made him and his kids happy. Not an easy feat when he rarely made it off the island.

As long as it didn't interfere with Sam's position at the resort, then what difference should it make if he slept with Charlotte? There was no hard-and-fast rule about it, even if he considered it one to live by.

Although, if he happened to catch one of his

employees trying to pick up a guest, he'd be certain to have a talk with him or her.

But this was different. He'd never pursued Charlotte and as far as he could tell, she hadn't done anything overt to get his attention, either.

They'd merely been drawn to each other by fate.

What harm could befall them by simply acting on their desire?

CHARLOTTE HAD HURRIED to her room, her mind spinning, refusing to consider whether sleeping with Sam was a good idea or not. She altered the familiar advertising slogan that kept running through her head. "What happens on Sapodilla Cay stays on Sapodilla Cay." Why not enjoy her time here with an opportunity she couldn't resist?

As she showered off the chemicals from the hot tub, the thought in her head switched to "Maybe he's not Mr. Right, but he's a really hot Mr. Right Now." She needed no convincing that having a sizzling affair with Sam would be the highlight of her week. If sex with him didn't wash away her cares, even temporarily, then she didn't know what would.

As for leaving him behind when she left the island…she would deal with that when the time came.

Maybe being here was relaxing her, after all.

She exited the shower and toweled off, her hands shaking as she slipped on the hotel robe that hung on the back of the bathroom door. She had no idea what to wear since she was flying without a net. Deciding to dry her damp hair first, she removed her hotel shower cap. Her hair had gotten a little wet at the hot tub, but it didn't take much to dry and style it again. She couldn't help remembering how it had gotten wet. She'd been so clumsy when she'd nearly fallen belly first into the water, but look what it had led to. She shivered at the memory of Sam's strong arms catching her and not letting go. The way his mouth covered hers so naturally, he made her forget everything else but him.

Snapping out of her delicious reverie, she moisturized her face and body, then added a light touch of makeup. Her dark lashes were okay bare, but she added some color to her cheeks even though she was flushed from both the shower and in anticipation of what they were about to do.

Charlotte was still wearing the thick, white hotel robe and nothing else when there was a knock on the door. She adjusted the robe to make sure it was secure and looked through the peephole.

"Hey," she said as she opened the door to Sam. "I didn't have a chance to get dressed after my shower. I'll just be a minute." When he en-

tered the room, she closed and locked the hotel
door, then turned to go into the bathroom. Sam
grabbed her elbow and pulled her into his arms,
flat against his body.

"No need to get dressed." Even the deep tone
of his voice was sexy. "Clothes will simply slow
us down."

She shivered at his words, and then he kissed
her. Long and slow and sexy. No rushing. They
had all the time in the world.

Or did they?

She reluctantly pulled away from his kiss to
ask, "Are your kids okay?"

"Mmm-hmm. Sleeping." He captured her
mouth again.

She drew back. "What if they wake up and
you're not there?"

He turned his hips slightly and poked her ribs
with something hard on the side of his belt. He
released her mouth and said, "They each have a
radio to reach me directly."

"Oh."

Her response was punctuated by his mouth
closing over hers. He slid the robe from one
shoulder and traced her neck to her collarbone
with his fingers, dipping one finger to where the
robe plunged low over her breast and barely covered her nipple. Then he worked his way back
up to her shoulder and down her arm to where
the robe hung at her elbow.

She trembled again. Not cold. Definitely turned on. She lifted his T-shirt until he stripped it off over his head and threw it to the side in one easy motion. She kissed his chest, loving the feel of his hands tangling in her hair. She touched him with her fingertips, exploring every angle and plane of his upper body until she reached his waistband. His mouth was on her neck when she teased him by sliding her fingers along the inside of his waistband and dipping as low on his abdomen as she could reach.

In retaliation, he bit her playfully on the neck.

"Ouch!" She laughed and adjusted the robe to cover herself again.

He spoke into her ear. "You're playing with fire." Then he nipped her earlobe, followed quickly by him taking it into his mouth.

Her legs grew weak with wanting him. He must have sensed it because he led her to the bed. He threw off the decorative pillows and comforter, leaving crisp white sheets that called out to her.

Holding her gaze, he kicked off his shoes and let his khaki shorts fall to the floor. Her heart beat wildly as he stood in front of her in his dark gray boxer briefs, which bulged overtly with his erection.

Feeling braver and sexier than she'd felt in a very long time, Charlotte stood at the end of the bed and faced him. She untied the thick belt of her robe. She allowed it to hang freely and the robe fell open slightly. She luxuriated in the desire in his eyes as he watched her.

He took a step in her direction. "You know you're killing me, don't you?"

"Not before I have my way with you," she teased and then slowly let the robe slip off her shoulders and down her arms. Ever so slowly, it finally dropped to the floor at her feet.

He covered the ground between them. She was off her feet and flat on her back on the cool sheets before she could do more than gasp. He was on top of her, his hands cupping her breasts, followed by his mouth sucking and licking and teasing each in turn. Somewhere along the way he'd shed his underwear, because she was extremely aware of his hot, smooth penis on the inside of her thigh.

More than anything, she wanted him inside her. She wiggled her lower body, trying to guide him into her, which made him chuckle.

"What's so funny?" she breathed. Instead of answering, his hand was suddenly between her legs and she gasped as he explored her intimately. She arched her back when his fingers teased her mercilessly until she nearly screamed as she climaxed.

He took her mouth then, stopping only to say, "You haven't seen nothin' yet."

SAM AWOKE WITH a start. His eyes wide open in the dark, it took him a few seconds to remember where he was.

Charlotte's room.

Charlotte's bed.

And her head lay on his chest as if he were her pillow.

What time was it? He needed to get back to his apartment. He'd never left his kids alone all night. He was a much better parent than that. Even if he was just one floor away from them in the same building, that was too far.

He turned his head and squinted to see the time on the bedside clock. Just after two. He'd only planned to be gone an hour, maybe a little more.

He lightly ran his fingers through Charlotte's soft hair. She'd worn him out. He never would have guessed she was such a vixen in bed. Her proper behavior in public belied her true personality.

His touch must have woken her because she stirred. "I need to go," he whispered, reluctantly guiding her head off his chest and onto a pillow.

"Mmm," she moaned without opening her eyes. She rolled onto her stomach and clenched the pillow under her head with both arms. He was actually jealous of the pillow.

Emma and Oliver. He needed to leave. He thought he was home free until her hand grasped his arm. He leaned over her and kissed her cheek. He wanted to say he'd see her later in the morning or he'd have breakfast with her, or something. But he wouldn't make promises he couldn't keep. Whatever this was, it needed to stay under wraps. He had no idea when he'd be able to be with her again.

Or if there would even *be* a next time.

"Don't go," she whispered, eyes still closed.

"I don't want to, but I have to," he said. "I need to be there when my kids wake up."

She nodded sleepily. "Right. I forgot."

He couldn't help himself. He touched her shoulder and then ran his hand under the sheet covering her. His hand moved freely down her smooth back until he cupped her backside.

"Are you leaving or starting all over again?" The humor in her voice came through clearly.

He moved her hair aside and kissed the back of her neck and scrambled to be closer to her. He rubbed his now-hard erection against the back of her thigh. "Maybe once more for good luck."

She chuckled and caressed his outer thigh. "Sounds like I'm the one with all the good luck."

MORNING CAME WAY too quickly for Charlotte. She'd awoken during the night to use the bathroom and to get a large glass of water for her parched throat. When she'd returned to bed, she realized Sam had left. The bed was cold except

for where she'd been sleeping, but she understood he didn't want to leave his children alone.
Somehow being a good father made him even
more attractive in her eyes.

She'd set her alarm on her cell phone and gone
back to sleep, deciding to forgo her nightshirt
and sleep naked. Thoughts of Sam's skill at love-
making kept her awake until her body and mind
finally both shut down.

Now her alarm was going off and she didn't
want to get up.

She dragged herself out of bed and into the
shower. A little while later, she headed down
for breakfast where she was nearly accosted by
Veronica.

"You'll never believe what happened," Veronica cried at the same time she took Charlotte's
elbow and led her away from anyone who might
overhear them. "You were right!"

As much as Charlotte loved hearing she'd been
right about something, she was confused. "Right
about what?"

"About Jared! He was sick. That's why he
didn't show up last night at the luau. Isn't that
great?"

Charlotte pursed her lips. "I'm not sure. Should
I be happy he's sick?"

Veronica laughed. "No, no. I meant that the
reason he didn't show up wasn't because he was
avoiding me. He was not feeling well enough to

come downstairs. He said he had an upset stomach. Maybe a bug, or something he ate."

"Well, I'm glad you solved the mystery," Charlotte said. "So you talked to him last night or this morning?"

Veronica looked about to burst. "That's what's so great. I went to his room last night when he didn't sound very good on the phone. He didn't want to let me in because he was so sick, although he didn't look that bad. Only a little flushed. I said I'd check on him this morning and he said, 'Don't come too early.' So I just came from there and he seems to be doing great."

Charlotte listened intently to the woman's explanation, wondering if there was more to the story that Veronica wasn't telling. Charlotte didn't know Jared very well—or Veronica, for that matter—so she wasn't one who could judge whether he was being truthful or not. It seemed quite possible that Jared had a woman in his room when Veronica showed up and he hadn't wanted her to know.

But maybe he was truly sick. She hoped for Veronica's sake that he'd told her the truth. She didn't want her new friend to get hurt.

"Nice to hear he's feeling better," Charlotte said. "I'm going to get some coffee. Want some?"

"I've already had two cups. I'm moderating a workshop this morning, so I need to run. Let me know when you get the presentation from Allie and we'll go over it if you want."

"That would be great. I haven't heard from her, but I know she has a big meeting today."

They each went in different directions, and Charlotte was putting a plastic lid on her to-go cup when she heard a deep, familiar voice behind her. "Good morning."

She spun around and her heart beat wildly at the sight of Sam in his usual uniform of khaki pants and navy resort polo. "Good morning," she said, unable to control her grin. "How are your kids?"

"Not happy that their tutor is back today. Otherwise, they're fine. They're used to me coming and going in the middle of the night." At her raised eyebrows, he added, "Because of resort emergencies."

"Oh. Right." She had to take his word for it because she didn't like the picture in her head right now of him with another woman.

"Sleep well?" He poured himself a cup of coffee, then gave her a sideways glance and winked.

"I guess so," she said with a nonchalant shrug of one shoulder and what she hoped was a taunting look. "You?"

"I slept great." He stretched his arms and rolled his shoulders. "I think my time in the hot tub tired me out."

She'd been about to sip her coffee and her eyes

widened at his teasing comeback. She feigned sarcasm as she retorted, "I guess I should have stayed in there longer. I probably could have used something to *really* wear me out."

He was grinning when he turned around to see if anyone was nearby. He sidled up to her as if to reach for something in front of her and under his breath he said, "I guess I'll have to work harder next time so you get a better night's sleep." Their scintillating banter was nearly as exhilarating as their romp in her bed last night.

Her face and entire body heated at his words. "Next time?" She cleared her throat and whispered, "Pretty sure of yourself, aren't you?"

Again, under his breath, he said, "Do you know how much I want to drag you upstairs right this minute and have my way with you?"

"Pretty sexist comment," she countered a little louder than she'd planned. She pictured the brazen scenario and couldn't help craving it, too.

"And what sexist comment would that be?" Donna Patterson had appeared behind them as if from nowhere.

Charlotte spun around to face Donna, trying to come up with a logical explanation for her comment, but her brain wasn't cooperating.

Sam quickly stepped in. "I was repeating what I heard on a radio talk show this morning. Something about women being better at reading facial cues than men are."

"That's hogwash," Donna snapped as she added several packets of a sugar substitute to the coffee she'd just poured. "Men would be better at it if they paid more attention."

Charlotte and Sam looked at each other, eyes wide, each trying hard not to burst out laughing.

"That's very true," Charlotte said when she could control herself. "Men would be much better at a *lot* of things if only they paid attention." She stared straight at Sam when she spoke, knowing he could read the humor in her eyes from the way those sexy lips of his fought off a smile. He was a perfect example of a man who clearly paid extra-close attention to a woman's needs.

"True, very true." Donna took her coffee and left them alone again.

"Are you saying I didn't pay enough attention to you last night?" he asked in a serious tone.

"Shh!" She spun around to make sure no one heard him. One close call was enough. "Of course I'm not saying that."

He grinned then, and she realized he'd been teasing her. "Maybe I need another chance to prove I can pay better attention," he suggested, raising his eyebrows to punctuate the idea.

She swallowed with difficulty. "On second thought, maybe you do."

"I'll catch you later," he promised with a wink and then headed in the direction of his office.

You can bet on it, she thought as she watched him walk away. *You can catch me and have your way with me. As long as you don't stop until I tell you to.*

SAM WENT ABOUT the rest of his morning with a spring in his step. He caught himself thinking about Charlotte at the most inopportune times.

So instead of walking around with a stupid grin on his face, he found himself spending a lot of time in his office, answering email, returning phone calls, dealing with guests who had been theft victims.

Not until midafternoon did he have a chance to wander around the resort, hoping to run into Charlotte. With the way his hormones were raging, he almost felt as if he was back in high school. He wouldn't be surprised to see a pimple forming on his chin the next time he checked a mirror.

Finally, he headed to the beach. His kids, and several other students who were resort employees' offspring, were to the left of the boardwalk with their tutor. Monica understood that the kids needed to spend time outdoors as much as they needed to learn math, science and reading.

Sam looked to the right of the boardwalk. There, way down on the edge of the pier sat Charlotte. He recognized her immediately by the way she brushed her windblown hair from her face. Her bare legs dangled over the side of the dock, and she had a hand to her forehead to block the sun.

He followed her gaze and saw the school of fish. They were bobbing in and out of the clear water as they moved away from the shore.

When they couldn't be seen any longer, Charlotte picked up her things and began the long trek back to shore along the pier. She wore a short skirt and a top that revealed her bare midriff. About halfway to the sand, she saw him in the distance and waved.

He waved back. A restless feeling came over him and he walked in her direction.

"Hi," he said lamely when he was close enough for her to hear.

She smiled and his hormones kicked in again. "Hi, yourself."

"Get any good pictures?" He pointed to the camera bag slung over her shoulder.

"I think so. I was shooting so fast I didn't stop to look at all of them." She motioned with her head to the other people on the beach. "Are you sure you should be talking to me?"

He shrugged. "If anyone mentions it, we ran into each other. Can I carry something for you?" She held multiple bags of things besides her camera bag.

"Thanks." She handed him part of her load. Their hands touched and sparks ignited.

"I guess kissing you right here on the beach wouldn't be a good idea."

She laughed as they began walking toward the resort, a sound he couldn't imagine tiring of. "I think that would defeat the purpose of us being discreet."

A thought popped into his head. He knew somewhere they could go and not be seen. "I've got an idea. Unless you're on your way somewhere?"

She shook her head. "No. I was just going to put these things in my room. I told Veronica I'd meet her for dinner at six. She's gathered a bunch of people to play cards afterward." She glanced at him. "What's your idea?"

He checked his cell phone for the time. Not even four o'clock. "There's a place down the beach on the other side of the pier that's private. It's an inlet with some large rocks that have been worn smooth by the ocean. I run past it all the time, but I've never checked it out. It's only visible at low tide and we're almost at that now."

"So I'll meet you there in, what? Fifteen minutes?" Her excitement showed on her face. He hadn't been sure if she would be receptive to the idea or not.

He gave her specific directions to the inlet. "Fifteen minutes it is. Look for the two sapodilla trees that guard the entrance or you'll go right past it." They'd reached the point where the boardwalk to the resort met the beach.

"Thanks for your help. I'll take these to my room." She took the bags he'd carried for her.

"I know I'm repeating myself, but do you have any idea how much I want to kiss you right now?" He'd blurted out the question before considering how desperate he probably sounded.

She smiled a smile that said she was loving the power she had over him. "I'm counting on you showing me in about fourteen minutes from now. Besides, I'm not so sure you want to do that when your kids are right there on the beach."

He didn't have to turn his head to see them. He already knew they were there. "That's why I'm going to walk away now before I have to explain why I'm walking around in this condition."

Her eyes narrowed and then realization dawned. She glanced at his fly and then back up to his face. "Let's make it ten minutes so we can make sure your condition is well taken care of."

CHAPTER TWELVE

CHARLOTTE WAS SO excited that she wanted to skip back to her room. She locked up her valuables and touched up the light makeup she'd put on that morning. Ten minutes was really very little time to get back to meet Sam.

There was something exhilarating about their secret affair. If she'd been home in Newport, she probably wouldn't have felt the same way. She'd have wanted to share her happiness with everyone she knew. But except for Veronica, there was no one else on the island she considered a confidante. And she didn't even know Veronica well enough to disclose anything about Sam.

She wasn't even sure she was ready to tell Allie about Sam yet, although Charlotte shared everything with her sister. Maybe if Allie and Sam didn't have a history, Charlotte might have felt differently.

From the corner of her eye, she saw the sketch she'd made that morning. She rarely drew people in her work, preferring natural and man-made structures, but this piece included Sam.

Suddenly, she could see the finished work and it wasn't just black and white. *It had color.* She saw the deep brown of his hair and his blue eyes with gold flecks, the navy in his resort shirt and the khaki of his pants.

She nearly wept when she realized how her perspective had changed practically overnight. Correction: definitely overnight. She credited her bursting from black and white into the rainbow colors of the Land of Oz to last night when she had given herself to Sam with complete abandon.

She'd known she'd go back to color someday, had prepared for it by always having her pastels available. But this was the first time she truly wanted to use color. She'd tried to force herself before, but she couldn't visualize her work other than in shades of black and white.

She wanted to dance around the room and then pull out her pastels to get to work. But she didn't. She had someone waiting for her. Someone who had been the catalyst for her to move forward in both her work and hopefully in life.

Charlotte took a deep breath and held her head high as she left her room.

She walked swiftly down the beach after avoiding anyone who might want to have a conversation with her in the lobby. She still had a way to go to get to the inlet, so she sped up her pace, which was not easy on sand. She had removed her sandals, but decided she could go faster if she moved closer to the water where the sand was wet and easier to navigate.

By the time she saw the sapodilla trees and reached the inlet, she was disappointed to see that Sam hadn't arrived yet. She wanted to tell him about her breakthrough, yet she wanted to surprise him with the finished piece.

She looked around to make sure she was at the right place. It was definitely an inlet, and from the wet sand, she could tell high tide would cover this area completely. A large crevice in the sand from the ocean to the inlet was carved out from the water as it filled the inlet at high tide. Smooth rocks that were worn down by the tide made a place to sit, so that's what she did.

She folded her hands on her lap and drank in her surroundings. The inlet provided shelter for several kinds of sea grass, making Charlotte feel as if she were in the middle of nowhere. Unless someone came by here on the beach to explore, which was highly unlikely, no one would find them here.

"Wow! You made it!" Sam appeared between the two sapodilla trees. "I thought I'd beat you here." He came forward quickly and she stood to put her arms around him as he pulled her close. "You are so beautiful," he breathed in her ear. "This place was made for you."

She wanted to ask him to repeat what he said earlier about not checking out the inlet before now, but she held back. She preferred to think of it as their own special place and not somewhere he'd brought other women before. She might come back tomorrow with her camera once she figured out when low tide occurred again.

He kissed her, long and slow and as passionately as ever. He deepened the kiss and their tongues clashed fervently. She wanted him and let him know by sinuously rubbing her pelvis against his already bulging erection.

"I can't believe how much I still want you after all we did last night," he breathed, locking her tightly against his body with one arm around her waist. He cupped her breast with his other hand, leaned his forehead against hers and groaned. "No bra?"

"Uh-uh." She'd thought about him as she'd chosen her clothes for the day. She wasn't overly endowed, always considered herself average, so being able to go braless was empowering. She reveled in her ability to both surprise him and have him want to come back for more. At least until he found her nipple through her shirt, and then she was the one moaning. He pinched and teased her nipple through the cotton fabric, covering it with his mouth. His teeth bit down lightly on the hardened pebble and she hurriedly unbuttoned and unknotted her shirt so he could have complete access to her breasts.

He pulled her in close again, making sure her

pelvis was pressing against him when he leaned her back to take her bare nipple into his mouth. His tongue teased it before he sucked gently.

A fire burned steadily in her core and she needed release. She gasped when his hand moved from her breast to the back of her thigh. His fingers inched up the inside of her skort and pushed aside her skimpy underwear to palm one cheek.

His hand slowly edged around and over her hip bone, his thumb leading his hand lower to where she wanted him to touch her.

"What the heck are you wearing?" he asked.

She laughed. "It's a skort. Shorts with a skirt over it."

"No wonder I was having trouble and my hand got stuck." He released her and sat down on one of the smooth rocks that formed a low wall. He maneuvered Charlotte sideways onto his lap, similar to how they'd started in the hot tub last night.

She wound her arms around his neck. Her shirt hung open slightly and he ran a finger down her sternum, the back of his hand brushing her naked breast.

"This isn't nearly as comfortable as I'd hoped," he joked.

"But it's private," she said.

"That it is." He kissed her lips while his hand rested high on her bare upper thigh. "So how has your day been?"

She smiled. "Pretty good, and even better now." She kissed him. "I got some work done and feel like I can get enough completed before my show." She was dying to tell him about her desire to use pastels, but didn't want him to think her sudden about-face in her work correlated to feelings for him. They had sex. Really, really good, toe-curling sex. That was it. She would be going home in a few days. "How was *your* day?" she asked instead.

He grinned and seemed to color a little. "Besides being more tired than I normally am, thanks to you…" He touched her closed lips with the tip of his index finger, effectively stopping her from reminding him of his earlier comment about the hot tub making him tired. Their gazes locked and she knew he was reading her mind.

He grinned that sexy grin. "Basically, it was the usual stuff. Working with the insurance adjuster to get the kitchen back to normal, a few other maintenance issues. The good news is there have been no more thefts. Reported anyway."

"That *is* good news. Hopefully, there won't be any more at all. Have there been any breaks on who's responsible? I know it's a long shot, but I'd love to get my driver's license back."

He shook his head. "Nothing new. I'm still waiting on the results of the background checks. As much as I'd like to search every room of the resort, I can't legally do that."

"How would someone make it off the island with everything they stole? It must be quite a haul by now."

"Good question. Although the majority of things that have been stolen—tablets, laptops, credit cards, jewelry, camera equipment—could easily fit into a large suitcase or two."

"So someone could simply smuggle everything in a suitcase when they check out and no one would be the wiser?"

"Hopefully we'll find them before that happens." He changed the subject. "So you're playing cards tonight?"

She shrugged. "I told Veronica I would."

"Sounds exciting," he teased. "And you won't play too late, right?" His eyes twinkled, and she could read his thoughts because they were the same as her own.

"I don't know." She ran her thumb over the shell of his ear. "I might as well, since I have no other plans."

He nibbled her neck, giving her the good kind of chills up and down her spine. "But you *do* have other plans."

"I do?" She tried to sound innocent. It was difficult to catch her breath with the things he was doing to her.

"Yeah," he whispered and then told her exactly what he had in mind. His fingers found their way up the inside of her skort to push her underwear to the side. Then he teased her mercilessly until she was wet and throbbing and she would have agreed to most anything he suggested.

BY THE TIME Charlotte made it back to her room on shaky legs, she had very little time to get herself put back together for dinner. She showered quickly and put on a long black-and-white-striped skirt with a white tank top. She was zipping the back of her second gladiator-style sandal when there was a knock on her door.

She checked the peephole and saw it was Veronica. Charlotte opened the door, shocked to see that the woman was crying.

Charlotte pulled her inside and put an arm around her. "What's wrong?"

Veronica sobbed and Charlotte led her to one of the two upholstered chairs. Charlotte sat in the other one and waited for Veronica to speak.

Finally, after hiccuping and wiping her eyes and nose with a balled-up tissue, Veronica tried to form words. "It's Jared."

Just as Charlotte suspected.

"He's—"

Expecting to hear he'd been with a woman last night, Charlotte waited for Veronica to spill it.

"He's sick. Too sick to stay here."

"What?" Did Veronica say sick? "What's wrong with him? I thought he had food poisoning or a stomach bug. Did he get that much worse?"

Veronica nodded her head. "He was still sick this morning and he's really in pain. They're taking him to a hospital on the mainland because they think it's his appendix."

"Oh my gosh. I'm so sorry. Are you going with him?"

Veronica looked at her. "No. He's going alone. They might have to do surgery if that's what it is."

"Don't you think you should go with him? He should have someone along to make sure he's being well taken care of, and who better than you?" Charlotte was glad Jared hadn't been lying to Veronica, but having to go through surgery as an alternative wasn't what she wanted, either.

"I don't know." Veronica seemed torn. "He didn't ask me to go."

"Wouldn't you want someone—him—there if it were you going through this trauma?"

"Of course. But he doesn't even know how I feel about him."

"What better way to show him than to be there for him during this time?"

Veronica seemed to be considering Charlotte's idea. "I guess you're right. I should go. It's not like I need to be here for anything the rest of the week." She covered her mouth with both hands and her eyes widened. "But you need me here. I promised to help you get ready for your presentation."

"Don't worry about me. I'll do fine." Charlotte didn't believe the words any more than Veronica did, but she stood up and Veronica joined her. "Jared is much more important than a presentation." Charlotte opened the door. "Now go be with him and keep me updated."

Veronica left and Charlotte closed and bolted the door. She leaned her back against it, wondering what she would do now that Veronica was gone. Who would help her practice Allie's presentation? No one else at the conference knew her real name or that she had zero experience in the advertising field.

And she couldn't tell anyone else because of the off chance that Raymond Foster might find out she was not who she said she was.

"THE GUEST MADE it to Fort Lauderdale," Katie reported to Sam about the conference attendee with possible appendicitis. "I heard from the charter captain that he was loaded into an ambulance and is on his way to the local hospital."

Sam nodded from behind his desk. "That's good. I was told someone from here wanted to go with him, but the boat we chartered had already left?"

"That's right. She was pretty distraught. I told her I'd keep her informed on his condition. We've already notified his brother who is his next of kin."

"Excellent. You've handled the situation well, even though it's not technically part of your job description."

Katie smiled. "As assistant conference manager, I try to be prepared for anything that comes up."

"You've certainly done that. I appreciate it." He'd been at the inlet with Charlotte when all this took place. "Just notify me as it's happening and don't wait until afterward to let me know."

"I will. I'm sorry about that. My first priority was the guest. When our EMT said he suspected appendicitis, I thought getting the guest to the hospital before it burst was the highest priority."

"Thank goodness we didn't have a disaster like that happen." Two of his security team were also certified EMTs, but a burst appendix needed more expertise than they possessed. His phone rang. "Oh, one more thing. Please make sure the woman who wanted to accompany the guest is okay." He would bet it was Charlotte's friend Veronica, since Jared had been the third point of their triangle all week.

"Will do," Katie said before giving him privacy to answer the phone.

As soon as he hung up, he texted Charlotte to find out how Veronica was doing. He didn't get an answer right away, so he pocketed his cell phone and headed to his apartment to figure out dinner before his kids ate everything in sight and ruined their appetites.

A while later, the three of them were eating the pork chops he'd thrown in the oven when Emma blurted, "I saw you today with that woman."

Startled, Sam had no idea what to say. He held a finger up while continuing to chew his bite of food, taking time to collect his thoughts. "That's right," he finally said. "She's a guest at the resort."

"But you were being nice to her."

"Yeah, Dad, you were nice to her," Oliver echoed.

"I try to be nice to all of our guests. It's called hospitality."

"But she's bad," Emma said. "She causes trouble."

Sam wanted to remind Emma that Charlotte wasn't Allie. She was different from her twin sister. But he didn't. In the back of his mind floated the thought that Charlotte was being dishonest to many people while she pretended to be Allie. They weren't in grade school switching places. This was real life, adult stuff.

Instead, he said, "She's a guest and as long as she stays out of trouble, then everything's okay." He got up from the table to put his plate in the dishwasher. Both Emma and Oliver did the same, none of them speaking anymore about Charlotte.

His phone vibrated on the counter where he

had left it during dinner. Emma picked it up and checked the display. "Who's Charlotte?"

Nothing like a preteen daughter to keep tabs on everything he did. "She's the guest we were just talking about. Remember I told you she was Charlotte and her sister, Allie, is the one we met in Charleston."

Sam picked up his phone, glad he had set it to Password Protected. He had a bad habit of leaving his phone out where people could easily read the screen.

"And you gave her your private cell phone number?" Emma stared at him until he felt as if she could see right through him.

The kids had never seen him date. He'd kept his sparse romantic life private to spare Emma's and Oliver's feelings. This—whatever this was with Charlotte—would remain private, as well.

He told them as much truth as possible. "Charlotte's friend was taken to the hospital in Fort Lauderdale because he was very sick and might need an operation. Charlotte—Ms. Harrington—would like me to keep her updated on his condition."

The answer seemed to satisfy Emma, even though it was a half truth, and Oliver didn't appear to care one way or the other. Sam and Charlotte had actually exchanged phone numbers when they'd run into each other on the beach that afternoon so they could contact each other if they ran late getting to the inlet.

His body reacted immediately when he thought of their inlet. *Their inlet.* That's exactly what he would always think of it as, long after she was gone from the island.

"Don't you guys have homework?" The requisite moans came from both of them, but they left him alone in the kitchen to read Charlotte's text.

Veronica's not good. I talked her into still playing cards to take her mind off Jared. Please let us know if you hear anything about him. See you after cards…

He grinned, glad his kids had left the room. Dot dot dot was just about the sexiest thing Charlotte could have written.

CHARLOTTE COULD BARELY concentrate on the card game with Veronica and a few of her DP friends. She wanted to go off with Sam for an encore performance of last night. Playing hearts with near strangers just didn't cut it.

"We need another round of drinks." Gary, the tall man with a comb-over, announced at the end of a hand.

"Absolutely!" That came from Veronica, who

was drowning her sorrows from what Charlotte had witnessed.

Not that any of the others were sober. How they could still play cards, she didn't know.

"I'll have another." The fourth in their group spoke up. Barb was a petite woman in her forties who had stripes on her long fingernails. Charlotte glanced at her own naked nails. She had trouble using one solid color. She couldn't imagine having the ability or the time to paint stripes on her nails.

"What about you?" Gary was looking at Charlotte.

"No, thanks. I'm fine." She sipped her gin and tonic, the only alcoholic drink she'd consumed that evening. It was pretty weak now that the ice had begun to melt. She'd never been a big drinker, even back in college.

As the evening progressed, her companions became more and more rowdy, laughing hysterically at jokes that made no sense. She couldn't help being drawn into their hilarity and found herself having a great time.

"Lesh get some music going," Veronica slurred when their game ended. "I want to dance." Gary made it his mission to do her bidding.

This was Charlotte's cue to excuse herself. "I'm pretty tired. I think I'll head up to my room." She started to rise from her seat.

"Oh no." Veronica grabbed Charlotte's arm. "You're not going anywhere."

"I should get to bed…" *With Sam* was the rest of Charlotte's thought.

Veronica shook her head violently. "No way. You need to stay here because Jared's not." Tears formed in her eyes. They flowed down her cheeks in rivulets, taking her mascara and eyeliner with them.

Charlotte grabbed the napkin from her drink and dabbed gently at Veronica's cheeks. "Jared will be fine. There's nothing to worry about." Veronica didn't look convinced, and Charlotte couldn't bear to leave her new friend. "Okay, let's dance."

As if by magic, music came through the lanai speakers and Veronica began dancing with abandon. Charlotte reluctantly joined her, feeling guilty for wanting to leave to be with Sam. Gary and Barb joined Veronica and Charlotte, and the four of them danced and became sillier by the minute.

Charlotte didn't know how much time had elapsed when she eyed Sam in the lobby next to the staircase. He was watching with great interest and she wanted to pull him into their fun. She motioned to him to do just that, but he shook his head.

As soon as the song ended, Charlotte made her way to Sam. "Come on. Have some fun with us." She grabbed his hand to lead him to the lanai, but he pulled it back. She stopped short. "What's wrong?"

His brows drew together. "What are you doing?"

"I'm dancing," she said, twirling around to show him. She swayed to the right and giggled like a schoolgirl, but caught her balance just in time.

"What happened to being discreet?" His tone was serious, intense, as he glanced around the lobby.

She tilted her head. "You danced with me the other night. What's changed?"

"How much have you had to drink?"

She glared at him. "You think I'm drunk, don't you?"

"Aren't you?"

She froze. "I'm not drunk." She wondered why she felt the need to explain when he was being a jerk, but she did so anyway. "I've had one drink."

He raised one eyebrow.

She cocked her head. "It's true. Why would I lie? We're just having fun and I wanted you to join us." She turned away so he wouldn't see how his brusque manner had stung. "Never mind." She started to walk away, thinking she might go up to her room. She didn't feel much like dancing or partying now. And she didn't want to experience any more of Sam's attitude, either.

"Wait."

His command made her stop and turn to face him. "Now what?"

Expecting an apology, instead he said, "I just got word that your friend, Jared, is having emergency surgery. They confirmed appendicitis, so they're operating right away."

She swallowed her hurt feelings, as well as her pride, because he was treating her as if nothing had happened between them. "Thank you for the information. I'll let Veronica know." She was about to walk away and find Veronica when she added, "I'm sorry I made you so uncomfortable."

If he didn't catch the sarcasm in her tone, then he was absolutely dense.

CHAPTER THIRTEEN

SAM WATCHED CHARLOTTE walk away from him.

One drink? Sam was hard-pressed to believe that. He'd seen her after one drink, and her behavior tonight contradicted her words. She'd nearly toppled over right in front of him.

That was exactly how his ex-wife had behaved. He'd divorced her when her excessive drinking— and lying about it—had begun to affect Emma and Oliver.

Maybe he'd made a mistake by getting involved with Charlotte.

He'd been looking forward to spending more time with her, both in and out of bed, but he couldn't afford to get any closer to her than he already had. And he especially couldn't allow her to make him start feeling something again. Look how bad his marriage had turned out. He couldn't let that happen again to himself or his kids.

He decided to call it a night, figuring the staff would contact him if he was needed. He'd asked Monica to stay with the kids when he'd thought he'd be spending time with Charlotte later. But now he could relieve the children's tutor early. She was probably exhausted after her long weekend away celebrating her parents' anniversary and might appreciate an early evening.

He rode the elevator to his apartment. When the doors opened, he saw that Monica had dozed off on the couch, covered by the silky throw the kids liked to curl up under. The book she'd been reading was open across her chest.

The elevator doors shut after he stepped out and the noise woke her. "Hi," she said sleepily, raising her head from the pile of throw pillows. "What time is it?"

"Not that late," he said. "It's quiet downstairs, so I decided to come up and relieve you." Saying he'd canceled his plans would have caused her to ask questions he didn't want to answer. "You must be tired after your trip. I really appreciate you staying with the kids."

"You know I never mind being around Emma and Oliver." Monica sat up, marking her page with a bookmark. "The trip was pretty exhausting, but certainly worth it."

"I'll bet." He removed his radio from his belt and placed it on the end table. "How were the kids? I hope they didn't give you any trouble."

"They never do." Monica stood to leave. "Not like some of the others I'm tutoring."

"Really?"

"Yeah, there are two boys—brothers—who

think they're pretty tough. They're older and don't want to be with the younger kids."

"That's probably hard for them." Oliver was one of the youngest in the class at nine, but Sam knew there was also a seven-year-old. That was a big age gap.

"True. But that's no excuse for not listening or interrupting when I'm speaking."

"Can I do something? Talk to them or maybe to their aunt?" Sam was familiar with the teenagers' home situation, which wasn't ideal.

She shook her head. "Their aunt? They're living with their uncle. He's young, early twenties. Too young, I think, to be raising boys who are twelve and fourteen. I've spoken to him and he just says he'll talk to them. A lot of good that's done."

"Uncle? What happened to their aunt?" He had an urge to know more about these boys, since they were with Emma and Oliver almost every day.

"You remember their mother worked in Housekeeping at the resort. Jenny Boyle. She was killed in a motorcycle accident, along with her boyfriend, in Miami last summer. She was only in her midthirties."

"Right," he said. "What a tragedy. And their dad is in prison. Their aunt came to take care of them, and I told her they could stay in their resort apartment for a year or until they found somewhere else to live."

"Well, somewhere along the line, the aunt left and the young uncle took over," Monica said. "I definitely saw a difference in the boys' behavior when that happened."

He needed to be more vigilant regarding his employees. He should have been more supportive when the boys lost their mother. "So what does their uncle do for a living?" Except for a few small shops that had been allowed to do business on Sapodilla Cay, everyone else was a resort employee. "Does he work for the resort?"

"He's a crew member on one of the ferries that goes back and forth between here and Fort Lauderdale. I would have thought he would have needed your permission to move in since the apartment is owned by Blaise Enterprises."

"He would." Sam walked to the dining room buffet and pulled out paper and pen. "Let me get the details written down so I can look into the situation." He'd offered the boys and their aunt a place after their mother's death and wouldn't ask them to leave until they had a place to go, but their uncle should have notified the resort about the change in occupancy.

"There's one more thing before you take drastic action," Monica said when he'd written everything down.

"What's that?" His pen was poised to write.

"Your daughter has quite a crush on the older boy."

AS MUCH AS Charlotte wanted to go directly to her room and have a good cry to rid herself of the humiliation she'd endured from Sam, she didn't. She owed it to Veronica to fill her in on Jared's condition.

Veronica was sitting at a table with the others who'd played cards. Charlotte waved her over when she caught her eye.

"What is it?" Veronica asked. "Is it Jared? Is he okay? Tell me. I need to know."

"Calm down. I don't know much. Just that he was taken into surgery."

Veronica covered her open mouth with both hands. "I knew it. I knew he'd need surgery. And here I am, stuck on this island, playing cards and having fun."

"Don't beat yourself up," Charlotte advised. "You couldn't do anything for him if you were at the hospital. At least here you have something to occupy your time."

Veronica closed her eyes and breathed in and out several times. "What else?"

"That's all I know. They confirmed it was appendicitis and decided to operate right away."

"They're not waiting until morning," Veronica

pointed out. "They're treating this like an emergency. This is bad, very bad." She covered her face with her hands.

Charlotte took Veronica by the shoulders and waited for her to uncover her face. She patted Veronica's shoulder. "It'll be okay. If I hear anything else, I'll let you know. In the meantime, go back and have fun. Do something to take your mind off Jared."

"That's impossible."

"Then try harder." She gave Veronica what she hoped was a comforting smile and squeezed her hand. "I'm going up to bed. I'll talk to you in the morning. By then, we should know how Jared made out in surgery."

She watched as Veronica walked away, her shoulders hunched and her stride unsteady as she rejoined her friends. Feeling better about leaving her, Charlotte headed for her room.

Except that she didn't want to go to bed. If she went upstairs now, she was sure she'd lie awake for hours being upset about how she and Sam left things. If given half a chance, they could have worked things out. Instead, Sam was being so bullheaded.

Charlotte wasn't even sure what Sam was so upset about. Grabbing his hand to have him join her new friends on the lanai was one thing, but he seemed to have a real problem with her besides that. She'd let down her hair, determined to have fun. After all, this was her vacation. As long as she wasn't hurting anyone, why would Sam have a problem?

She shook her head. His loss. Right this minute they could have had a repeat performance of last night. In her bed. She refused to think about it because then it would become her loss, too.

She walked out the front door that led to the boardwalk they'd used upon arrival. Perhaps strolling to the end of it and gazing at the ocean would be exactly what she needed to clear her head.

She'd barely begun walking in that direction when she ran into a man coming toward her. "Nice night," she greeted him.

"That it is," he responded. "You be careful if you're walking to the end of the pier. I'm working security here and I wouldn't want to find out you fell into the water."

She smiled. "I'll definitely be careful. Good night." She continued on her way, thinking she'd never seen the man before. Sam must have brought in some security reinforcements with all the trouble the resort had been experiencing.

Walking along the boardwalk alone, she breathed in the salt air. She listened to the lapping water, the insects, the other sounds of the night that she couldn't distinguish. The moon wasn't visible, but the water glowed with blue neon lights, reminding her of stars.

She stopped at the sound of voices. There was no one on the boardwalk between her and the end where the boats docked. She spun around. There was no one behind her, either.

She listened closely. At least two people were speaking. The sound came from the woods. The voices weren't loud, and she couldn't make out the words, but the tone sounded as if they were having a disagreement.

She carefully stepped off the boardwalk to investigate, holding her long skirt so it wouldn't catch on anything. There wasn't much undergrowth around the palm trees. Sandy soil kicked up and into her sandals as she walked, but she couldn't risk taking off her shoes and getting cut on something in the dark.

There had been occasional lights along the boardwalk, but her eyes needed to adjust to the darkness in the woods before she walked any farther. She stood quietly for a moment, focusing on which way to go.

Not long after that, she walked in the direction of the conversation, concerned their disagreement might escalate. As she got closer, she realized they were fairly young from their voices. A boy and a girl. The girl pointed a flashlight at the ground, enabling Charlotte to barely make them out.

Her heart beat faster. Was the girl in trouble? Charlotte crept closer, careful to remain quiet so they wouldn't discover her. She needed to know whether or not a problem was brewing, and then she'd give them their privacy.

A branch broke under her foot, loud enough that their heads turned in Charlotte's direction. She froze. If the girl moved her flashlight a little to the right, they'd see her.

"Is someone there?" The girl's voice was familiar.

"It's probably just an animal," the boy said. "Maybe we should get back inside. Your babysitter might wake up and figure out you're not in bed."

"I don't know why my dad insists on having our tutor stay with us. I'm old enough to take care of Oliver. In fact, that's what happened last night and everything was fine."

Tutor? Oliver? The girl must be Sam's daughter, Emma. What was she doing sneaking around after dark like this? And who was the boy with her? Charlotte listened to see if she could gather any more clues.

"You're right about her waking up," Emma said. "I should get back." She touched the boy's arm. "Please promise me, no matter what else your uncle wants you to do, please don't."

"I can't promise that." The boy, not much taller than Emma, sounded resigned. Could they be moving and he didn't want to go? The boy leaned down and kissed Emma quickly and awkwardly. "I'll see you tomorrow at school."

Charlotte waited until the two went their separate ways. Emma passed Charlotte on her way to the boardwalk. The boy walked in the opposite direction, going deeper into the woods.

Listening closely until she could no longer hear footsteps in either direction, Charlotte cautiously took the same path as Emma. By the time she reached the boardwalk, the girl was nowhere in sight.

Charlotte had originally planned to go to the end of the boardwalk to enjoy the silence, but she was concerned about Emma. She was obviously making poor choices by sneaking out to see that boy. Charlotte needed to let Sam know.

Because if Emma were her child, she'd certainly want to be told.

AFTER GETTING MONICA into the elevator, Sam checked on both kids. Typical Oliver was lying sideways on his bed, his feet hanging over the side. Sam grinned, knowing better than to touch the boy and risk him kicking or slapping at Sam while asleep. He'd suffered that enough over the years, and the boy was getting bigger and stronger, able to cause damage without being aware of it.

Emma was the opposite kind of sleeper. Sam couldn't even make out her head in the covers piled over her. He closed her bedroom door quietly and went into his own room.

He brushed his teeth and was about to strip down for bed when he received a text message on his cell phone.

Charlotte.

He wasn't sure if he wanted to read it, but he did. She needed to speak to him.

He didn't feel like it.

He had just gotten into bed and turned off the bedside light when another text came in. Thinking he'd turn off the phone completely, he read Charlotte's second text before doing so.

Need to talk to you about Emma. Very important.

What could she want to say about Emma? His daughter was fast asleep, and as far as he knew, hadn't had any more contact with Charlotte.

He reluctantly replied. Why?

She responded immediately. Come to my room and I'll explain. Too much for text.

Sam stared at her text for a few minutes, trying to decide what to do.

His children were the most important people in his life. If Charlotte needed to tell him something important about Emma, then he couldn't ignore her.

He dressed and stopped by Emma's room

again. This time her head was slightly visible
from under the covers. What did Charlotte have
to tell him about his daughter?

He rode the elevator to Charlotte's floor and
raised his hand to knock on her door. He hoped
this wasn't a mistake.

She answered his knock quickly and let him
in. "Thank you for coming," she said stiffly, and
pointed to the pair of chairs across the room.
"We can sit over there."

He couldn't help remembering last night in
this room. How they'd enjoyed each other, with
no hesitation.

Look at them now. Acting like strangers.

Charlotte still wore her long skirt from earlier.
She sat across from him and slid one leg over
the other, revealing bare feet with pink polish
on her toes.

"What's this all about?" He needed to take his
mind off Charlotte and her body and focus on the
subject at hand. "What about Emma?"

Charlotte bit her upper lip and finally spoke.
"I went for a walk on the boardwalk out in front
of the resort. You know, after we spoke." She
looked at her hands. "I needed to clear my head
and thought I'd walk to the end."

"Go on."

She shot him a look that spoke volumes. She
would tell the story at her own pace.

"Anyway, I was walking down the boardwalk

and first I ran into someone I assumed was one of your new security guys."

He nodded. "We've added to our security team, yes."

"So then I walked some more, enjoying the peace and the sounds of nature, when I heard voices."

He narrowed his eyes. "Voices?"

"Yes, they were coming from the woods."

"I still don't understand what this has to do with Emma."

"I'm getting there. Don't be so impatient." She uncrossed her legs and leaned forward. "It sounded like an argument, so I stepped off the boardwalk and into the woods to investigate. That's when I found Emma with a boy."

"Impossible." He rose from his seat. "That doesn't make sense. She's asleep in her own bed. She couldn't have been outside with a boy."

"She might be there now, but she wasn't when I saw her in the woods."

He paced across the room and back. "Why would you make up a story like this?"

She stared at him, and her jaw literally dropped open. She closed her mouth and stood, her eyes on fire. "Get out." When he didn't move, she repeated. "Get out! I was trying to tell you what your daughter is up to, but you'd rather stick your head in the sand than take me seriously."

She was definitely angry. Like her unfettered behavior in bed, this anger was a new side of her.

"Why are you so angry?" he asked.

"Get out. Don't make me call your security to usher you out. That would be more embarrassing than to discover your daughter is slipping out at night to meet a boy and do who knows what."

She had his attention now. "Why would you think that?" he asked. "She's not even thirteen yet."

"They kissed. That's all I saw besides them disagreeing about something. I wasn't close enough to hear enough of their conversation."

He sat on the edge of Charlotte's bed and ran his hands through his hair. "This is impossible. She's in her room, asleep. I've checked on her twice in the past hour."

"I'm telling you that she might be there now, but she was in the woods earlier. About half an hour ago. She even mentioned sneaking out when her babysitter dozed off."

Monica *had* been asleep when he'd returned earlier. "Let's say she was where you say she was." He held up a hand to prevent her from saying anything. "How could she have gotten back into the apartment without me hearing the elevator?"

"I don't know. I'm simply telling you what I *do* know." She tilted her head. "If there's a fire and you can't use the elevator, there must be a stairway from your apartment."

He nodded. "There is, but you need the key to get into the apartment that way. My kids don't have that key."

"Who *does* have access to it?"

"I do. I keep it on a hook near the stairway door inside the apartment. You don't need it to go downstairs, only if you plan to come up that way, because it locks automatically. I have a spare in my office in case there's a power outage and I can't use the elevator."

"So she could have taken it when she left and put it back when she returned? Sounds like you wouldn't have noticed it being gone."

He was beginning to see how Emma might have fooled him into thinking she'd been asleep in bed all evening. Coming through that stairway door, maybe while he brushed his teeth, would have been a much quieter option than the elevator.

"I can see from your expression you're beginning to believe me." Charlotte stated it as a fact, not a question.

Sam rubbed his hand along his jaw. "I'm saying it's possible. What I don't understand is why. It's not like she asked to meet this boy, whoever he is, and I said no."

"Maybe she didn't have a chance to ask you."

"What do you mean?"

"Maybe the opportunity arose while you were out of your apartment, and she decided to sneak out rather than ask the babysitter for permission."

His earlier conversation with Monica ran through his head. She'd mentioned that Emma had a crush on one of the troublemaker boys. The older one. Fourteen, he thought she said. Monica definitely would have said no if Emma had asked to meet him, leaving the decision up to Sam. "How old was the boy? Could you tell?"

"I'm not very good at kids' ages. I'm just not around them enough."

"Did he seem a lot older than Emma?" Fourteen was bad enough. He hoped the boy wasn't in his later teens. That would make this scenario worse than it already was.

"I would say he was maybe a little older than her, but it was dark. He was slightly taller, too." Her eyes widened. "Oh, and I noticed he seemed a little awkward when he kissed her. More like a young teenager, I think."

"He kissed her!" He'd ignored that fact the first time because he hadn't thought it was Emma that Charlotte had seen. "What else haven't you told me?" His heart beat wildly at the thought that his daughter was growing up way too quickly for his liking.

"Calm down. It was just a kiss. A quick, chaste kiss. That's all."

His eyes were drawn to Charlotte's mouth, remembering for an instant how their kisses had been anything but chaste.

He mentally cleared his head. "She was okay with his kiss? He didn't force himself on her?"

She shook her head. "No, it seemed mutual."

The way their kisses had been.

Sam didn't know what to say. "I need to talk to her," he decided. "Find out what's going on. Her tutor has been having some trouble with a couple of the older boys in the class."

"What kind of trouble?"

"Nothing big, just not listening to her and disrespecting her. They don't like being in class with younger kids."

"That must be hard on them."

"True, but there's no other option besides one tutor for all of them. Sending them to school on the mainland would make for a very long day, as well as being a possible safety hazard with them riding the ferry more than an hour each way."

"Talking to Emma is a good idea," Charlotte said. "If I can make one suggestion, let her speak."

"What does that mean?"

"You tend to jump to conclusions and don't let

people explain their actions. Listen to what your daughter has to say."

He mulled over her advice. "You're talking about tonight, aren't you? When I didn't believe you?"

"Let's not rehash the argument. You obviously have some reason for not taking me at my word."

Her hurt came through and he wondered for the first time since they parted earlier whether he should have given her the benefit of the doubt.

"I guess I've been burned so many times in the past, I'm extremely wary when it comes to taking people at their word."

CHAPTER FOURTEEN

"Do you think that's fair?" Charlotte asked Sam. "Never giving people the benefit of the doubt? Not even your daughter." She hoped if he realized what he was doing and why, then he might not be so hard on the people around him. Including her.

"That's not true."

"What about when you thought I was drunk? I had one drink tonight. Period. End of story. Anything you seemed to witness me doing that made you think otherwise is purely conjecture on your part." She drew in a breath after her pronouncement. "I was just having a good time." She should have ended there, but added, "And you ruined the evening we had planned." His distrust made her angry all over again.

He didn't say anything, and she didn't know what to expect. Finally, he said, "You're right. I jumped to conclusions. You were having a good time and appeared to be intoxicated. But what was I to think when you nearly lost your balance right in front of me?"

"Even cops give sobriety tests before accusing someone of an offense."

"Point taken."

Silence.

"Why?" she asked.

"Why what?"

"Why don't you feel you can trust people?" Her frustration was off the charts, and her voice rose in volume. She was having a hard time staying calm. "What happened in your past to make you be so suspicious of everyone?"

He hesitated. "If you had known my ex-wife, you might understand."

"So make me understand."

His throat worked as if he was swallowing with difficulty. "First of all, she was an alcoholic. So I'm pretty sensitive about alcohol consumption."

She nodded. "I kind of figured something like that. Did she have an alcohol problem when you married?"

"No, it started shortly after her mother died. Rebecca couldn't stop blaming herself for not being there for her mom when she got sick, even though she couldn't do anything for her. They'd been very close, but her mother kept the extent of her heart problems to herself. Not until the very end did any of us realize how sick she'd been."

Charlotte didn't want to interrupt. She had her

own demons involving her mother. She waited for him to continue.

Sam ran his hands through his hair, looked at her with sad eyes. "For a long time, Rebecca was very good at hiding how much she was drinking. Collecting wine bottles and throwing them out somewhere other than the recycling bin. When she bought bottles, she hid them in the trunk of her car. One day, I saw a case of wine in her trunk and asked her about it. She claimed it was for a neighbor who was having a surprise party for her husband, but I found out later that was a lie. In fact, it was at couples therapy that I found out some of what she'd been doing behind my back."

"Is that why you divorced?"

"Partly. As time went on, I became more and more aware of how big the problem had become. I tried to get her individual help, but she didn't really want it. She wanted to bask in the pain of losing her mother. I thought she was getting better because she stopped drinking when she got pregnant with Oliver. She took care of herself for his sake, but soon after he was born, her drinking became even worse. She switched from wine to hard liquor. I never realized it, thinking she'd gotten the problem under control. Then I started noticing liquor store purchases on the credit card. When her drinking began to affect the kids, that's when I decided things needed to change."

Charlotte wanted to know details, but hesitated to push him too hard. "What kind of things was she doing?"

"Probably a lot more than I know. She would forget to pick up Emma from preschool, and one time she left both kids home alone to go to the liquor store. Emma was only three at the time and Oliver was a newborn. We were lucky child services didn't find out. A neighbor was in the yard and saw Rebecca leave without the children. She'd left the door unlocked, so the neighbor stayed with the kids until I could get home from work. That was the last straw."

"What did you do?"

"I had been working with Rebecca's dad to get her help, and when I called him, he agreed we would all be better off if she came to live with him. Away from the kids until we were sure she could handle them again. But every time we thought she had her disease under control, she'd fall off the wagon. I finally divorced her so the kids and I could start fresh."

"But you said she died?"

"Yes, that was a few months after the divorce was final. She'd been going to AA meetings and seeing a counselor. We all thought she'd turned the corner. She and I had gone out to dinner that night, hoping for a second chance, but taking it slow."

He stopped talking, and swallowed. "Later that night, about three in the morning, I got a call from the police. Rebecca still had my address on her driver's license. She had gone to several bars after we parted, got plastered and then drove herself into a telephone pole. She died instantly. Thankfully, she didn't take anyone else with her."

"I'm so sorry." She wanted to grasp his hands in hers, but held back.

He nodded. "That was a long time ago. Another lifetime. I guess I never got over being lied to, especially that last night when she assured me she was doing well and planned to stay sober."

"You know it wasn't your fault, right? She would have done it that night or some other night."

"That's what I learned in counseling, but I'm not sure I believe it even now. Looking back, I'm pretty confident she'd been drinking before we met for dinner. I should have remembered that the anniversary of her mother's death was coming up in the next week and been more observant."

"That explains why you didn't believe me when I said I'd had only one drink."

He nodded. "I'm sorry. Old habits..."

"I understand." She could kind of relate after

dealing with her mother's deceit. She still had no idea how to reconcile what she now knew about her mother's actions. Sam probably felt the same way about what happened to Rebecca. "So now what?" Not wanting him to think she was asking him to resume romantically where they'd let off before—though she would if he wanted to—she added, "Will you give Emma a chance to explain?"

"I will. Thank you for the advice." He rose from the end of her bed. "And thank you for letting me know what Emma has been up to." He headed for the door.

She touched his arm and he stopped. "You're welcome. I hope everything works out okay. I'm sure Emma has a good reason for sneaking out."

He laid a hand on hers. "I hope you're right."

And then he left, making her wonder whether or not this would be their last time alone.

AFTER A RESTLESS NIGHT, Charlotte woke early Wednesday morning. She showered and dressed, anxious to work on the picture of Sam. Her first piece in pastels in over a year.

She wasn't usually so sentimental, but if they were going their separate ways, she'd like to be able to have the completed piece as a reminder of their time together. She could show it with her other works, but she'd put a sold sign on it to keep it for herself.

Just before eight o'clock, her cell phone rang. Caller ID showed it was Allie.

"Hey, Allie. I hope you have some good news for me."

Her sister laughed. "I do. I hope I didn't wake you."

"I've been up for hours."

"Good. I just emailed you the pitch for Raymond Foster. It's a PowerPoint presentation, and I also have a script for you. Then there's a thirty-second sample TV ad I'd like you to play for him during the pitch."

"So you have the words you want me to say written down?" That made the idea of pitching to the man much more palatable.

"That's right. You don't need to stick to the script I wrote word for word, but it'll give you an idea of what needs to be said where in the presentation."

They talked more about the specifics of the pitch and then Allie told her, "I got your duplicate driver's license yesterday."

"Oh! That's wonderful news! I've been so worried about not being able to fly home on Friday." What a relief.

"I tried to overnight it to you, but the post office said it would take two days to get to the island. So you won't have it until Thursday."

"As long as I get it before my flight Friday, then I'm happy. Thank you so much for taking care of it for me."

"It's the least I can do after you offered to pitch to Foster."

"I hope I don't mess it up." Charlotte's nerves jangled. "Somehow I think this guy's going to be able to see through me and know I'm not a professional."

"You'll be great. I'm sure of it. Take a look at what I sent and we'll go over it later."

They hung up soon after that and Charlotte went downstairs to the resort's business center to download and print the materials Allie had emailed her.

As she reviewed the presentation while it printed out, Charlotte liked it more with each page. Her sister was talented and innovative, creating a new animated "family" from Raymond Foster's many brands. She'd combined them into one TV ad to showcase his large portion of the marketplace. Each brand was represented by a "family member." The dad was Foster's men's shaving products. The mother was their healthy frozen-food line who tried to get one of their snack-line children to make better food choices, such as the sibling who characterized Foster's frozen-vegetable line. Charlotte could see how the campaign could be expanded into a series of advertisements.

She ran upstairs to her room to drop off the presentation and then decided to find Veronica. She was most likely at breakfast. Charlotte hadn't heard anything more about Jared, but maybe Veronica had.

Charlotte was grabbing a quick cup of coffee at the kiosk when Veronica came up behind her.

"There you are," she said. "I just went searching for you in your room. Have you heard anything about Jared?" Veronica held a small bowl with yogurt, fruit and granola. Her hand visibly trembled.

"I must have been in the business center when you checked my room." Charlotte pointed to nearby seats. "Let's sit down. I haven't heard anything about Jared. I was hoping you had."

Veronica shook her head and gave Charlotte a look that broke her heart. "I don't know how long I can wait to hear something. I'm going crazy. I barely slept last night."

"I understand." Charlotte sipped her coffee, thinking she needed to get some food, but first she needed to find out about Jared. "I'll go see if Sam has heard anything. He might be in his office by now."

"That would be great. I wish I had a phone

number for Jared's brother. He must have heard by now if Jared made it through surgery okay."

"I'll see if I can get that from Sam." Charlotte headed for Sam's office, trying to forget the other times she'd been in this hallway and their emotional encounters in his office.

Unfortunately, his office was empty.

"May I help you?" a woman's voice asked.

Charlotte spun around. "I was looking for Sam. Mr. Briton."

"I'm Gayle, his assistant. He called to say he would be delayed this morning."

Charlotte hoped his kids were okay. She wondered how his talk with Emma had gone, or maybe that's why he was late for work.

"I wanted to talk to him about Jared, the man who was taken to the hospital. Some of us were wondering how his surgery went. We were hoping Mr. Briton had heard something by now."

"If he did, he hasn't mentioned it to me," Gayle said. "You can leave him a note with your cell phone number or room number and he can contact you when he comes down."

Sam knew both her cell phone and room numbers already, but Gayle didn't need to know that. "Thank you. I'll do that."

She wrote the message on the notepaper Gayle provided and then attached its sticky side to Sam's phone where he'd be sure to see it.

Charlotte had barely reached the end of the

hallway when she nearly plowed into Sam in her haste to get back to Veronica.

"I left you a note." She was a little out of breath, possibly more from his nearness than from exertion. "Gayle said it would be okay. Veronica needs an update on Jared. Have you heard anything? She's a basket case right now."

"Nothing new." He continued to his office and she followed.

She enjoyed the view of his broad shoulders, narrow waist and firm butt. Touching was out, so looking would have to do.

"I'll give the hospital a call to see if they'll give me an update."

"That would be great."

He sat down behind his desk, checking his computer for what Charlotte assumed was the number for the hospital. She took the seat across from him, folding her hands on her lap.

He dialed, then asked for information about Jared's condition. "No, I'm not a relative. I'm the manager of the resort where he was staying when he became ill. He has a lot of friends here who would like to know how he's doing." Sam listened and then said, "I understand. Thank you." He hung up and looked at Charlotte.

"They couldn't tell me much," he said. "Only that he's in critical condition after his operation."

She narrowed her eyes. "That doesn't sound good, does it?"

"No, it doesn't." He pursed his lips.

She racked her brain to figure out how she could get more information for Veronica. "Do you have a number for any of his family members? The hospital would surely give them an update."

"I don't," Sam said. "I wish I could help, but I don't know what else I can do."

Charlotte nodded. "It sounds like he's not well enough to answer the phone if we called his room."

"Agreed. He's in ICU according to the woman I spoke to."

"Something must have happened for him to be there and not in a regular room on the surgical floor. Maybe his appendix burst?"

"That's possible. Could be why he went into surgery so late at night."

Charlotte's eyes widened. "That's true!" How could she find out for sure? "I've got it. I'll call the hospital and pretend to be his sister to get information."

Sam stiffened. "I don't think that's a good idea."

"Of course it is. It's a perfect idea. Yes, it's a lie, and I know you don't like deceit, but it's not going to hurt anyone. It's not like Jared's famous and I'm trying to get a medical update so I can post it all over the internet. This is to help Veronica calm down and stop worrying so much about him."

He didn't say anything, but she knew he didn't agree.

"Do you have a better idea?" she finally asked.

"No, I don't, but I think it's wrong for you to lie to the hospital."

She tilted her head. "I don't agree. I'm doing it for the right reason. For Veronica."

"It's a slippery slope. You're pretending to be your twin sister, now you're also going to pretend to be Jared's sister. What's next?"

Anger bubbled in her midsection. She leaned over his desk and lowered her voice. "And you fooled around with a resort guest. How honest does that make you?"

He stared at her, saying nothing.

His words had been like a knife to her midsection, causing her to strike back. She'd lick her deep wounds later. She drew in a deep breath and spoke from her heart. "Listen, I would never do something to hurt someone. That's just not me. In fact, most of my life has been spent doing the right thing. Somehow, ever since I've been here, I've been pushed into doing things out of my comfort zone, but it's all been to help other people. If you don't like my actions, then maybe we have nothing more to say because I'm getting pretty tired of you acting like my conscience."

He ripped a piece of paper from a tablet on his desk and wrote quickly. He held it out to her.

"Here. The number for the hospital. Do what you want. That's what your sister would do."

SAM WAITED UNTIL Charlotte was way down the corridor and couldn't hear him. He pounded a fist on his desk. "Damn!" What he hated most was that she was absolutely right. He'd done something he shouldn't have. He'd slept with a resort guest.

The problem with admitting it was that he wasn't sorry. If not for their seemingly distant points of view about honesty, he'd spend more time with her in an instant.

Needing to get his mind—and body—far away from the subject of Charlotte, Sam picked up his phone and called Gayle. "I need a phone number," he said when she answered. "There are two brothers that Monica is tutoring and I need to get in touch with their uncle. Can you get that for me?"

"Sure thing. I'll do it right now."

He'd call the uncle and check out their story. If the uncle really was working on a ferry and wasn't a resort employee, then Sam would have to do something about their living situation. The boys also wouldn't be able to have Monica tutor them, as that was a free perk for resort employees only. Sam wasn't about to kick them out with nowhere to go. He would be sure they had another home first.

Thinking of the boys made him remember his morning with Emma. He'd wanted to talk to her about sneaking out last night, but it turned out to be a morning where they'd all been running late. His phone battery died during the night, so the alarm he set on it never woke him, and both kids slept through their alarms.

Emma had been determined to have her hair maneuvered into a special braid she'd seen on the internet while visiting her grandfather, but she couldn't do it herself. And Sam was all thumbs when it came to Emma's hair. She'd had a meltdown, and then he hadn't had enough time to confront her about last night.

Those were the moments that made him angry at Rebecca for not being around. Emma needed a mother, a woman in her life. Monica was good up to a point, but she and Emma didn't have the maternal closeness that Emma needed.

Now he'd have to be the bad guy when he talked to her after school. He was tired of always being the bad guy. Someday, he'd love to be the good guy in her life, but there was no one else but him to keep her out of trouble.

Gayle popped her head into his office. "No luck. We have nothing in our files and I checked with Monica. She doesn't have a phone number for them, either. She said the boys told her their uncle has a cell phone, but they don't know the number."

"Thanks, Gayle." What was he going to do now? He rose from his desk. He needed to have Monica get better information about her students in case of an emergency. "I'm going to their apartment to visit their uncle. I need to verify that he doesn't work for the resort while living on resort property. Text me if anything comes up."

"I'll do that." Gayle left and Sam headed out of his office and through the lobby. He'd go out to the garage and grab a golf cart instead of walking to the boys' apartment. It would be much faster. They had built the paths wide enough to run the carts around the island.

He drove along the path, palm trees on either side of him, in the direction of the two-story employee apartment building. According to the records he found, the uncle and brothers lived in apartment 2C, the apartment listed under his deceased sister's name.

He parked in front of the building and turned off the golf cart. He rarely had a reason to come here, but he was glad he had. The building was well kept, at least on the outside. The stucco walls were in good shape, as was the paint on the trim. The landscaping was being well taken care of, too. He would mention that to his maintenance staff. They should know he was aware of their good work.

He climbed the outside flight of stairs that

would take him to the boys' apartment. He knocked on the door of 2C. No answer.

He knocked again, putting his ear to the door to listen. Nothing.

"Looking for your daughter?"

Sam spun around to find Millie, one of the kitchen staff who worked early mornings. The older woman held a broom, her apartment door wide open.

"My daughter? No, she's in school right now." Seemed like a strange thing for her to ask. "I'm looking for the man who lives here. The uncle of two boys?"

Millie nodded, her thinning, frizzy gray hair bouncing. "Right, the uncle. Rick is his name."

Sam nodded as if he knew she was correct. "Have you seen him? He's not answering the door."

"He works long hours, a mechanic on the ferry, I believe. The boys are home alone quite a bit. I try to feed them dinner when I know there's no one to cook for them. They're growing boys. Always starving."

Not a good situation with so little supervision. No wonder Monica complained about them giving her grief during class. They were practically raising themselves.

"I'm glad you're here for them," he said. "If you see the uncle, would you have him call me?" He handed Millie his business card.

She glanced at it. "This about your daughter coming here?"

Sam's mouth went dry. "She's been here?"

"Oh, yes, several times. Nice young thing she is. Very polite. You should be proud."

All news to him. "Would you do me a favor, Millie? Would you give me a call the next time you see my daughter here?"

Millie smiled. "I'm guessing this is new information for you."

"Something like that." This recent development, combined with meeting a boy in the woods last night, did not bode well for Emma's teenage years. How would he ever survive them?

"I'll do that, Mr. Briton."

"Thanks. I'd appreciate it." He took another business card and wrote a quick note on it, asking the uncle to call him. He stuck it in the space where the door met the frame.

"You take care," Millie said as he left.

"You, too." He waved and slid into the golf cart, wondering why life had to be so complicated.

CHAPTER FIFTEEN

CHARLOTTE COULDN'T DECIDE if she was more hurt or angry after she left Sam's office. How dare he be so opinionated about her actions when he was just as guilty of deceit.

She had to admit the one thing her time on the island had accomplished was that she was experiencing emotions besides betrayal—her reaction to her mother's dishonesty. Even if it happened to be anger at Sam, it was another emotion. And she'd certainly run the gamut of emotions this week, from attraction and passion to hurt and anger.

Charlotte strode directly from Sam's office to her room to call the hospital about Jared. She picked up the phone and hesitated. Was Sam putting this situation in the same category as his ex-wife's lies about her drinking?

She hung up the phone.

What else could she do? She quickly picked up the receiver and dialed the hospital. "Hello, I'm calling for information about a patient," she said after she was transferred to ICU.

"Are you a relative?"

Exactly the question Charlotte had expected. "No. I'm a...friend."

"I'm sorry, but I can't give out more than the patient's condition. He's critical at the moment."

"I understand that," Charlotte said. "I know his brother is there and I was wondering if you would give him a message."

"I can do that."

Charlotte gave Veronica's name and cell phone number. "I really appreciate it."

When they disconnected, Charlotte took a few deep breaths, feeling good about finding a way to help her friend without being deceitful.

Charlotte left her room to look for her new friend. She finally found Veronica alone on the beach in a lounge chair, eyes shut. Charlotte hated to disturb her, but she knew Veronica was waiting for answers.

"Veronica?" Charlotte didn't speak very loudly, but her friend's eyes popped open and she sat up straight in her chair. She blinked a few times before her focus settled on Charlotte.

"Did you find out anything about Jared?" she asked. "Is he okay?"

Charlotte propped herself on the edge of the lounge chair by Veronica's legs. "I wasn't able to find out anything more than that he's in ICU in critical condition, but I left a message for Jared's brother to call you. I figured he could fill you in on the details."

Veronica clapped both hands over her mouth. "ICU? That's terrible." She picked up her cell phone. "I have a missed call. Probably from Jared's brother. I must have drifted off and didn't hear it." She stood. "I'm going inside to listen to it. I'm not sure I'll be able to hear him out here."

"Let me know what you find out," Charlotte called to her back.

"I will!"

Charlotte headed back to the lobby much slower than Veronica, who had found a quiet corner to listen to her message. Not liking the serious look on Veronica's face, Charlotte found a seat across the way to wait for her.

"I should have made him get medical help sooner," Veronica lamented when she finished telling Charlotte that Jared was on massive antibiotics in ICU because his appendix had burst. "He just kept telling me he didn't feel well and that it was some sort of stomach bug."

"You couldn't have known how sick he was." Charlotte experienced a twinge of guilt that she had doubted that Jared had been sick at all. She'd worried he'd had a woman in his room and that she'd be comforting a brokenhearted Veronica.

They spoke a few more minutes and then Charlotte said, "I should get back to my room.

Allie sent me the presentation for tomorrow and I've only skimmed it."

"Maybe we can go over it later," Veronica said. "After you've had a chance to review it."

"Sounds good. Will I see you at lunch?"

"I haven't had much of an appetite, I don't know. You go ahead without me."

Charlotte could commiserate with how she was feeling, so she left Veronica and headed for the staircase. She decided to make a quick stop in the ladies' room first, and was surprised to see Emma. They made eye contact in the mirror. The girl's eyes were puffy and red.

"Are you okay?" Charlotte couldn't help asking the question, even with the way the girl had acted the first time they'd met.

Emma nodded. "I'm fine." She stood in front of the mirror, trying to get her hair to do something. But from the frustration on her face, it wasn't doing what she wanted.

Charlotte spoke up again. "I'd be glad to lend you a hand, if you'd like."

Emma narrowed her eyes. "I don't want your help."

Charlotte took a deep breath, feeling the need to explain. "I know you don't like me because of my sister, Allie. She's done some things she's not proud of, but she's a very nice person now."

"My dad said you were twins, but I didn't believe him. You look exactly like her."

"No kidding," Charlotte said lightly. "You should have seen us when we first met at a wedding a few months ago. Her brother was marrying my date's cousin, and everyone kept confusing us."

Emma's lips twitched. "You really didn't know you had a twin sister?"

"I wish so much that I had known, but no, I had no idea." She swallowed the lump in her throat and tried not to let herself get overly emotional.

"That must have been a huge surprise," Emma said. "To find out you have a sister. I've always wanted a sister."

"I've always wanted a sister, too. So finding Allie was a wonderful surprise."

Emma fooled with her hair some more, finally dropping her hands to her sides. "Maybe you can help me. I'm trying to do this." She pulled a ragged, folded-up picture of a girl's hairdo from her back jeans pocket. The girl's braids were pinned to the side of her head in the shape of hearts.

"Let me see what I can do. I grew up as an only child, but I had several close girlfriends, and we were always braiding each other's hair." She undid Emma's tangled hair, then finger combed it before dividing it into sections. "You have gorgeous hair, so thick and long."

"Thank you. My dad says it's just like my mom's was."

Charlotte steered the conversation away from Rebecca. She couldn't imagine growing up without a mother. At least Charlotte had her mother growing up, even if she had kept secrets. "It's so much easier to braid someone else's hair than your own."

"I know," Emma said. "And my dad is hopeless when it comes to my hair."

"I'll bet he is." Although he could do many other wonderful things with his hands. Her face heated at the memory and she forced herself to concentrate on braiding.

Charlotte finished with Emma's hair a few minutes later, happy with the results. "How's that?" Their eyes met in the mirror. Emma might have a few of her mother's attributes, but she definitely had her father's eyes. Charlotte wouldn't forget them any time soon.

"Perfect!" Emma turned her head this way and that to see as much as she could in the mirror.

"I'm here until Friday morning if you need any more help before then."

"Thanks." Emma seemed sincere. She opened the restroom door to leave and looked back at Charlotte. "I'm sorry I didn't believe you at first about who you were. My dad was right. You *are* a nice person."

AFTER SAM RETURNED from visiting the uncle's apartment, he was looking over some paperwork at his desk when Emma peeked her head around the corner.

"Hey, ba— Emma, what are you doing here?" She rarely came to see him in the middle of the day.

"Can't a daughter drop by her father's office without so many questions?" Sometimes she really did sound like an adult, rather than an almost teenager.

He held his hands up in surrender. "Sorry, what was I thinking? Oh yeah, maybe that you rarely stop by to see your good old dad unless you want something." He grinned at her blush.

"Really, Daddy. I was coming down to get lunch and thought I'd stop by to see you. If you don't want me here—" She turned to go.

"Wait!"

She faced him once again.

"Get back in here." He pointed to the chair on the opposite side of his desk. "Have a seat." Maybe this was the opportune time to talk about last night.

She sat in the chair, smoothing her hair as she got comfortable.

"I see you finally got your hair the way you wanted it. Very nice. I like it."

"I had some help."

"Oh, did Monica do it?"

She shook her head. "No, it was that twin lady, Charlotte? I don't remember her last name."

Sam gaped. "Ms. Harrington did your hair? When did you see her?"

"I ran into her in the lobby bathroom just now." Emma was nonchalant about it, odd since she was so adamant about staying away from the woman. "She's actually very nice. She offered to help me with my hair. She's much nicer than her sister was. Did you know they didn't grow up together? Isn't that weird? I can't imagine not growing up with Oliver, although sometimes it might be nice." She was going on and on, barely stopping to take a breath.

"I thought you were going to stay away from her."

Emma shrugged. "I know, but this was by accident. We were both in the bathroom at the same time." She touched the heart braid on the side of her head. "I guess maybe I'll give her a second chance. She *was* really nice to me. Isn't that what you're always saying, Daddy? Sometimes people aren't at their best and we should give them a second chance to be someone we want to be around."

"Uh-huh." He hated when his own words bit him in the butt. "I was usually referring to your brother when I said that."

"But it works with other people, too."

He sighed. "Yes, being nice to people is sometimes hard to do, but it's definitely the right thing." He knew that firsthand when it came to Charlotte.

"I agree." She patted her hair and stood.

"Wait a minute. I have something to talk to you about."

She sat again and looked at him expectantly. "I don't have much time left before our lunch break is over."

"Don't worry about that. I'll explain to Monica if necessary. I have a question to ask and I need you to tell me the truth. That's all I want. The truth."

She bit her lower lip. "Okay, Daddy."

He hated this. Hated being the disciplinarian, hated always being the guy with the rules to follow. "So, last night. Monica was staying with you and Oliver, right?"

She nodded, her eyes innocent round circles.

"And you two went to bed, right?"

She nodded again.

"And you stayed in bed all night, didn't get up and go outside, right?"

She stared at him, not blinking.

He tried again. "Did you meet someone outside after you were supposed to be in bed?"

She stared down at her folded hands and chewed her lip.

"Emma?"

When she finally looked at him, she was about to cry. "I'm sorry, Daddy. I had to meet my friend, Lucas."

"Why?"

"Because he needed me to."

"Is he your boyfriend?"

She blushed. "I don't know."

If he mentioned he knew the boy had kissed her, that might push his advantage. Right now, he had her worried about how mad he was, and she was willing to talk, at least up to a point.

"I don't want you going out after dark without letting me or someone know where you're going, is that understood?"

Her head bobbed up and down quickly.

"And I also don't want you going to anyone's house without permission." Emma had no idea that Millie had told him about her visits to the apartment, and he wasn't about to reveal details. He'd learned early on that parents should keep their sources private to keep their children off guard.

"I'm sorry, Daddy. He's my friend, and he needed me, but I won't do it again without asking." She swiped at the tears on her cheeks and wiped her wet hands on her jeans.

"That's what I'm counting on." He rose from his chair and came around the desk to take her in his arms. He squeezed her and kissed her neck.

"I love you, baby." She didn't even fuss at his use of the pet name.

Please stop growing up so fast.

RIGHT AFTER LUNCH, Charlotte spent time reviewing Allie's presentation. She hadn't heard from Veronica about helping her prepare, but she was sure her friend wouldn't break her promise.

The presentation was tomorrow at two. Where had the time gone? Thinking about it, her nerves began to rattle. It was one thing to practice in her room, quite another to present this thing well in front of a man who could make or break Allie's company.

When Charlotte couldn't practice speaking in front of the mirror anymore, she switched to her own work. She could have stayed on her balcony, but instead decided to take her art supplies to the beach. She included her pastels, because the first thing she planned to do was work on the drawing of Sam.

He was able to make her angry like no other person she knew, but she still wanted to finish the picture.

Trudging across the sand to a place where she could work in peace and not be interrupted by conference attendees on a break, she set up in a spot where the sand was damp and wouldn't blow up onto her work.

First, she set up the small folding desk she'd

bought years ago. The work area was just large enough, while the short folding legs made it useful anywhere. She unfolded a towel and put it on the sand behind the desk so she could sit cross-legged to work.

She pulled out her pastels, running a finger over the colorful cover. Her fingers remembered the numerous pieces she'd done over the years. She loved pastels. Loved the colors they left on her hands. The way they could be smudged into each other to blur a border, create a new color. Nothing stood out on its own. Everything blended from one thing into the next.

Charlotte had been working for a while, not paying attention to the time, when she heard young voices down the beach. She saw Emma with her tutor and the other children. They were stretching. The tutor was smart to bring them outside for fresh air and to get some exercise.

Charlotte continued to work, so involved in what she was doing, and so excited to be using color again, that she never heard Emma approach.

"Hi," the young girl greeted her.

Charlotte smiled. "Hi, Emma. You surprised me. I didn't hear you coming."

"Sorry."

"No, that's okay. I just lose track of time and everything around me when I'm involved in my work." She pulled a fresh wipe from her supplies to clean off her pastel-covered hands. "What are you up to?"

"We have a few minutes before we have to go back in for our math test." Emma made a face that included sticking her tongue out. "I noticed you over here and thought I'd come see what you were doing."

"I'm an artist and I have a show soon. This is one of the pieces I'm planning to show."

Emma leaned over Charlotte's shoulder to get a better look. "Is that my dad?"

Caught red-handed. "Yes, it is. Do you like it?"

Emma's eyes were wide with excitement. "I love it. You even have his expression exact. I can never get faces right."

"You enjoy drawing?"

Emma nodded. "I love it. I'm always doodling something. I've never used pastels, though. Do you always use them?"

"Most of my work is done in pastels. Some more recent pieces are charcoal." Emma didn't need details on why she'd made the switch. Or why Emma's dad was hugely responsible for her switching back to color.

"I watched a video once on pastels. I like how you use your finger to rub the colors together."

"That's what I've always liked, too." Charlotte pulled a tablet from her tote. "Would you like a lesson? I don't have another desk, but I think this will work okay."

"That would be great!" Emma looked back at her teacher and then at Charlotte. "Darn. I only have another minute or two before Miss Monica blows her whistle for us to come in."

"We can do it another time if you want."

"That's perfect. Maybe you can come to our apartment after dinner tonight. Unless you have something else you need to do."

Charlotte's schedule didn't matter as much as whether Sam would like her being in their apartment. "Why don't you ask your dad and let me know?"

Monica blew her whistle.

"I'll see you later!" Emma waved and skipped down the beach to join her classmates.

Meanwhile, Charlotte wondered how Sam would feel about her offer to spend time with his daughter.

LATE IN THE AFTERNOON, Sam was surprised once again by his daughter.

"School's over already?"

"It's been over for a *long* time, Daddy." Her preteen sarcasm was punctuated by an eye roll.

"So, twice in one day you come to see me. You must want something."

She put an arm over his shoulders.

"Now I *know* you want something," he teased. He slipped an arm around her waist and pulled her tight. "Fess up, what is it?"

"Well…" She drew out the word as if trying to think how to say what was on her mind. "I kind of invited someone to our apartment for after dinner tonight. I probably should have asked you first, but I was so excited I didn't think."

Was this the boy Charlotte had seen her with? The boy who might be a boyfriend?

"Is this someone special?" he asked.

She nodded. "She's an artist, Daddy. A real artist who has art shows and everything."

Sam would have been dumb not to recognize that Emma was talking about Charlotte. He wasn't sure who would have made the worst guest, Charlotte or the maybe boyfriend. "Are you talking about Ms. Harrington? Allie Miller's twin sister?"

"Yes, that's her. So you already know she's an artist. She's *so* good! She even did a picture of you. I'm going to ask her how she does people so well. Maybe there's a trick to it."

Charlotte drew a picture of him? He didn't know what to think. He only hoped she'd drawn him dressed if his daughter had seen it. "Why do you want to invite Ms. Harrington over? And why would she want to come over?" She must still be fuming after their last encounter, whether she'd drawn him or not. She might merely be planning to use the picture to throw darts at.

"I told her how I draw all the time and that

I've never used pastels, so she offered to teach me. Isn't that great?" Emma's preteen excitement was difficult to ignore.

"It certainly is." He didn't know what to say to her request. If he said yes, then avoiding Charlotte would be impossible in his own home. But if he said no, then he'd come off as the jerk dad in both Emma's and Charlotte's opinions.

"So is it okay if she comes over tonight? Please, Daddy?"

"Tonight? Doesn't she have something else to do?" He could hope.

"No, I already asked her." She raised a hand. "I know, I know. I should have checked with you first. But I was so excited about using pastels—"

"I get it." Sam inhaled and exhaled slowly. He had no choice in the matter. He could probably manage to be around Charlotte for the next forty-eight hours if that made his daughter happy. "She can come over after dinner, as long as you have your homework done first."

She squeezed his neck and kissed his cheek with a loud smack. "Thank you, Daddy. I'll go do all my homework right now, even my thirty minutes of reading."

She was out the door before he could say anything else, much less change his mind.

On second thought, maybe that's exactly why she left so quickly.

CHARLOTTE HAD BARELY stepped into her room with her art supplies when the room phone rang. She hurried to answer it.

"Hello?"

"Ms. Harrington? This is Emma Briton."

"Hi, Emma. How are you?" As much as Charlotte knew she would enjoy teaching Emma, she wasn't sure how comfortable she'd feel in Sam's apartment. He'd surely be there. And he wasn't the kind of parent who would just let his daughter go to a near stranger's room for an art lesson. Sure, they'd slept together, but they barely knew each other outside of bed.

"I'm good. My dad says it's okay for you to come over tonight as long as you're okay with it. You're okay with it, aren't you?"

Charlotte grinned. "Yes, I'm very okay with it. What time should I come up?"

"I can meet you at the third-floor elevator at seven o'clock. I'll have the elevator key to get us up to our apartment. Is that okay?"

"That's perfect. I'll see you then."

Charlotte checked the time. She had about two hours to freshen up and eat dinner with Veronica. They could review the presentation, and with any luck, Charlotte would feel more comfortable with it. She was pretty sure Veronica wouldn't mind if Charlotte didn't do anything with her after dinner. Veronica seemed to have lost her partying spirit once Jared had gotten sick.

Charlotte was actually grateful to have plans with Emma so she could take her mind off her nervousness for a little while.

Her cell phone rang. Allie.

"Hey, Allie. What's up?"

"Hi, Charlotte. Just checking in. Have you looked at the presentation yet?"

"I have."

They spent the next few minutes going over it, and Allie pointed out some things she wanted Charlotte to emphasize.

"I'm sure you'll do great tomorrow," Allie told her.

"I hope so. I don't want to let you down."

"It's not the end of the world if Raymond Foster doesn't want to move forward with my company."

"Really? I thought this account would be extremely important to you."

"Oh, don't get me wrong. I really, really want it. But I think Jack's rubbing off on me."

"How's that?"

"I don't know. I began to realize that things like business aren't as important as family and friends. If you want to back out of doing the presentation, I'd completely understand."

Her sister had come a long way in the few months she'd known her. "I'm doing it," Charlotte told her. "It's out of my comfort zone and maybe that's good."

"You could at least let Foster know who you really are. You don't need to pretend to be me."

"Easier said than done," Charlotte admitted. "Almost everyone here thinks I'm you. Don't worry. It'll all be fine." She tried to sound more confident than she was.

"Oh," Allie said. "I almost forgot. I emailed you another slide to add to the presentation."

She explained how it fit into the pitch while Charlotte pulled up Allie's email on her laptop. She scanned her new emails and one caught her attention. She skimmed it. "Oh my gosh." Charlotte's mouth went dry.

"What is it? Is something wrong?"

Charlotte could barely speak. She swallowed with difficulty, desperately needing a drink of water. "You know all those emails and Facebook messages I sent to everyone who might be related to us? Hoping to find our biological relatives?"

"Yes…"

"Well, I just got a reply, and it says it's from our biological aunt. Barbara Sherwood was her younger sister, and as far as she knows, no one in the family even knew Barbara was pregnant, let alone carrying twins that she gave up for adoption."

"Wow, that *is* amazing. Wait a minute. How do you know for sure we're related to her? She might be pretending to be related in case she can get something out of this."

"I don't think so. She brought up how Barbara was incarcerated and her drug use. I never mentioned those things in any of my messages or emails." Charlotte's hands shook.

This email might be her chance to discover a piece of her own history.

CHAPTER SIXTEEN

"Ms. Harrington is coming at seven," Emma told Sam as she helped him clean up after dinner. He hadn't even asked her to help, so this was a near miracle. "I'm going to meet her at the third-floor elevator and bring her up."

"You have your elevator key?"

"Yes, Daddy." Surprisingly, there was only a hint of frustration in her reply.

Both kids had keys to the elevator so they could come and go when necessary. Oliver had finally gotten old enough that Sam trusted him with his own key. So far so good. No lost keys.

"Oliver and I will stay out of your way," Sam told her. Oliver had headed straight into his bedroom to finish his homework when Sam had promised to play video games with him afterward. "You and Ms. Harrington can work at the kitchen table." He looked to Emma to see if she approved.

"That's what I was thinking." She straightened things on the kitchen counters as she walked around. "Pastels get dusty, so I'll clean up when we're done." She skipped to the couch and fussed with the throw pillows, placing them exactly where she wanted them.

He hadn't seen Emma so excited about something in a very long time. She had always been an upbeat child, but this exuberance was way above the usual.

He had to admit he was a little wound up himself at the thought of Charlotte inside their apartment. She seemed to have that effect on him, and he didn't know what to do about it.

"I'm going down now," Emma told him a few minutes later when it was barely five minutes before seven. "I don't want her to have to wait."

"Okay, see you in a few."

Not two minutes passed before Sam heard Emma chattering in the elevator. Poor Charlotte. His daughter had no on-and-off button.

He grinned at the thought, just as he and Charlotte made eye contact.

"Hi," she said, giving him a tentative return smile.

His grin refused to go away. "Hi." He was glad to see her, no matter what had transpired between them. He lowered his voice so Emma wouldn't hear from where she was getting drinks for Charlotte and herself. "I should apologize for my daughter. I hope she hasn't already talked your ear off."

Charlotte set her things down at her feet. "Oh, no, I'm enjoying her a lot."

"I'll leave you two alone then." He turned to go into his bedroom.

"Wait."

He spun back around.

She wet her lips with her tongue and his blood heated. "Thank you for letting me come over tonight. You and I don't see eye to eye on many things, but Emma was really excited about learning how to work with pastels."

He nodded. "My daughter's very important to me and this means a lot to her. So I'm the one who's grateful." Their gazes locked.

"Here we go." Emma set two glasses of ice water on the kitchen table. "We can work over here, Ms. Harrington."

Charlotte turned her complete attention to Emma, while Sam headed to his bedroom.

Any connection he'd had with Charlotte was broken.

CHARLOTTE ENJOYED WORKING with Emma immensely. The girl was a quick learner and possessed an artistic eye.

First, Charlotte started with different techniques. Emma was fascinated with how you could use your finger to smooth the chalk pastels and also blend the colors together.

"It's like crayons, only better," she commented excitedly.

"That's right. Messier, too." Charlotte used wet wipes to clean the color from her fingers as she worked.

They used a sunset photo that Charlotte brought with her as a guide. She'd downloaded it from her camera to her laptop and then printed it in the resort business center. The print quality wasn't very good, but it did its job.

"Let's see if we can each do this sunset. We'll go step by step, beginning with the sky." As Charlotte drew an arch with a piece of darker blue pastel on its side, she felt as if she was back home again. Not physically, but artistically.

Emma copied her motions, very intent on what she was doing.

"You're an excellent student," Charlotte told her a little while later.

"This is fun." Emma pursed her lips as she concentrated on blending just right, reminding Charlotte of Sam.

Every once in a while, Charlotte would hear Sam and Oliver playing a video game in Sam's bedroom. She grinned at their bursts of excitement. Meanwhile, she and Emma chatted as they completed their sunsets.

By the time they finished and were cleaning up, Sam joined them. "Oliver is brushing his teeth. You're next, missy."

"Oh, Daddy, we had so much fun. Ms. Harrington is such a great teacher." She held up her finished product. "See what I made?"

"Wow," Sam said. "You did that all yourself?"

"Every bit of it," Charlotte confirmed.

He stepped closer for a better look and Charlotte got a whiff of the woodsy-scented deodorant he used. A scent she would always associate with him.

"This is wonderful, Emma. I'm very proud of you."

Emma blushed. "I just did what Ms. Harrington told me to do."

Sam's voice took on a teasing tone with his daughter. "Well, if I tried to do something like that, it would probably turn out to look like a blob of nothing."

"Oh, Daddy." She kissed his cheek. Then she turned to Charlotte. "Thank you so much for this lesson. I'm going to save my allowance to buy some pastels to practice with."

"I'll tell you what," Charlotte said. "You're such a good student that I'll order some online and ship them directly to you. Some good paper, too."

Emma's eyes were as round as saucers, and she suddenly ran over to Charlotte and put her arms around her waist, hugging her tightly. "Thank you, thank you, thank you," she whispered.

Charlotte hugged her back, knowing the two

of them had made a special connection tonight. Her eyes were moist when Emma released her. "You're very welcome, Emma. And I'd love to see what you're able to create with them. Maybe your dad can send them to me by email."

Emma nodded, her eyes glassy with emotion, also. "Good night," she whispered and left Sam and Charlotte alone.

"I should get going." Charlotte avoided eye contact with Sam while she gathered her art supplies. He didn't need to see how emotional she was about Emma.

"You don't have to leave." His words made her head swivel in his direction. "Would you like a glass of wine?"

"Are you sure? Our last conversation made it seem like we had nothing more to talk about."

"My daughter obviously thinks the world of you, and that makes me happy. The least I can do is offer you a glass of wine. Red or white?"

She smiled, tentative. "Red would be nice." She set her things down next to the elevator doors while Sam opened a bottle of wine in the kitchen.

She sat on the sofa and he brought two glasses, which he set on the coffee table in front of her. "Let me say good-night to the kids and I'll be right back."

She nodded and took a glass from the table. Her first sip told her it was going to be a very nice glass of Malbec. And the company wouldn't be so bad, either.

Before long, Sam rejoined her and picked up his glass of wine. He sat on the other end of the sofa, his body turned toward her. He rested one foot on the opposite knee. "Thank you again. And also for helping Emma with her hair. I'm lost when it comes to that."

Charlotte smiled. "I enjoyed it. All of it."

"Is there something bothering you?" he asked. "You seem a little sad."

"I don't know. I guess I've been a little more emotional than normal today. It was really fun working with Emma."

He peered at her. "It's something more than that. What's going on?" He raised a hand slightly. "Or maybe you don't want to confide in me. I understand. Our time together has been a bit rocky."

Her lips twitched. "That's an understatement." She brushed her hair back and took a sip of wine. "I think I'm afraid to talk about what's going on because I don't want to get all emotional and start bawling like a baby."

"It's that bad?"

"Actually, it's that good."

"Now you have me curious."

She swallowed. "I've been searching for biological relatives for a while now. Even before Allie and I met, I wanted to find out my medical history. My mother's illness was what made me think to do it."

"Makes sense. Go on."

"Today I received an email from someone claiming to be my mother's older sister."

"That's great!" He clinked his glass against hers in a toast. "So now what?"

"I wrote her back and asked if she had any pictures of my mother. She's going to copy some and send them. My biological mother died in her early twenties, so I figured the pictures would be of her as a young girl, but at least that would give me something. She was only nineteen when she had Allie and me. According to the aunt—Mary is her name—no one in their family knew about my mother's pregnancy, so she's as surprised to find me as I am to find her."

Sam blew out a breath. "That's incredible to hear."

"She told me my mother ran away from home with her boyfriend when she was sixteen. They didn't know what happened to her until someone contacted them to say she died of a drug overdose. My mother happened to have a piece of paper in her wallet with her mother's address. She must have somehow known that someday someone would find her dead and wonder who she belonged to."

"I'm so sorry."

Charlotte nodded. "I am, too. She led a tough

life, probably living on the streets as a teen, spending time behind bars, giving up her children, using drugs. I have a hard time imagining that I came from her."

"That's quite a background, so different from the way you said you grew up."

She nodded. "I wish I could thank her for giving us up instead of subjecting us to the life she led."

"I think you've already done that by leading such a good life and being a successful artist."

"Thank you. That means a lot. I hope she somehow knows how Allie and I turned out. Especially that she and I found each other."

They both sipped their wine, quiet for a few minutes.

Finally, Sam asked, "Is there something else?"

"Something else?"

"I sensed it when you were working with Emma. You were so intent you didn't notice when I came through the living room to get a different video-game controller."

"You're right. I never saw you."

He nodded. "Anyway, you had a look on your face that I can't quite describe. Somewhere between being happy and emotional and sad at the same time."

She swallowed. "You're right. I was all those things while working with Emma." She sipped her wine and decided she'd already told him about the email from her aunt, so she might as well tell him everything. "You know I'm an artist. That's what I do for a living."

He nodded. She had his full attention.

"And I told you about my mother, how she fell ill and died not long after."

"Right."

"Well, ever since she was diagnosed with cancer, I've been unable to use color in my art. I've been using charcoal because I haven't been able to see my art in color. Everything in my head has been black and white and shades of gray."

"But you used color today." He cocked his head.

She nodded. "This afternoon was the first time."

His eyebrows rose. "Wow! What happened? What made you choose color again all of a sudden? Was it the email from your aunt?"

"I'm not sure what caused the change in my head, but it was before I got the email." She didn't want to say it was him because she wasn't sure it was entirely true. Plus, she didn't want him to think she'd somehow fallen for him in their short time together. How she felt about him was something she couldn't put into words yet. "I kept my pastels nearby, always hoping I would have a breakthrough. And I guess I finally did. There's something about this island. I've had more ups and downs here than I've experienced in quite a while. I think I've purposely avoided those ups and downs since my mother's diagnosis. I worked in my house in Rhode Island and basically avoided life."

He looked at her over his glass of wine as he took a drink.

She continued, feeling as if she was spilling her guts. But it felt good. "You and your daughter and this island and Veronica and Jared. All those things made me realize that I haven't really been living since my mother began dying."

She wasn't aware she'd been crying until the tears fell down her cheeks. Sam rose and grabbed a box of tissues.

"Thanks." She took one and wiped away her tears.

He sat down right next to her this time, the heat from his body transferring to hers where their legs touched. He took her hand in his. "I'm sorry you've been having such a difficult time." He brought her hand to his mouth and kissed the back of it. "I'm also sorry that I've contributed to that difficult time."

She chuckled through her tears. "That's true. You have been a pain. But you've also been wonderful." She dabbed her cheeks again. "I think that was part of my growth this week, to experience all the ups and downs, and come through it all." Their eyes met. "And the good news is that now I'm back as an artist."

His gaze traveled to her mouth and he leaned in to kiss her.

CHARLOTTE TOUCHED HIS mouth with her fingertips and stopped him within a few inches of her lips. "Is this a good idea?" she asked. "We've had quite a rocky week." Their eyes met.

She was right. Well, his brain agreed with her. His body had definite doubts.

He pulled back slightly. "Probably not." He picked up his wineglass and sat back against the cushions, taking a healthy swallow.

"I was kind of hoping you'd disagree with me," she admitted.

His head spun in her direction. "You were?"

She nodded, smiling slightly, appearing a little sheepish.

"Then why did you stop me from kissing you?"

She shrugged. "I guess I wanted you to be sure. I didn't want you to do something on the spur of the moment that you'd regret later."

He set his drink next to hers, deciding to be as honest as possible. He placed a hand on her knee, then leaned in close to her ear to speak quietly. "Truthfully, there's nothing that happened between us this week that I'll ever regret."

She gave him a tentative smile. "That makes

me very happy. I feel the same." She held up a finger. "Except for some of the verbal sparring we've done."

"Absolutely. And also that first kiss in my office." He ran his fingers through his hair. "I'm so sorry about that. I let my anger and my immediate physical attraction to you combine into someone I didn't recognize."

"That *was* kind of a strange beginning to the week." She picked up her glass and sipped. "But I can't say I didn't enjoy it." Her shy smile nearly did him in.

He winked and took her free hand in his. "I can't say that, either."

She glanced down at their hands. "The week is almost over."

"And what a week it's been," he added, not as happy about the week going by so fast as he'd once been.

A few contemplative moments passed until Charlotte broke the silence. "So are you sure?"

He narrowed his eyes. "Sure about what?"

She tilted her head. "Sure about whether kissing me is the wrong thing to do?"

He grinned and took her wineglass. "There's no question about it. Kissing you is *always* the *right* thing to do." He set her glass down next to his before his mouth claimed hers with a scorching passion.

Her mouth was hot and sexy, and she tasted like the wine they'd shared. Her tongue battled with his as their fervor grew with every second.

Her hands cupped his face and then moved down to his neck. Her fingers traced his ears and slid into his hair on the back of his head. Her touch was magic, urging him on.

He pulled her onto his lap without breaking their kiss. His hand found her breast and she moaned when he gently squeezed. His thumb teased her hardened nipple through her clothes.

Breathless, he pulled his mouth from hers. He tasted the underside of her chin, down her neck to her collarbone. His heart raced. His blood was on fire. He wanted her more than he'd ever wanted anyone or anything in his life.

He leaned her back in his arms, enabling him to capture her nipple between his teeth. He wanted to remove her T-shirt and bra, wanted her completely naked, wanted to be inside her.

He stopped.

"What's wrong?" Charlotte lifted her head to look at him.

His whisper came out hoarse. "My kids."

"Oh my gosh!" Charlotte quickly sat up. She removed herself from his lap and straightened her clothes. "I'm so sorry," she whispered. "I completely forgot they were right down the hall."

He grinned. "Me, too."

She stood and finger combed her hair. "I should go."

That wasn't what he wanted her to do, but he knew it was the right thing. "I'd invite you into my bedroom, but it's no more private than us being right here."

Charlotte nodded. "I agree. I wouldn't want your kids wondering what we were doing in there."

He waited for her to invite him to her room. Instead, she walked to her art supplies and pressed the elevator button.

"You're leaving just like that?" he asked, dumbfounded. How could she turn passion on and off so easily?

She smiled at him. "If I stay here one more minute, you know what's going to happen."

He sidled up to her, standing close enough to feel the heat radiating off her body, but not close enough that they touched. "Tell me what would happen."

She blushed. "Well," she teased in a whispery voice. "First, you would take off my top and you'd see that I'm wearing a lacy pink bra that reveals my hardened nipples, which are begging for you to suck on."

He moaned. "Then what?" His own voice was raspy.

She smiled, obviously getting into the fantasy. "Then I would strip off—"

The elevator doors opened. Neither paid attention to the waiting cubicle and the doors shut again.

"Yes? Go on." He sucked in a breath. "You'd strip off—"

"Your T-shirt and throw it on the floor."

"Oh." He didn't care about his own clothes.

"And then I'd rub my body against yours and you'd be so turned on that you'd quickly remove my bra so we could be skin to skin."

"I like that." He leaned forward until their foreheads met. "As much as I want you to continue, I'm not sure I can take any more when you're standing right in front of me and I want you so much."

She kissed him quickly and then whispered in his ear. "But we haven't even gotten to the really good stuff yet."

He swallowed. "Okay, what's next?"

Instead of speaking, she touched him. Her thumb traced his throbbing erection through his khaki shorts before cupping him with her entire hand.

"You're killing me," he gasped. When he could speak, he said, "I'll meet you in your room in a few minutes. Let me make sure the kids are settled first."

She pushed the call button for the elevator again and the doors opened immediately. Her answer to him was a knowing smile and a finger wave before stepping into the elevator.

ALLIE COULDN'T SLEEP, which meant Jack wasn't sleeping, either. She tossed and turned for the umpteenth time.

"What's wrong?" Jack whispered from the other side of her bed.

She flipped onto her side to face him. "I'm worried about tomorrow."

"You mean Charlotte doing your presentation?"

"Yes. She's never done anything like this before, and I know she's nervous." She brushed her hair back from her face. "I should have told her no. She's only doing this to help me."

Jack took Allie's hand. "That's true. She wouldn't take no for an answer, though. She'll do the best she can. That's all you can ask for."

"I know. You're right. But Raymond Foster is a big deal. I know I'm being ridiculous, but I'm as nervous about her doing the pitch as I would be if I were there doing it."

He chuckled. "I can see that." He released her hand to run his finger up and down her arm. "When you talked to her earlier, she seemed to be okay. Confident, even. What changed?"

Allie shrugged. "I'm not sure. Maybe it's a combination of the pitch and Charlotte telling me about finding our biological aunt. I can't stop thinking about how we have these relatives out there that we've never met."

"That makes sense," Jack said, propping his

head on his bent arm. "You've barely gotten used to the fact that you have a twin sister and now who knows how many relatives will come out of the woodwork."

"Well, that definitely makes me feel even more anxious when you say it like that." She laughed, a nervous sound.

"Is Charlotte going to try and meet them sometime soon?"

"She didn't say. I'm not sure she even knows what she's going to do."

"What about you?"

"What about me?" she asked.

"Are you going to meet them?"

"I don't know. I never thought about it. We all share similar DNA, but they're strangers." She paused. "Do you think I should meet them?"

"I think you should do whatever feels right to you." He kissed her. "You know I'll support whatever decision you make."

"I know." She kissed him back and then wiggled her naked body closer until it pressed against his. "That's one of the reasons why I love you so much."

"I love you, too." He wrapped an arm around her, grasped her by her backside and pulled her even tighter against his awakening body. "So there are more reasons?" He kissed her neck.

"Mmm-hmm."

"And would you like to elaborate?" He was

breathing hard when he suddenly flipped her onto her back and pressed her into the mattress.

She giggled. "Nope." Her hand slid between them and wrapped around his erection. "I think I'm done talking for now."

"I think you're right." And then he slid down her body, tasting every inch before making sure they were both satiated enough to get a good night's sleep.

CHAPTER SEVENTEEN

THE NEXT MORNING, Charlotte overslept. She sat straight up when the sun came through the window. She'd planned to be up early, but the bedside clock read 8:32. An hour later than she'd wanted to rise.

As soon as she began to wonder why her alarm didn't go off, she smiled. Her body heated as she remembered her night with Sam. He'd left sometime after she'd fallen asleep, which explained why she never set her alarm.

She climbed out of bed, stretching and enjoying the little body aches due to her strenuous night. She was about to go into the bathroom when she spotted a piece of paper on the nightstand. A note from Sam.

Sorry I had to leave. Hope you slept well. Call me after your presentation. You'll do great! Sam

She smiled, running a finger over his words. She loved that he was considerate enough to leave a note and to remember today was the presentation, even if he disagreed with her pretending to be Allie. She tucked the note away to look at later.

She skipped a shower for the moment. There wasn't enough time. She merely dressed and cleaned up enough to meet Veronica for breakfast. She could get a shower closer to the time of her appointment with Raymond Foster.

"There you are," Veronica said when Charlotte brought a fruit-and-yogurt parfait and a cup of coffee to sit down with her.

"Sorry I'm late. I overslept." She placed a napkin on her lap and took a spoonful of yogurt. "Are you still able to go over Allie's presentation after breakfast?"

Veronica nodded. "I am."

"Good. Any word on Jared?"

"Actually, yes. He's too weak to talk on the phone, but his brother called me again. He said Jared asked him to call."

Charlotte smiled. "That's wonderful. Is he getting better, I hope?"

"Sounds like it."

"And?"

"And what?" Veronica's lips twitched before she grinned unabashedly. "Okay, so I'm happy he asked his brother to call me with an update."

Charlotte laughed. "Which means he cares

about you, too, or he wouldn't have thought about filling you in."

"That's true." Veronica sipped her hot tea. "And I can go see him tomorrow in person when we take the ferry to Fort Lauderdale."

Charlotte couldn't believe the week was over already. "Give him my best when you see him. By then, I don't care if he knows who I really am. This presentation to Foster is either going to go well or really stink."

"You'll be great. Are you almost ready to go work on it?"

Charlotte had finished her yogurt. She held up her coffee cup. "Let me pour this into a to-go cup and we can run up to my room."

"Sounds like a plan."

A short while later, Veronica said, "I don't think you need any more practice. You've got the pitch down cold."

"Thanks. I just hope I'm believable. You know, like I know what I'm talking about. If he starts asking questions, I'm not going to have any answers."

"Just fake it."

"How can I do that?"

"If he asks a question you don't have an answer to, get up and walk around the room." Veronica began walking around Charlotte's room to demonstrate. "At the same time, repeat his question in the form of a statement. Stop every once in a while to look at something closer. Then ask him a completely different question."

"That's crazy. It'll never work."

"Trust me. If you have his eyes following you as you move around the room, he'll never remember what he just asked." She walked again, her hips purposely swaying as she did so. "Ask me a question and I'll demonstrate."

"How long before you tell Jared you have feelings for him?" Charlotte raised her eyebrows while she waited for Veronica's answer.

Veronica said, "How long before I tell Jared I have feelings for him. That's a very intriguing question." She stopped to touch the bedside clock before wandering to the other side of the bed, her hips still moving and her chest sticking out provocatively.

Charlotte nearly fell off her chair laughing so hard. "That's never going to work."

Veronica got to the opposite side of the bed and said, "Oh, what's this?" She pointed to the floor. This time her eyebrows rose. "Want to tell me how a man's sock got into your room?"

"Okay, so asking me a completely different question did throw me off, but I'm not sure it'll work with Raymond Foster."

Veronica leaned down to the floor and then gingerly held up a man's sock. "No, I'm really talking about this sock. Whose is it?"

Charlotte was shocked into silence for several seconds. She had no answer but the truth. "It's Sam's."

"Sam's? As in resort manager Sam? The guy who thought you were Allie and treated you like dirt?"

"Uh-huh."

"You and him?" She pointed to the bed. "Here?"

"Uh-huh."

"Last night?"

"And two nights ago, too."

Veronica's jaw dropped.

"And you never mentioned it?"

Charlotte shrugged. "It's been so sudden and so up and down between us that I wasn't sure exactly what was going on. I'm still not sure."

"I can relate. Will you see him after the week is over?" Veronica waggled her eyebrows.

"I doubt it." Charlotte's chest constricted at the thought. "He hasn't mentioned anything about after I leave."

"Do you *want* to see him after this week?"

Charlotte hadn't thought that far ahead. "Yes, I think I do." They'd had their difficulties, but in a normal situation where they didn't have to sneak around, things might be different. She also wouldn't be pretending to be Allie, which Sam had never approved of.

"So what are you going to do about it?"

"Now you're sounding like me when I told you to let Jared know how you feel."

"Where do you think I pulled the question from?"

Charlotte laughed, not wanting to dwell on Veronica's question. "Come on, let's figure out what I'm going to wear to do this pitch."

CHARLOTTE HAD PLANNED to be early for her two o'clock appointment with Raymond Foster, but at the last minute, she realized she forgot the paper with the conference room location. She ran up to her room to get it, and by the time she reached the appropriate room, she was right on time. And breathless.

"Sign in here if you have an appointment." A fairly young man with reddish-brown hair and matching facial hair was stationed at a table outside the conference room.

"Thank you." Charlotte wrote Allie's name on the chart he pointed to. No turning back now.

"Mr. Foster is running a minute or two late, so you can have a seat over there." He pointed to a row of folding chairs set up against one hallway wall.

Charlotte took a seat and folded her damp hands on her lap. Her heart raced, and she was as nervous as when she had to give oral reports in high school. She reminded herself she was well prepared and would do fine.

That didn't help. She never should have suggested pretending to be Allie. Lying wasn't her strong suit. Maybe she could cancel. She shifted in her seat, prepared to stand.

The conference door flew open. A middle-aged man she'd seen around the resort exited, rolling a computer case behind him. He took the corner too sharply and the case hit the doorjamb and got stuck. He turned it, gave it a tug and hurried down the hallway.

"You're up," the young man who'd signed her in said.

"Thank you." She stood straight, wiped her damp palms on the sides of her long skirt and picked up her bag. *Remember to breathe.* She entered the conference room and closed the door behind her. The lone man in the room had his back to her and never acknowledged her arrival.

She remembered Allie's and Veronica's instructions and plugged the thumb drive containing the presentation into the laptop on the table so it would project on the screen.

Raymond Foster was still turned away from her. He tapped on his phone intently.

She waited patiently, and finally he put his phone down and turned to her. "I'm sorry to keep you waiting. I had something come up—" His eyes widened in surprise. "Charlotte Harrington!"

As soon as he had turned around, Charlotte recognized him. Now what? Did she keep to the pretense that she was Allie, or should she be honest with the man who was the very first to buy her work? It seemed ages ago that she met him at her first art show. Since then he'd bought several of her pieces, and had also commissioned one of his Connecticut mansions outside New York City.

She took a huge gamble. "R.J., how are you?" With a warm smile, she reached out to shake his hand, but he pulled her in for a bear hug. He was a large man, both tall and fifty or more pounds overweight. His head of white hair was still thick and trimmed neatly, and she'd bet his pin-striped business suit had been tailor made.

R.J. held her by the shoulders, taking in her appearance. "You're as pretty now as you were the first time I saw you." He pointed to a chair. "Have a seat and tell me what you're doing at this conference, pitching to me. Have you switched careers? I thought your art career had taken off."

She cleared her throat. "It's a long, complicated story."

He crossed his arms and sat back. "I'm in no hurry."

"To be honest, I was going to pretend to be my identical twin sister and pitch to you on her behalf. She and I didn't know about each other until a few months ago. Allie is the one in advertising and she decided not to come to the conference, instead giving me what was supposed to be an island vacation. I've been kind of down since my mother died more than a year ago, and she was trying to do something nice for me." Charlotte didn't want to talk about her mother's letter. "So you see, I haven't changed careers. In fact, all of this advertising business is new to me."

"A twin sister," he said. "And you never knew anything about her. What a story." He chuckled. "They say truth is stranger than fiction and you've gone and proved it."

She smiled. "Very true. If it's okay with you, I'd like to present Allie's pitch. I think it's very good, although you're the expert."

"Go right ahead." He sat back in his chair, prepared to listen.

Charlotte felt much more relaxed knowing she wasn't tricking R.J. into believing she was Allie. She finished the presentation and then showed him the short commercial spot Allie had made.

When she finished, she was pleased when R.J. clapped his approval. "Well done, Charlotte. Well done." He made a few notes in a notebook and then said, "I'm very impressed with what your sister can do. Tell me more about her company."

Charlotte did so, although there wasn't much to tell, since her sister had a one-person operation.

R.J. nodded his head. "I see." He kept nodding his head. "Let me think about this and I'll get in touch with her. You have a business card for her?"

"I don't." Charlotte panicked a little. She hadn't even thought about it. "But I can write down her information for you."

"Excellent." He tore a piece of paper from his notebook and handed it to her.

When she finished writing and handed it back, she asked, "What does the R.J. stand for? I never put together that the R. J. Wellington I met at my first art show was the same Raymond Foster who ran the conglomerate and the man everyone was excited to see this week."

R.J. grinned. "Wellington is my mother's second husband's name. He adopted me when they married. I've always been R.J. to my friends. It stands for Raymond Junior. My biological dad was Raymond Foster Senior. He died when I was young. I struggled to make both a career and a name for myself. That's why I want to be known as Raymond Foster in business. To keep my dad alive. He always told me to work hard and then work even harder to get where I wanted to go."

Charlotte smiled. "That's wonderful advice. I'm sure your dad would be proud of your accomplishments."

"I hope so." His face softened at the mention of his father.

"I'm glad we met like this," she told him. "It gives me a chance to thank you personally for all of my pieces you've bought over the years."

"I'm the one who should be thanking you.

You're extremely talented, and I love each and every one of them."

A warmth blossomed inside her, a feeling about her art that she hadn't experienced in a long, long time. "I appreciate you saying that." She rose to leave. "I think you have another appointment after mine, so I should probably let you get to it."

"Let's get together. Dinner tonight?" he suggested.

"I'd love it." She told him how the conference dinners worked and where and when to meet. "I'll see you later."

"I'll look forward to it," he said. "I want to hear what you've been up to besides finding a sister."

And Charlotte couldn't wait to tell that sister how the pitch went.

SAM WAS DEALING with a registration issue when he saw Charlotte hurrying through the lobby. "I'll be right back," he told Tom.

He followed Charlotte and when he was within earshot, he called out her name.

She stopped and spun around.

"From the smile on your face, I take it the pitch went well."

"It couldn't have gone better," she said. "And you'll be pleased to know that I began by telling him I wasn't Allie."

Surprising. "That was a risk."

"I know. It wasn't exactly by choice, but it was for the best. Listen, I need to call Allie and let her know how it went. Can we catch up later?"

"Sure. Want to do dinner?"

Her shoulders slumped. "I already have plans for dinner."

"I'm sure Veronica would understand."

"She would, especially since she found your sock in my room this morning." Her color heightened.

"Sorry about that." He had grabbed his clothes quickly after they'd spent longer in her bed than expected. He must have missed the sock in the dark because he'd slipped his shoes on without them. "So we're on for dinner?"

She shook her head. "I can't. I have dinner plans with someone else."

He wanted to ask who, but she would have said if she'd wanted him to know.

She looked around the lobby then leaned in close. "I'll tell you all about it later. How about we meet at that place on the beach? When is low tide?"

"I'll find out and text you," he said.

"Then it's a date."

"ARE YOU KIDDING ME?" Allie exclaimed loudly through Charlotte's cell phone. "Raymond Foster was the first person to buy your art? That's unbelievable. What a coincidence."

"That's what I thought, too. So you can see why I told him the truth. He thought it was a great story about how we found each other and he wants to hear more at dinner tonight."

"You're having *dinner* with him?" Allie's voice grew more excited as she spoke. "So I take it the pitch went well?"

"I think so. It's hard to tell. He asked me about your company after I finished the pitch, and then he wanted your contact information. So I expect you'll hear from him."

"That's wonderful, Charlotte. I don't know how to thank you."

"Don't thank me yet. You don't have the account, and it's not a guarantee."

"I know. But at least you made a good impression."

"True. I was so afraid I'd get you blackballed if I screwed up."

"I've already been through that before." Both women laughed.

By the time they disconnected, the afternoon was half over. Charlotte hadn't heard from Sam, so she took her art supplies and her cell phone and headed to the beach to work.

Noticing that the tide was fairly low, she decided to go to the inlet where she and Sam had met before. That way he could join her if he was able to get away.

When she got closer, she was surprised to hear voices. She listened a minute, recognizing Emma's voice, as well as a young boy's. She could barely make out their words, but she was pretty sure it had something to do with the thefts.

Charlotte's pulse throbbed at her temples. Did Emma know who had been committing the thefts, as well as who set the fire, and hadn't told anyone? Especially her father? Charlotte didn't want to believe it.

She backed away from the inlet's entrance and looked around for a spot to set up her work so she and Emma would run into each other when the young girl exited the cove.

She found the perfect spot a ways down the beach but before the boardwalk that led to the resort. Charlotte kept an eye peeled for Emma. Finally, she and the boy appeared. He headed in one direction and Emma walked slowly toward Charlotte.

Emma seemed distraught as she walked slowly toward where Charlotte had set up. The girl wasn't paying attention to anyone around her. In fact, she walked right past Charlotte without acknowledging her.

"Hi, Emma," Charlotte said at the last minute.

The girl stopped and turned. Her eyes were bloodshot and her complexion blotchy.

"Are you okay?" Charlotte knew the answer.

Emma shrugged, but stood in the same spot.

"Want to talk?" Charlotte patted the sand beside her.

Emma hesitated and Charlotte thought the girl might say no and go on her way. But then Emma walked over and sat down.

"I'm a good listener, if you want to talk." When Emma remained silent, Charlotte added, "Or if you want to just sit here and be quiet, that's okay, too."

Charlotte chose a gray pastel chalk to add depth to the sky she'd begun. She had barely touched the color to the paper when Emma spoke.

"I know who's been doing the thefts at the resort."

Charlotte wanted to look at Emma, but instead, continued to work, hoping she would elaborate.

"It's not Lucas's fault, though. His uncle is forcing him to do it." She sobbed and the sound tore at Charlotte's heart.

She quickly wiped off her hands and put her arms around Emma. "Why don't you tell me everything and we'll figure out what to do."

Emma sniffed. "It started when his uncle found the master key in their apartment last week. It was Lucas's mother's when she worked in Housekeeping. She must have accidentally brought it home from work. Then she was killed in a motorcycle accident last summer before she could return it."

Emma sucked in a breath and sniffed before continuing. "His uncle figured they could use it to rob people. He came up with different ideas, like moving video cameras so Lucas wouldn't get caught."

"What about the fire?"

"His uncle said he'd provide a diversion for one of the thefts. Lucas had no idea he'd start a fire and put everyone in danger. That's when Lucas finally said he couldn't do it anymore."

"So his uncle has been pressuring him to do this? He hasn't been a willing participant?"

Emma nodded, her head bobbing passionately. "That's right. He never wanted to do this. Ever."

"Then why did he? Why didn't he go to someone and tell them what his uncle was making him do?"

"Because his uncle said he was doing Lucas and his brother a favor by being their guardian after their aunt couldn't take care of them anymore because she was sick. He said Lucas and his brother owed him, and if Lucas didn't cooperate, then he'd let him and his brother be put into foster care and they'd probably be split up."

Charlotte was horrified that these two young boys were being treated in such a way, especially after losing their mother so recently.

"We need to figure out how to fix this so that doesn't happen," Charlotte said. "First of all, where are the things that were stolen?"

"I'm not sure."

"Then find out quickly before Lucas's uncle pawns it all. If we can recover everything or most of it, then the authorities might go easier on Lucas."

"I can do that. I'm going to tell Lucas that you're helping us." She stood and brushed the sand off herself.

"What about your dad?" Charlotte asked.

"What about him?"

"He should know what's going on."

"No!" Emma nearly shouted. "He can't find out. He'll make sure Lucas is punished, and that's not fair."

"I'm sure your father would understand just like I did."

Emma shook her head vehemently. "Oh no he wouldn't. He doesn't trust people. He'd assume Lucas wanted to steal those things. We can't tell him." She was on the brink of tears. "Please promise me you won't tell him."

Charlotte held up a hand. "Okay, I'll agree to that for now. You find out where the stolen items are and I'll come up with a plan for after that."

Emma leaned down and squeezed Charlotte tight. "Thank you so, so much," she whispered before releasing her and running toward the resort.

The text message alert on Charlotte's cell phone sounded. A text from Sam.

Almost low tide. Can't make it there right now. Does after dinner work? Or are you attending the final evening bash?

Charlotte desperately wanted to confide in Sam about Emma's revelation, but she was afraid Emma was right. Sam might blame Lucas for not coming forward, and then Emma would be even more upset.

She texted Sam back.

Probably not going to party tonight. Will text you after dinner.

She continued working on her art piece, but her heart wasn't in it. Besides, storm clouds were rolling their way. A sign of what was to come? She hoped not.

She quickly packed up her things and made it back to the resort's main building just as raindrops began to fall.

A bad omen indeed.

CHAPTER EIGHTEEN

SAM ATE DINNER with Emma and Oliver in their apartment. He had made spaghetti, one of the kids' favorites, but all three of them seemed to be in other worlds.

He and Emma were both quiet, but not Oliver. He talked continuously. Sam wasn't sure what the boy was saying half the time because Sam's mind was on Charlotte.

This was her last night on the island. Their last night together before she traveled hundreds of miles away.

Did she consider whatever was between them a vacation fling or something more?

Would she like to see him again after this week?

What would Emma and Oliver say about him seeing someone?

And who the heck was Charlotte having dinner with?

She hadn't spent time with anyone else this week. That's why he was so curious. He told himself he wasn't the jealous type.

He wanted to know all about her, and whether she shared the feelings he was beginning to have for her. He'd realized that as soon as she'd turned him down for dinner. He wanted to see her, be with her. He was feeling that fire deep down inside that ignites when two people make a connection.

A fire he hadn't felt since college when he'd met the mother of his children at a Blaise resort. They had both worked there part-time.

"Dad!" Oliver's voice rose as if he'd repeated the same thing over and over.

"What, Oliver?"

"I asked if I could have dessert. I ate all my dinner."

"Sure," Sam said. "Clear your plate first. I think there's some ice cream in the freezer. Do you want to fly your kite early tomorrow morning?" He'd been preoccupied with Charlotte and needed to make sure he spent enough quality time with his children.

Oliver's eyes widened in excitement. "Yeah!"

Sam turned to Emma, who was moving the spaghetti on her plate back and forth. "Not hungry?" he asked.

She looked at him, but didn't seem to focus on what he had said.

"Are you okay, Em?" He touched her forehead to see if she had a fever. Cool to the touch.

"I'm fine, Daddy. I'm just not hungry." She wiped her mouth on her napkin. "May I be excused?"

He assessed her demeanor and finally said, "Okay."

In robotic fashion, she cleaned up her dishes and then went into her bedroom, shutting the door behind her.

Sam sat at the table alone while Oliver fixed his ice cream, wondering if his evening would pick up. He'd arranged for a sitter for the evening so he could spend uninterrupted time with Charlotte. He'd told the kids before they sat down to dinner, so it would be no surprise when Nicky showed up around seven o'clock. If he hadn't heard from Charlotte by then, he'd go hang out in his office until she texted him.

By the time Nicky arrived, Sam had cleaned up the kitchen and was ready to leave. He'd already said good-night to both kids, but he was still very concerned about Emma. She had been on her cell phone when he'd checked in on her. She hadn't even looked up when he'd reminded her of the "no cell phone after nine o'clock" rule.

Was this how her teenage years would be? He wasn't sure he'd survive.

Sam rode the elevator downstairs. When he exited, he peeked out on the lanai. Only a few people were out there because of the rain. The area was covered, but the rain tended to blow underneath. One of those few braving the dampness was Charlotte. Her back was to him, but he could see her dinner companion. An older man with thick, white hair. Sam hadn't seen him before. He watched them for a minute, pretending to read something at the registration desk. They appeared to be having a good time, at least the man was, if the deep laughter coming from their direction was any indication.

Finally, deciding he was being ridiculous for acting like a jealous lover, he strode into his office and waited patiently for Charlotte to text him.

How sad was that?

CHARLOTTE WAS HAVING a wonderful dinner with R.J. He had great stories to tell, and she was enjoying her time with him immensely.

Her cell phone vibrated in her skirt pocket. "Excuse me, R.J., I need to see who this is. I'm expecting some information." She pulled her cell phone from her pocket and glanced at the screen. Emma.

Lucas says everything's at his apartment.

That was good news. The uncle hadn't pawned it yet.

"I just need to answer back," she told R.J. "I'm sorry about this."

"Quite all right. I do it all the time. My wife hates it, but certainly does enjoy the fruits of my labor." He took a long swallow of the straight-up, top-shelf whiskey he'd ordered from the bar before dinner.

When will uncle be gone so we can move it?

She sent it and waited for a reply.

"Trouble?" R.J. asked.

She saw no reason to keep the truth from him. He had nothing to do with any of it and he might give good advice. "Yes, actually. There's a young girl who needs some help with a friend of hers. He's in trouble through no fault of his own." She realized how convoluted that sounded. "Sorry, I'm trying to be discreet, but it probably sounds pretty mixed up to you."

"On the contrary, you're doing your best to mentor this girl so she can help this boy stay out of trouble. Do I have it right?"

Charlotte smiled. "Yes, you do." Her phone vibrated.

He leaves at four in the morning and works twelve-hour days on the ferry.

She replied.

Tell me how to get to apartment and I'll move it all to my room tomorrow. Then I can give it to your dad to return, no questions asked.

Emma texted back right away. That's perfect! I'll take you there myself. You're the best!

Charlotte wasn't sure that having Emma along was the best idea, but the girl was more familiar with the island than Charlotte. She might also need Emma to help carry the stolen items. Charlotte would take as many tote bags as they could gather and she'd have Emma bring her backpack, too.

She set her phone aside after relaying the information to Emma and making plans to meet at five tomorrow morning.

"All set?" R.J. asked.

Charlotte nodded, pursing her lips. "Yes, I think we have a plan."

A SHORT TIME LATER, Sam's cell phone vibrated with a text message. Charlotte. He grinned like a schoolboy and read her text.

In my room. Come up when you can.

He texted her back.

On my way.

He made a quick stop on his way upstairs, and as he stood at Charlotte's door with his hand raised to knock, his stomach flipped. He hadn't been this nervous about seeing a woman in years.

No one could blame him, though. It had been a very long time since he'd told a woman he had feelings for her.

No wonder he was anxious.

He knocked and she answered almost immediately.

"Hey, beautiful," he greeted her, then held up a bottle of champagne and two glasses.

Her smile widened, although she seemed almost sad. "I like the way you think."

He kissed her quickly on the lips, wanting to spend more time doing that, but he knew they needed to talk. This might be his last opportunity before she left tomorrow. "Then you'll really love what comes after this."

She didn't comment, merely led him to the balcony. She wore a formfitting top cut low in the front and a midthigh length skirt that showed off her long legs and bare feet. "Is outside okay? The rain seems to have stopped and I wiped down the chairs. I love the smell of the air after a rainstorm."

"This is perfect." He set the glasses on the small table and then popped the champagne. He poured them each half a glass and put the bottle on the concrete floor.

"What shall we toast to?" she asked in a slightly melancholy tone.

"To a great week. And to new friends." He wanted to say more, but the words wouldn't come.

She clinked her glass against his and they both drank. He watched her over his glass and couldn't help noticing her eyes. Something was definitely wrong.

"Let's sit down," he suggested. When they were settled in the lounge chairs, he said, "Now tell me about the presentation and then dinner." He refused to ask outright who the man was.

"The presentation went great," she said, her body becoming more relaxed as she relayed what happened.

"I can't believe he's the same person who bought your first artwork."

"I know. And he can't believe I have a twin sister." She sipped her champagne. "I'm kind of bummed that he told me he won't be able to go with her firm."

"Really? That's too bad. Did he say why?" That could possibly explain why Charlotte had seemed so down when he arrived.

"He said he really liked her presentation. Really, really liked it. But he needs a larger company to take care of his advertising needs. He wants a full staff, able to work hard and fast."

"I guess that makes sense for the size of his conglomerate."

She nodded. "The good thing is he's going to spread the news about Allie's talent."

"That's great. So it isn't all bad."

"I guess not. I was just hoping he would pick Allie's firm." She sipped her champagne. "Anyway, that's why I couldn't have dinner with you tonight."

"So you chose him over me," Sam teased.

"I couldn't turn him down," she explained. "He's not only the first person I sold my work to. He bought several other pieces after that and told his friends about me, too. Many of them have bought pieces over the years. R.J. is largely responsible for my successful career."

"And now he's going to do that for your sister. Sounds like a good guy." He took a swallow of champagne. "Although I have to disagree about him being responsible for your success. I've seen your work and I think you would have made it even if he hadn't bought a single piece."

Her eyes softened. "Thank you. That's nice of you to say."

"I mean it."

She nodded. "I know. And I like hearing you say it."

There were more things he wanted to say, like having feelings for her and wanting to see her after the week was over, but she stood and set her glass on the table. Then she took his and put it next to hers.

"Scoot over," she requested before curling into him with her one leg settled intimately between his, and her breasts pressing against his chest. "I hope this is a sturdy chair," she joked, running her foot seductively along his bare calf and her thigh reaching his rapidly bulging crotch.

"Don't worry if it breaks. I know the manager." That earned him a giggle.

He sucked in a breath when she unbuckled his belt, followed by the button on his shorts. Slowly, ever so slowly, she lowered his zipper. Slipping her fingers into the flap in his underwear to reveal his rock-hard shaft, she grasped him with her hand. He moaned. She moved her fingers over and around him, stroking lightly until he stilled her hand with his own.

"You keep that up," he choked out, "and this will be over before it begins."

He frantically kicked his shoes off in surrender when she released her hold on him. They could talk later, much later.

With one arm around her to hold her tight against him, his free hand roamed her body. He explored her curves, down her back, over her hip and butt to the back of her thigh. When he reached the edge of her skirt, his hand continued his exploration beneath it.

She gasped when he palmed her butt cheek and

he got his own surprise. "Commando? You're killing me."

"Actually, a thong." She chuckled deep in her throat. A sexy sound that urged him on.

"Even sexier." Sam brought his hand around to her front to reach between her legs, finding her hot and wet. He slid his fingers in and out of her, taking her to the edge several times before allowing her to finally climax. His mouth clamped over hers to quiet her release, and in time, she relaxed again.

Keeping her in his arms, he stood and carried her inside and onto her bed, where they made love like he'd never experienced before.

Much later, just after midnight, according to the bedside clock, Sam reluctantly removed himself from Charlotte's embrace and got out of bed. He watched her sleep for a few moments, taking in her sheet-covered body and her dark hair spread out like a halo on the pillow.

An angel. That's exactly what she was. An angel who'd come into his life to make him live again.

He gathered his clothes strewn around the floor next to the bed and took his time dressing. Charlotte was still sound asleep—she hadn't moved a muscle since he'd left her bed—and this wasn't the time to wake her to express his feelings.

He'd see her tomorrow and they'd make plans to be with each other then.

BY EIGHT O'CLOCK the next morning, Charlotte had already been up for hours. A short period of sleep after incredible sex with Sam.

Emma had, indeed, gone with her to Lucas's apartment to retrieve the stolen items. Looking back on it, Charlotte wasn't sure how she could have managed without the girl's help.

Emma knew where to get a golf cart so they could travel faster, as well as knowing her way around the island. Charlotte would surely have gotten lost both coming and going on her own. The golf cart allowed them to take everything back to the resort in one trip. Lucas and his brother made the loading up a breeze. Before she left the boys, she reminded them to be sure to stay at the resort after school and go directly to Emma's dad's office. He would make sure they were safe and cared for.

Charlotte had just showered and was all packed to leave when she headed out the door to meet Veronica for breakfast. She made sure the do not disturb sign was in place, so even if the housekeeping crew didn't realize she was checking out today, they wouldn't go in and see the stolen goods in her room.

She would hopefully run into Sam downstairs and tell him the story about the thefts. But first he needed to promise he'd make sure Lucas didn't get into trouble and that he and his brother would get a proper guardian.

"Hey, there," Veronica said when Charlotte joined her. "Ready to go home?"

She shrugged. "I guess. You know, as much as I desperately wanted to go home a few days ago, now I could stay here for a long, long time." Part of that was how good she felt here, away from reminders of her mother's deceit, but mostly, it was because of Sam.

He'd left last night while she'd slept. She'd wanted to ask him how he felt about seeing each other after the week was over, but she never got the chance. He had ways of distracting her that made her forget everything except what he was doing to her body.

"Well, I'm certainly ready to get out of here." Veronica's words brought Charlotte back to the present. "I can't wait to see Jared."

"You'll keep in touch, right?" Charlotte didn't want to lose her new friend.

"Of course. I'll text you as soon as I see Jared and let you know when we'll be back in Connecticut."

Charlotte nodded. "Good. We'll get together as soon as Jared's up to it."

"What about Sam?"

"What about him?"

"Are you going to see him after this?"

Her insides clenched. "I don't know. He hasn't mentioned anything."

"Then you should say something. Make sure

he knows you're interested." Veronica smirked. "Isn't that the advice you kept giving me about Jared?"

"You mean the advice you never did take?"

"Hey! I would have if he hadn't gotten sick." Veronica's mouth turned down.

"I know, I know. I'm just kidding." She was also trying to move focus away from a touchy subject. She checked the time. "I better go make sure I'm packed and all set to go." Veronica didn't know about the stolen items in Charlotte's room and she wasn't going to tell her any of it until they were on the ferry.

"I'll see you in about an hour at the ferry dock."

Charlotte hurried to her room. She hadn't seen Sam downstairs, so she'd need to text him to come to her room for the stolen goods.

First, she removed everything from the bags to make sure nothing was damaged. She put laptops, cell phones, tablets and camera equipment on the bed, then she placed jewelry on the bedside table. There were a few wallets, and she located her own credit cards and driver's license. She looked at everything all spread out. Lucas's uncle had gathered quite a haul with little effort.

She couldn't believe he had used his young nephew like that.

She was typing Sam a text message when a knock sounded on her door.

Peering through the peephole, she was glad to see it was Sam. She opened the door wide and said, "Come in! I was just texting you."

"And I was personally delivering this. Your replacement driver's license." He smiled broadly, handed her an envelope and stepped inside her room. He stopped abruptly and his smile disappeared.

"What the hell is all this?" he asked in a loud voice.

"Isn't it great? This is everything that was stolen this week. Well, I think it is. I don't have a list to compare, but I think we got it all." She smiled.

He stared at her, turned his head to look at the bed filled with stolen electronic equipment, then he looked back at her. "Where did you get it? Have you had it hidden in here all this time?"

Her face heated. "Of course not. What are you talking about? I recovered all this. I found out who took it and got it back."

"You *stole* it back?"

"Technically, I guess you could say that."

"So tell me, *technically*, how you managed to do this."

"Why are you so mad at me? I thought you'd be happy that people will get their things back."

"Of course I am, but I can't believe you knew what was going on and didn't tell me." He ran his hands through his hair as he looked around again. "You kept this from me."

"I haven't known about it for that long. I found out yesterday."

"How *did* you find out?"

"I can't say." She wasn't about to give up Emma as an accomplice. It was up to Sam's daughter to let him know her involvement.

"What do you mean, you can't say? Is it because you're neck deep in this?"

"How many times do I need to explain to you that I didn't know anything until yesterday?" She was getting madder by the second—as mad at him as he was with her. And she still wasn't sure why he was so angry.

"Right. And you didn't pretend to be your sister all week. What makes you think I'm ready to believe you weren't always aware of who was stealing things since you never came to tell me what you knew?"

Through gritted teeth she said, "I told you I have my reasons for not telling you. If you can't accept that, then we have nothing else to talk about." She sucked up the emotions threatening to spill out and grabbed her packed suitcase and carry-on, then swung her purse strap onto her shoulder. She glanced quickly around the room to make sure she hadn't missed any of her belongings, and then handed him a piece of paper with the uncle's address on it. "Protect Lucas and his brother from their uncle because he's going to be really angry. The boys are coming directly to your office after school." Sam could figure out the rest, and Emma would make sure he took care of Lucas and his brother.

Charlotte strode out of the room without another word.

Not until she reached the boardwalk did she feel her tears, cooled by the ocean breeze, running down her cheeks.

CHAPTER NINETEEN

As soon as Charlotte shut the door behind her, Sam pulled out his cell phone and called his head of security. He didn't want to broadcast this news on his radio.

"George, we've got a break in the thefts. Come to room 323."

"Be right there."

"And bring the complete list of stolen goods." He wanted to compare the list to the items in front of him.

While he waited for George, Sam stared at the stolen goods. How had Charlotte found all of this and never thought to let him in on her discovery? He hadn't wanted to believe she was in on the thefts, but what was he supposed to think? She had refused to give him any other explanation.

The one flaw in that idea was the big question of why she would return everything if she was in on it. Of course, the other flaw was that he didn't truly believe she was involved. But he couldn't get past the feeling that she had betrayed him by not letting him know everything before now.

The paper in his hand was a huge clue. Sam had recognized the address immediately. He'd already been there once this week.

A knock on the door was George. "Come in."

"Holy crap!" George was wide-eyed as he looked around the room.

"My feelings exactly."

"Have these things been here the entire time?"

"Probably not, but I don't have all the details." He waved the paper with the address. "I think this is where everything's been." He handed the paper to George. "There are two boys and their uncle who live there."

Slowly, Sam put the pieces together. He needed to speak to his daughter. She not only knew the boys who lived at the address, but she'd been there. "Listen, take care of this stuff. I'd love to give everything back, but then we have no evidence for an arrest." He considered it. "Take it somewhere safe and I'll let you know what to do with it next."

"I'll take pictures before I pack up, that way we'll have those if you decide to give everything back before guests depart the island."

"Good idea." Sam left George to deal with the stolen goods and he went in search of his daughter. His first stop was the small conference room where Monica tutored them.

He stuck his head in the door. "Sorry to interrupt. I need to speak to Emma." His daughter exchanged a worried look with the boy he thought was Lucas.

"Come with me," he requested when she was outside in the hallway. They went to his office and he closed the door.

They took seats across from each other and he looked directly into her eyes. "I need the truth, Emma. It's very important. What do you know about the stolen things that were in Ms. Harrington's room?"

Emma's eyes filled with tears. "Please don't be mad, Daddy. We were trying to help my friend, Lucas. He didn't want to steal anything, but his uncle threatened him."

"First of all, *we*? You were involved in this?" He hadn't wanted to believe that before now. "How long have you known who was doing the stealing?"

"I found out a few days ago. That's why I snuck out to meet Lucas. He was really upset about the fire his uncle started." She filled Sam in on the details.

"Why didn't you come directly to me?"

Emma bit her lower lip. "I know how much you hate it when people aren't honest, Daddy. I was afraid you wouldn't believe Lucas, and then he would get into trouble. That's why I told Ms. Harrington yesterday and she figured out a plan to get everything back."

Was that how his daughter saw him? A ruthless dictator with no feelings? Someone who saw guilt before the evidence was in?

"I'm sorry, Emma. I'm sorry you weren't comfortable enough to come to me with this. I promise I won't judge so harshly."

Emma nodded. "What's going to happen now? Will Lucas get into trouble? He and his brother need a place to go before his uncle gets home." Her voice broke. "He's not a nice man, and I'm afraid for them."

"Don't worry. We'll keep them here until everything is straightened out." He needed to call the authorities to find out if the boys could stay with them and what would happen when their uncle was arrested.

"That's what Ms. Harrington said you'd do. She's really great, Daddy. I'm going to miss her."

So would he.

He checked the time on his cell phone and realized the ferry must be docking. "Listen, you go back to class and I'll take care of everything. Tell Lucas and his brother to come to my office after school. Right now, I have some apologizing to do."

He hurried out of his office, down the hall and across the lobby to the boardwalk. He began running toward the ferry that had docked at the end, but he was too late. The ferry and Charlotte were on their way to Fort Lauderdale.

Out of his life.

And it was his own fault she had left without knowing how he felt about her.

CHARLOTTE SAT ON the ferry as it pulled away from the dock. Away from the place that had changed her life forever. She wanted to curl up and forget what had just happened between her and Sam.

"Are you okay?" Veronica sat beside her.

"No."

"Was it Sam? Did he just brush you off like a piece of lint from his clothing?"

"Worse."

In ragged phrases, Charlotte relayed everything that had happened, ending with him thinking she knew all along about the thefts.

"How could he think that of you? Is he blind? You're the nicest person I've ever met. You wouldn't hurt a fly."

Charlotte appreciated Veronica's view of her. "I'm not *that* nice."

"Yes, you are. Look what you did for that little girl and her friend. You didn't have to. You could have said no or called the authorities or who knows what else. But you didn't, because you're a good person."

"If I'm so good, then why does Sam think I'm so bad?"

Veronica mulled it over. "Maybe he was looking out for his kid. You know, the parental bond and all that. He wants to protect her, and if you stood in his way like between a mama bear and her cubs, then he's not going to stand idly by."

Maybe Veronica had a point. Sam was a single parent raising two kids. Of course he'd protect them from everything he could. In a moment of clarity, Charlotte realized that's exactly how her mother had behaved. She'd protected Charlotte from her biological family because her mother believed she was doing the right thing.

"Maybe I should have gone to Sam when Emma first confided in me, but she made me promise not to tell him."

"Why didn't she want Sam to know?"

"Because she was afraid he wouldn't believe Lucas didn't want to be involved in the thefts. She said her dad hates dishonesty and wouldn't like that Lucas didn't ask for help to get out of the situation." She knew firsthand what it felt like when Sam didn't believe you were telling the truth.

Veronica threw up her hands. "He's a kid. He probably had no idea where to go for help."

"*We* know that, but you can see how Emma's mind works. And she's right about Sam, although I thought he'd turned the corner when he finally believed me about being Allie's twin."

Charlotte had been sure she'd regained his trust, but then she'd lost it when she'd kept her promise to Emma.

Before long, the ferry arrived at Port Everglades where she and Veronica would part ways.

"Keep in touch," Veronica told her as they embraced.

"You, too, and give Jared my best."

Veronica nodded as they separated. "Do yourself a favor."

"What's that?"

"Don't count Sam out yet. I've seen how you two look at each other. There's something there. Don't let it slip away like I almost did with Jared."

Charlotte gave her a sad smile. She couldn't help it. "But you still haven't told Jared how you feel about him."

"Who says?"

Charlotte's mouth dropped. "When did this happen?"

"When we talked on the phone. Right after he told me he was in love with me, I told him I felt the same about him." She blushed. "He said being so sick made him realize how he was wasting time by not spending every moment with me. Of course, he's on painkillers, and he might not remember the conversation, but that's okay. I've had practice now, and the next time I tell him I love him won't be quite so scary."

"That's wonderful." Charlotte gave Veronica another quick hug. "Good luck and let me know how it goes."

They each went their own way, Veronica toward the car rentals and Charlotte to find transportation to the airport.

While waiting to board her flight, Charlotte checked her phone for emails. When she hadn't gotten even a text from Sam, she'd hoped for maybe an email, although she wasn't sure if he knew her address. She couldn't remember if she'd given one when she registered at the resort.

There *was* an email from Mary, her biological aunt. She was inviting Charlotte and Allie to visit with her and other family members in two weeks. They were anxious to meet the two sisters. Charlotte thought she'd talk to Allie about it before replying, but didn't think Allie would want to go. She was loyal to the family who'd raised her, and she had never been interested in finding any biological family.

Charlotte's art show was that weekend, so she'd be pretty busy. She could invite everyone to the show. It was taking place at a small gallery in Providence, and her biological family lived in Massachusetts. That would give them a little time to get together, but they wouldn't have to spend every minute with each other in case they didn't have much to talk about. It was a good idea. She needed to keep her mind off of Sam, and what better way than to be around new people?

People who actually wanted to be around her.

A few hours later, Charlotte saw the Newport Bridge through the window of the town car, which was driving her home from the Providence airport. She thought being home would feel good, but instead, she felt worse.

She paid the driver and dragged her suitcase up the stairs to her front porch. The sun was low in the sky, reflecting off the windows. She unlocked her front door and was greeted with a strong floral smell. Then she saw the flowers on the coffee table.

She left her things near the front door to check out the bouquet. For a second, she thought they might be from Sam, but then realized they would be sitting on the porch if they were.

She picked up the card and read the handwritten note.

Just a small token of my appreciation for what you did for me this week. Thanks for being such a wonderful sister. Love, Allie

Tears sprang to Charlotte's eyes, blurring her vision. She needed to focus on what she had and not what she'd lost.

There was a knock on the metal frame of her screen door and Charlotte quickly wiped the moisture from her eyes before turning.

Allie opened the door and entered. "I saw you

arrive. Jack and I took off work early since it was such a nice Friday afternoon. We were both anxious to see you, too."

They hugged and Allie held Charlotte away from her to peer into her face. "What's wrong? Are you okay?"

Now that she was home and in the company of her sister, Charlotte crumbled, both physically and emotionally. "No, I'm not okay."

Allie led Charlotte to the sofa and sat down next to her, holding her hand. "Do you want to talk about it or wait until later?"

Like floodgates that were suddenly opened, Charlotte spilled her guts. She told Allie everything, not leaving out a single detail. Including the fact that she was falling in love with Sam.

"I remember Sam and how rigid he was," Allie said. "You probably don't want to hear this, but it sounds like maybe you dodged a bullet."

Allie might be correct, but it didn't feel like it at that moment.

"I really thought he was coming around, and that he trusted me." She covered her face with her hands and sobbed. "I can't believe I was so wrong about him."

SAM TRIED SEVERAL times to call Charlotte in those first hours after the ferry departed, but his calls always went to voice mail. He didn't know if she was simply not answering, or if she couldn't receive calls while on the ferry or if her phone was turned off because she was on the plane. He never left a message. What could he say that would make her forgive him? He'd hurt her badly and didn't know how to make up for it.

That evening at dinner, Lucas and his brother, James, joined them. Sam had contacted the authorities and they were waiting for the boys' uncle when he came home from work that evening. The boys would stay at the resort until the situation was resolved and another guardian could be located. Emma made Sam promise that the boys wouldn't be separated in foster care and he told her he would do his best not to let that happen.

"What's wrong, Dad?" Emma asked as they put the last of the dishes into the dishwasher. "Are you still mad at me?"

He immediately hugged his daughter. "Of course I'm not mad at you. Do I wish you had come straight to me with the problem? Yes. Do I understand why you didn't? Again, yes."

"I'm sorry, Daddy. I didn't know what to do, and then Ms. Harrington was there and she was so nice and wanted to help me." Her expression was sad. "I miss her already."

He hugged her again. "I know. Me, too."

Emma looked at him. "You do?"

He nodded.

"I thought you were mad at her."

"I was at first, but I understand now why both of you did what you did." He didn't want to speak poorly of Emma's mother, but Sam would always know that Rebecca was the one who had changed him into such a distrustful person.

"I'm glad." She kissed his cheek. "Do you think we'll see Ms. Harrington again? I really like her."

"I don't know, Em. I hope so. I really like her, too."

Emma raised her eyebrows. "Do you mean *like her* like her?"

He grinned. "Yes, I mean *like her* like her. How do you feel about that?"

She floated from the kitchen to the living room, her arms outstretched. "That's the best news I've had all day!" She spun around and around.

"Be careful," he warned. "I don't want to have to use my sewing kit to stitch you up."

"Oh, Daddy." She laughed and skipped down the hallway to Oliver's room to join her brother, Lucas and James who were playing a board game. She stopped suddenly and turned to face him. "You better work hard to make sure Ms. Harrington still likes you, too, Daddy." She disappeared into Oliver's room.

He shook his head. How did he get so lucky to have such a smart daughter?

The rest of the weekend, Sam called and texted

Charlotte, but she never responded. He even re-trieved her email address from registration and wrote her an elaborate apology.

Still no reply.

By the next Friday morning, as he sat in his office, he was beginning to lose hope that she'd ever give him a chance to beg her for forgiveness.

His office phone rang and he picked it up. "Sam Briton."

"Hey, Sam, it's John."

Hearing from his former father-in-law was usually good, except when he was hoping it might be Charlotte calling.

"What's up? This is an early call."

John chuckled. "I know. I was just wondering how everything was going now that the thefts have stopped. What's the story with the broth-ers? Is there another guardian?"

Last Friday, Sam had filled John in imme-diately after contacting the authorities. "No guardian yet, but they're fine here for now. I've brought up cots, and the boys are sleeping in Oli-ver's room with him. Luckily, his room is large enough to accommodate them and the cots get folded up during the day."

"Sounds like a good temporary solution, but not a permanent one."

"Exactly. I'm going to make a call this morn-ing to find out what's going on. I'm also won-dering if their next-door neighbor might be interested. I saw Millie the other day. She's an older woman who works in the resort kitchen, and she said she's been feeding them when the uncle's gone. So she knows them well."

"That might be a good solution for them."

Sam also knew that would make Emma happy because then the boys could stay on the island.

"There's something I need from you." John changed the subject. "I want to thank the woman who helped Emma retrieve the stolen goods. Can you give me her information? I meant to call you earlier in the week, but I haven't had cell service until now." John tended to go out fishing on a whim to places where he couldn't be reached. It was his way of getting away from work.

"Sure. I can give you her contact info." She'd be much happier to hear from John than she would from Sam. He pulled her address and read it to John.

"Thanks. I'll let you go."

"Wait."

"Yes?"

"When you speak to Charlotte, would you tell her I really need her to return my calls?"

"She's avoiding you? Why?"

Sam knew John would be curious, but he would do anything to hear her voice again. To know she forgave him.

"Because I was angry that she didn't come

to me when she found out who had committed the thefts."

John was silent for several seconds. "Is there something going on between you two?"

Sam swallowed the lump in his throat. "Would you be upset if there was?"

"Don't answer a question with a question. You know I've wanted you to move on with your life. You and the kids need a woman in your lives. Not that I condone getting involved with guests, but I'm sure you were discreet."

"Yes, we were." His own daughter never even suspected, and she always seemed to be able to read his mind.

"Then what are you doing to rectify the situation, son? Where does she live? Are you going after her?"

"I don't know what to do. She lives in Rhode Island, and even if I flew up there, I'm not sure she'd see me."

"Do you have honest feelings for her, not just as a hot body for the week?" John was nothing if not a straight talker.

"Yes, I definitely have feelings for her."

"Then you know what you need to do." He paused. "Tell you what. You keep trying to contact her, and then you and the kids can come with me on the boat up the coast when I have a board meeting in Boston next week."

"I'm sure the kids would love that—"

"Don't mess around, Sam. Life is too short to lose people we care about even before they're taken away from us for good."

Sam didn't need to be reminded that John would always miss Rita, his wife and the love of his life, who was taken from him way too soon.

CHAPTER TWENTY

ALLIE WAS NEARLY ready to go to Charlotte's art show in Providence when Jack called to her from downstairs. "There's a guy at Charlotte's house. Looks like he's delivering flowers. I'm going over to get them so he doesn't leave them on her front porch to die."

"Okay. I'm almost ready to go." She'd chosen a fitted purple dress with silver accents and silver heels borrowed from Charlotte.

When she came downstairs, she saw that Jack and the deliveryman were deep in conversation on Charlotte's porch. The guy was still holding on to the flowers and was dressed in a suit and tie. Odd clothes for a deliveryman.

She walked outside to investigate. She was crossing the street when she realized who the man with the flowers was.

Sam Briton.

"It's about time you showed up," she called. For the past week, her sister had locked herself into her workroom to prepare for tonight's art show, but Allie knew part of the reason she had done so was because Charlotte had been devastated by Sam's treatment.

His head spun in her direction and he did a double take. "Allie?"

She'd give him points for knowing the difference between her and her twin. But she was not happy with him.

She joined them on the porch. "Long time no see," she quipped. "Although you can't say I haven't done what you asked and stayed away."

Sam's complexion darkened. "Can we put all of that in the past? I'm here to see Charlotte."

"Why?"

Jack tugged on her arm. "Sam's intentions are good."

Allie disagreed. "That's not what I hear."

"I want to apologize to Charlotte. She won't answer my calls or texts or the email I sent her. I care about your sister and want to tell her."

Allie softened like a marshmallow. "You do? You really have feelings underneath that hard exterior?"

"Allie." Jack's tone said a lot.

Sam held up a hand. "It's okay, Jack. She's got every right to talk to me like that. I owe her an apology, too."

Allie smiled. "Thank you, Sam. That means a lot. And I'm sorry for the things I said and did back then." She took Jack's hand and looked up at him when she spoke. "I've come to realize that my methods in the past haven't always been me at my best." Jack winked at her.

"According to Charlotte, you've changed since then, and I see that's true." Then he added, "So where is Charlotte?"

"She already left for her art show. She's been at the gallery all day, making sure everything was hung just the way she wanted."

Sam nodded. "I didn't realize that. Can you give me an address for the gallery?"

Allie pulled a business card and a pen from her small clutch and wrote down the address on the back of the card. She held it out to him. "I can't guarantee she'll be happy to see you. She was pretty hurt by the way you two left things."

His expression was solemn. "I know. But I need to try my best to make things right."

CHARLOTTE WAS NERVOUS. She thought she'd left her jitters behind years ago, but here they were, front and center.

She'd gotten used to walking around unnoticed at her shows, listening to strangers compliment or criticize her work. But tonight would be different. She had special people coming to see her work for the first time.

Her biological aunt, Mary, was bringing her husband, Dave, as well as her widowed sister, Nancy. Charlotte had met them last night at dinner at her house. Allie and Jack had been there, too. They'd been amazed at how much Charlotte and Allie looked like their biological mother, Barbara. And Charlotte and Allie commented about how much Mary and Nancy looked like them, so all three sisters must have been similar in appearance.

Charlotte smoothed her black cocktail dress over her hips and thighs in a movement to cover up the fact that she was actually drying her damp palms. She flipped her head back to get her hair away from her face and that's when she saw him.

Sam.

He stood in the gallery doorway looking as good as she'd ever seen him, resplendent in his dark suit and pale blue tie. He held a bouquet of flowers. And he was looking right at her. Her body temperature soared.

She couldn't move her legs. She should stop staring and figure out why Sam was here. Everything he said to her before she'd left the island flooded back, giving her the momentum to turn her back on him.

"Charlotte, dear, would you like us to get you a glass of that wonderful champagne?" Aunt Mary, as Charlotte had begun to refer to her, appeared from nowhere. Uncle Dave stood right behind her.

"That would be nice. Thank you." She could feel the heat of Sam's gaze on her back, although it sounded ridiculous when she thought about it.

Aunt Mary and Uncle Dave took off to get Charlotte a glass, and now she was left alone again. She took a single step forward and heard Sam's voice behind her.

"Charlotte?"

She didn't take another step, but didn't turn to him, either.

"Please talk to me." His voice was just loud enough for her to hear.

She finally turned around. "This isn't a good time." She motioned to the people milling in the gallery.

"You look beautiful tonight." He held out the flowers.

She swallowed. "Thank you." She accepted the bouquet and their hands touched for a second. Long enough for her to feel that physical reaction once again.

"I'm sorry to interrupt," a woman she'd never met said to her. "I understand you're the artist?"

"Yes, that's right." From the corner of her eye, Charlotte noticed Sam retreat while the woman asked a few questions.

"Here's your champagne," Aunt Mary said and the woman with the questions moved on.

"Thank you." Without conscious thought, Charlotte peered about the room for Sam. She didn't see him anywhere. Aunt Mary was saying something to her. "I'm sorry, what did you say?"

"I said your young man is over there." She

pointed to the corner of the room where Sam spoke with Uncle Dave.

"You've met him?" Charlotte asked.

"He introduced himself. He could see the resemblance between us and figured out who we were." Mary's eyes welled up. "I'm so glad we all found each other." She took Charlotte's hand. "I wish we had known about you from the beginning. So many lost years." She wiped a tear from her cheek. "I'm sorry to get so blubbery. Dave says I can get emotional at the drop of a hat." She released Charlotte's hand and took the flowers from her. "I'll take care of these." Then Aunt Mary grasped Charlotte's upper arm, turning her toward Sam. Her aunt gave her a little shove. "You enjoy all of this attention and go talk to that nice young man."

The momentum carried Charlotte several steps toward him, who immediately ended his conversation with Uncle Dave to walk toward Charlotte.

His smile was tentative, and she knew he had no idea how she felt about him being there. She hadn't been ready to speak to him when he'd called, texted and emailed. He'd made several apologies over the past two weeks, but she had refused to be sidetracked from her work. She'd vowed to wait until after this show to deal with her feelings for Sam.

Now, in the midst of the fruits of her hard

labor, she finally thought she was able to listen to him.

They stopped a foot from each other, staring into each other's eyes.

He took her hand and his touch made her want to weep.

"I've missed you," she admitted in a whisper.

"Not as much as I've missed you." He brought her hand to his lips, keeping eye contact. "I'm so sorry, Charlotte. I said terrible things to you. Please forgive me."

She blinked. "I should have come right to you when Emma confided in me."

He shook his head. "No, she was right about how I would have reacted. Your way was better."

"How are the boys?"

"The older woman next door, Millie, is now their foster parent until she can become their legal guardian. She'd been feeding and watching over them for a while now. When she heard about what the uncle had been making Lucas do, she was upset the boy hadn't come to her, and especially that she hadn't noticed what was going on."

"I'm sure she was. I'm glad they're taken care of. And the uncle?"

"In jail, awaiting trial, where he belongs. Not only for the thefts and the fire, but child-related charges for using Lucas to carry out the illegal activity."

"What about Emma and Oliver? How are

they?" She barely knew Oliver, but she missed Emma terribly.

"They're actually close by."

Charlotte's eyes widened. "How close?"

"John Blaise brought us all up the coast with him on his boat. He has a board meeting in Boston on Monday. They dropped me in Providence, where I rented a car and they're going on to Boston."

"You should have brought them tonight. I'd love to see them."

He squeezed her hand. "I thought about it, but decided we had too much to talk about before bringing them into it." He paused. "I know I've sent texts and emails and called you. I've apologized and promised to be more open-minded and less distrustful. But there's one thing I've been saving to say in person."

Her heart fluttered in her chest.

He took a deep breath then continued speaking. "Charlotte, I have no idea where the two of us are headed, but for the first time in a long time, I want to take a chance with you. I know we've only spent a week together, and it's only been three weeks since we first met, but I'm falling in love with you."

"I don't know what to say." Actually, she did know what to say. "You hurt me with your distrust." She pulled her hand from his.

"I know. And I can't emphasize it enough that I'll do whatever it takes to make it up to you."

"What about next time?"

"Next time? There won't be a next time." He took her hand in his and she didn't resist. "I trust you completely. If I didn't, then I wouldn't want you around my kids."

She knew how important his children were to him and admired that trait, among others. She felt herself soften and she cocked her head. "So, are you ready to prove you trust me?" Her tongue wet her bottom lip and she had his complete attention.

He waggled his eyebrows. "Tell me what you want me to do and I'll do it."

She spoke quietly in his ear. "Anything?" Her breasts grazed his arm.

He coughed and she laughed. Then she turned serious. "Ever since I got home, I've been trying to tell myself I couldn't possibly be in love with you after one week. But here you are, telling me exactly that." She touched her lips to his and then gazed into his eyes. "I love you, too."

EPILOGUE

April, six months later

"THIRTY YEARS OLD," Charlotte said to the mirror. Who could have guessed she would be this happy today? In the past year, she'd met her twin sister and Allie's adoptive family, as well as several of their biological relatives on their mother's side.

Right before Christmas, she and Allie had gone to visit their biological grandmother, who was in a nursing home in North Carolina and unable to travel. It was through meeting her, a strong woman who still had her mental faculties, even if her body couldn't keep up, that Charlotte was finally able to completely forgive her adoptive mother.

She'd watched each of her biological relatives forgive Barbara for the choices she made as a teenager: running away and forced to live on the streets, using drugs and going to jail, getting pregnant and then giving up her twin daughters. All without telling a soul about their existence. If they could forgive so easily, then Charlotte could chalk up her mother's deceit to loving Charlotte with all of her heart.

She applied lipstick and flicked a piece of fuzz from her sleeveless, deep blue dress. She and Allie were having a combined birthday party. Their first birthday together, and it was being held at the Grand Peacock Resort on Sapodilla Cay.

"You almost ready?" Sam came up behind her and put his arms around her waist. He rested his chin on her shoulder. "The new manager has everything under control. The room and food are ready, and the guests are beginning to come downstairs." Sam had asked for a transfer to the Blaise property in Boston to be closer to Charlotte. They'd been able to spend more time together, and his kids now attended a regular school.

Charlotte teasingly wiggled her behind against him. They held eye contact in the mirror and he separated his body from hers. "Don't start that or you'll never make it to your own party."

She grinned. "We can't have that. Let's go. I'm anxious to see everyone."

John Blaise had brought several of the guests to the island on his yacht and others had come by plane and ferry. Sam and Jack had made all the arrangements, keeping the details and guest list secret from both Allie and Charlotte.

Walking down the staircase to the lobby, she

saw Allie and Jack waiting for them. The two women smiled and ran to hug each other.

"I love your dress," Allie told her.

"Yours, too," Charlotte said, and they both laughed. They'd purposely bought identical dresses since they'd never had the chance to dress alike before.

Charlotte removed herself from Allie's embrace and grabbed her sister's left hand. Then she looked from Allie to Jack and back at Allie again.

"You're engaged?"

Allie nodded vigorously. "Jack asked me last night on the beach." She held her hand out to admire the ring. "I don't want to take focus off our birthday, though, so we're not going to announce it until later."

Allie had certainly come a long way—in the past, she would have put herself first. Charlotte smiled and hugged her again. "I'm so happy for you!"

She put a hand on her abdomen and hoped Allie would feel just as happy for Charlotte when she shared her own good news. Sam had been talking marriage for weeks, but even he didn't know about her positive pregnancy test.

"Let's go," she said. Then, arm in arm, the two women headed to their very first joint birthday party.

"Happy birthday!" everyone shouted as the

women entered with Jack and Sam right behind them.

Charlotte took in the sight of everyone she held
dear. There were Emma and Oliver, who had
accepted her presence in their lives wholeheart-
edly. They stood next to Lucas and James, while
the boys' guardian, Millie, hovered nearby as
they all precariously balanced plates of appetiz-
ers. Then there was Sam's former father-in-law,
John, standing next to Aunt Nancy, Aunt Mary
and Uncle Dave. John and Aunt Nancy, both widowed at a young age, had hit it off when'd they
met over the holidays.

Allie's entire adoptive family was there, too,
including almost four-year-old Sophie and her
baby brother asleep in his dad's arms. Veronica and Jared held hands. Charlotte hadn't seen
them since they'd all gotten together right after
the new year. Her new friends had been living
together since shortly after they'd returned to
Connecticut. Charlotte hadn't been surprised.

She looked at Allie and Jack, then at Sam,
with whom she exchanged knowing smiles. "I
love you," she whispered.

"I love you, too."

She held up the glass of champagne that someone had handed her when she walked in. The
room was quiet as she spoke. "I can't believe how
lucky I am." She sucked in a breath to keep from
breaking down. "I started life as an only child

of a single mother, and look how things have changed in such a short time. I can't thank you enough for the love and support you've shown both of us." She raised her glass to Allie and shouts of *"Hear! Hear!"* rang throughout the room. She pretended to take a sip and then set the glass down.

As the noise level rose, she and Allie turned to each other, the men in their lives at their sides. "Happy birthday, Allie."

"Happy birthday, Charlotte." Then Allie added, "And thank you, Barbara Sherwood, for loving us enough to give us up so we could have better lives."

"And to the parents who chose us." Charlotte's voice broke. "For loving and caring for us the best they knew how."

* * * * *

LARGER-PRINT BOOKS!
GET 2 FREE LARGER-PRINT NOVELS PLUS
2 FREE GIFTS!

HARLEQUIN®

Romance

From the Heart, For the Heart

YES! Please send me 2 FREE LARGER-PRINT Harlequin® Romance novels and my 2 FREE gifts (gifts are worth about $10). After receiving them, if I don't wish to receive any more books, I can return the shipping statement marked "cancel." If I don't cancel, I will receive 4 brand-new novels every month and be billed just $5.09 per book in the U.S. or $5.49 per book in Canada. That's a savings of at least 15% off the cover price! It's quite a bargain! Shipping and handling is just 50¢ per book in the U.S. and 75¢ per book in Canada.* I understand that accepting the 2 free books and gifts places me under no obligation to buy anything. I can always return a shipment and cancel at any time. Even if I never buy another book, the two free books and gifts are mine to keep forever.

119/319 HDN GHWC

Name _____ (PLEASE PRINT)

Address _____ Apt. #

City _____ State/Prov. _____ Zip/Postal Code

Signature (if under 18, a parent or guardian must sign)

Mail to the **Reader Service:**
IN U.S.A.: P.O. Box 1867, Buffalo, NY 14240-1867
IN CANADA: P.O. Box 609, Fort Erie, Ontario L2A 5X3

Want to try two free books from another line?
Call 1-800-873-8635 or visit www.ReaderService.com.

* Terms and prices subject to change without notice. Prices do not include applicable taxes. Sales tax applicable in N.Y. Canadian residents will be charged applicable taxes. Offer not valid in Quebec. This offer is limited to one order per household. Not valid for current subscribers to Harlequin Romance Larger-Print books. All orders subject to credit approval. Credit or debit balances in a customer's account(s) may be offset by any other outstanding balance owed by or to the customer. Please allow 4 to 6 weeks for delivery. Offer available while quantities last.

Your Privacy—The Reader Service is committed to protecting your privacy. Our Privacy Policy is available online at www.ReaderService.com or upon request from the Reader Service.

We make a portion of our mailing list available to reputable third parties that offer products we believe may interest you. If you prefer that we not exchange your name with third parties, or if you wish to clarify or modify your communication preferences, please visit us at www.ReaderService.com/consumerchoice or write to us at Reader Service Preference Service, P.O. Box 9062, Buffalo, NY 14240-9062. Include your complete name and address.

HRLP15

LARGER-PRINT BOOKS!

HARLEQUIN

Presents®

GET 2 FREE LARGER-PRINT NOVELS PLUS 2 FREE GIFTS!

YES! Please send me 2 FREE LARGER-PRINT Harlequin Presents® novels and my 2 FREE gifts (gifts are worth about $10). After receiving them, if I don't wish to receive any more books, I can return the shipping statement marked "cancel." If I don't cancel, I will receive 6 brand-new novels every month and be billed just $5.30 per book in the U.S. or $5.74 per book in Canada. That's a saving of at least 12% off the cover price! It's quite a bargain! Shipping and handling is just 50¢ per book in the U.S. and 75¢ per book in Canada.* I understand that accepting the 2 free books and gifts places me under no obligation to buy anything. I can always return a shipment and cancel at any time. Even if I never buy another book, the two free books and gifts are mine to keep forever.

176/376 HDN GHVY

Name	(PLEASE PRINT)
Address	Apt. #
City	State/Prov.	Zip/Postal Code

Signature (if under 18, a parent or guardian must sign)

Mail to the **Reader Service**:
IN U.S.A.: P.O. Box 1867, Buffalo, NY 14240-1867
IN CANADA: P.O. Box 609, Fort Erie, Ontario L2A 5X3

**Are you a subscriber to Harlequin Presents® books
and want to receive the larger-print edition?
Call 1-800-873-8635 today or visit us at www.ReaderService.com.**

* Terms and prices subject to change without notice. Prices do not include applicable taxes. Sales tax applicable in N.Y. Canadian residents will be charged applicable taxes. Offer not valid in Quebec. This offer is limited to one order per household. Not valid for current subscribers to Harlequin Presents Larger-Print books. All orders subject to credit approval. Credit or debit balances in a customer's account(s) may be offset by any other outstanding balance owed by or to the customer. Please allow 4 to 6 weeks for delivery. Offer available while quantities last.

Your Privacy—The Reader Service is committed to protecting your privacy. Our Privacy Policy is available online at www.ReaderService.com or upon request from the Reader Service.

We make a portion of our mailing list available to reputable third parties that offer products we believe may interest you. If you prefer that we not exchange your name with third parties, or if you wish to clarify or modify your communication preferences, please visit us at www.ReaderService.com/consumerchoice or write to us at Reader Service Preference Service, P.O. Box 9062, Buffalo, NY 14240-9062. Include your complete name and address.

HPLP15

LARGER-PRINT BOOKS!
GET 2 FREE LARGER-PRINT NOVELS PLUS
2 FREE GIFTS!

⟨H⟩HARLEQUIN®

INTRIGUE
BREATHTAKING ROMANTIC SUSPENSE

HILP15

YES! Please send me **The Montana Mavericks Collection** in Larger Print. This collection begins with 3 FREE books and 2 FREE gifts (gifts valued at approx. $20.00 retail) in the first shipment, along with the other first 4 books from the collection! If I do not cancel, I will receive 8 monthly shipments until I have the entire 51-book Montana Mavericks collection. I will receive 2 or 3 FREE books in each shipment and I will pay just $4.99 US/ $5.89 CDN for each of the other four books in each shipment, plus $2.99 for shipping and handling per shipment.*If I decide to keep the entire collection, I'll have paid for only 32 books, because 19 books are FREE! I understand that accepting the 3 free books and gifts places me under no obligation to buy anything. I can always return a shipment and cancel at any time. My free books and gifts are mine to keep no matter what I decide.

263 HCN 2404   463 HCN 2404

Name _____ (PLEASE PRINT) _____

Address _____ Apt. # _____

City _____ State/Prov. _____ Zip/Postal Code _____

Signature (if under 18, a parent or guardian must sign)

Mail to the **Reader Service:**

IN U.S.A.: P.O. Box 1867, Buffalo, NY 14240-1867
IN CANADA: P.O. Box 609, Fort Erie, Ontario L2A 5X3

MMLPBPA15